MURDER AT THE TOWER

MURDER AT THE TOWER

Teresa Collard

SEVERN SH HOUSE

This first world edition published in Great Britain 1991 by
SEVERN HOUSE PUBLISHERS LTD of
35 Manor Road, Wallington, Surrey SM6 0BW.
First published in the U.S.A. 1991 by
SEVERN HOUSE PUBLISHERS INC of
271 Madison Avenue, New York, NY 10016.

British Library Cataloguing in Publication Data
Collard, Teresa
  Murder at the tower.
  I. Title
  823.914 [F]

  ISBN 0-7278-4188-2

Printed and bound in Great Britain by
Billing and Sons Ltd, Worcester

For Susan and Christopher Venning

Acknowledgements

I acknowledge all the help I have received from so many people in the writing of this book, and wish to thank them. Tony Cornwell, Deputy Governor (Resources) of The Tower of London, for his unfailing support before ever a sentence was written. Peter Hammond, Deputy Master of the Royal Armouries for so generously checking the historical detail. Ed Baines who tried so hard to explain the mysteries of my Amstrad which has a mind of its own. Joe McGloin, Jon and Judie Jordan, Sheila Reader, Ann Reay, William Gibbs, and Rosemary Bromley, my agent, who has never lost heart.

PROLOGUE

Geneva July 1st 1990

The man sat high behind a desk. As he spoke an illuminated electronic currency converter, above and to his right, translated his words into figures.

'Thirty thousand.'

'Thirty five thousand.'

The converter read 35,000 Swiss francs

14,200 Sterling

25,000 Dollars

40,000 Marks

'Forty thousand . . . lady on the front row.

'Fifty thousand.'

'Sixty thousand.'

'Seventy thousand.'

'Eighty thousand.'

'Ninety thousand. A new bidder on the right.'

All eyes turned to look at a well-dressed man standing by the wall.

'One hundred thousand.'

Again the young man gave the slightest nod.

'One hundred and ten thousand. Lady on the front row.'
'One hundred and twenty thousand.'
'One hundred and thirty thousand.'
'One hundred and forty thousand.'
'One hundred and fifty thousand.'
A slight pause and then the young man gave an almost imperceptible nod.

'Going – going – gone.'

The man sitting high, behind a desk, brought down his gavel with a satisfied smile.

1

Chaos! Total chaos!

Harry Johnson, who'd called to return a book he'd borrowed, stared at the study in disbelief. Newspapers torn to shreds, the desk on its side, books strewn all over the study floor, and the picture, the Professor's favourite picture, smashed to smithereens. The broken frame, with its panel pins sticking out in all directions, had been aimed at the bay window; shattered glass bestrewed the Victorian chair and the large photograph, the Professor's pride and joy, was ripped to shreds.

This was no ordinary student prank. This was unforgivable vandalism.

Harry's first impulse was to tidy the room, clear the debris, not let the Professor see this mess, make it presentable for him. He was so angry that he felt like hurling the book he was carrying against the wall. Hot, angry tears coursed down his face. In all his thirty years in the college he'd never seen anything like this. If only he'd returned the book earlier, he might have got his hands on the bastards.

Most of the teaching staff at Princeton would have been able to take this in their stride. To them it wouldn't have mattered quite so much. They lived off the campus. They returned to their wives, their families or flat mates, but for Professor Lawrence Berkeley, whose whole life was centred in this room, who was unmarried, who had no loved ones, whose parents had been killed in a plane crash, this wanton destruction was heartbreaking. Strange, Harry thought, he's usually here at this time of the day, must be taking a shower in his apartment before going out for his evening meal. Like everyone else on campus, Harry knew the Professor's unvarying daily routine. 'Apartment' was a euphemism for the two rooms the Professor occupied, rooms normally reserved for visiting lecturers or V.I.P's, but the President had made an exception for Lawrence Berkeley, an academic who was constantly being offered chairs as far afield as Germany, Australia and New Guinea. It was not so long since Cambridge had offered him a crown, but the President in his inimitable way had dealt with the challenge. No one was going to poach on his territory. He'd done his homework. 'Take it Lawrence,' he'd said, 'but there's no fishing within a couple of hundred miles of Cambridge to compare with what we have on our own doorstep.' That, thought the President, had been the end of the matter.

Haven't seen the Professor for about ten days, thought Harry, not since he went to Yale for a symposium, neither have I heard any reason why anyone should want to do this. It's no good I shall have to ring him, and Security as well. I'd better not touch anything either, it's the first question the police ask when they arrive at the scene of a crime. *Have you moved anything?* Harry knew the procedure. Since his wife had died he'd done little else but read, because he couldn't abide the TV with its intrusive advertising which ruined every film. There was no tension in thrillers interrupted every fifteen minutes by ads for washing powder or dog food so he filled his empty days by occasional fishing, jogging and a diet of Deighton, Le Carré, Chandler, Seymour and Price.

He picked his way carefully over the debris, to the phone which lay on the floor behind the sofa. The black leather sofa was still in its usual place. The Professor liked to sit and gaze through the casement window at the trees, the red brick buildings and the students dashing hither and thither. 'I don't have to dash anywhere, Harry', he'd say. 'My world is here.'

Harry put his hand on the back of the sofa to steady himself as he picked up the phone, but as he straightened up he froze. The telephone fell to the floor and for some seconds, unable to move, he looked down on the recumbent figure of Professor Lawrence Berkeley. He's dead. Those bastards have killed him. In that moment of stillness Harry realised, for the first time, how close he was to this man. Lawrence Berkeley looked the same in death as he'd looked in life. Somewhat untidy, his long grey hair curling over the collar of his bright pink open neck shirt. His grey-green cotton trousers were too tight and his sandals had seen better days. His feet and arms were well tanned, but Harry knew, because he'd seen him swimming in the lake, that the rest of his body was as pale as on the day he was born.

Harry kept staring. He kept staring because there was something strange about this death. He looked too peaceful – and another thing – there was no blood, no bruises, no sign of a bullet wound. Dare I hope, Harry whispered to himself? Perhaps they hit him, not hard enough to kill him, just hard enough to knock him out?

He moved fearfully round the sofa towards the supine figure. Holding his breath he touched the right cheek. As he did so the Professor yelled 'Kettle'. Harry was so shaken he leapt backwards, and as he did so slipped on an empty whisky bottle, landing on his back. It was all too much for Harry. He couldn't believe that the Professor, who hardly ever drank when he was on campus, had polished off a bottle of whisky. Then it dawned on him. The Professor had returned to his study, found the mess, couldn't take it, and had drowned his sorrows.

'What are you doing down there Harry?' asked Lawrence Berkeley, as he sat up and stretched.

'Sorry Prof, but I thought you were dead. You gave me an awful shock when you shouted "Kettle".'

'Did I shout "Kettle"?'

'You sure did.'

Lawrence shook his head and said no more.

'Hadn't we better get security over right now before either of us touches anything?'

'Security! Whatever for?' demanded the Professor.

'All this mess, this senseless vandalism.'

'It isn't vandalism, Harry. Well yes, I guess it is, but I'm the vandal.'

Harry gazed at the Professor in astonishment. He'd known this man ever since they were young lads both visiting their grandparents during the holidays. The condominium in New Brunswick held happy memories for them both. Over forty years ago, and in all that time Harry had never seen him lose his cool. Must be ill. There was no other answer.

'You've been overdoing it, Professor. At Christmas you cancelled your skiing holiday in Vermont, and for the first time in years you didn't even spend time in your cabin in the hills.'

'Mountains, Harry, Adirondak Mountains.'

'Mountains then, whatever, but you shouldn't work all hours that God sends.'

'My problem, Harry, hasn't been caused by overwork, rather the reverse. You know that for the past ten years I've spent my leisure time holed up in the cabin. On many occasions you've been with me. Did I work, or did I fish?'

'You fished, but you thought a lot, didn't you? Isn't that how you work?' Harry was perplexed. How could fishing cause all this mayhem?

'Get up Harry, find yourself a chair', ordered the Professor, 'and I'll try to explain what havoc has let loose the dogs of war.'

Harry found himself a chair and sat down gingerly. His back was giving him hell again.

'It's a long story, but I'll need to start at the beginning.'

Harry tried to look attentive. After all he'd heard it all before.

He knew the Prof had majored in History, minored in English and to obtain his Doctorate had written a controversial thesis on Abelard and Heloise. Historians, so Lawrence had told him often enough, maintained that Fulbert, Heloise's uncle and a canon of Notre Dame was enraged when he discovered she'd been seduced by Peter Abelard, her tutor. Fulbert unaware of their secret marriage determined to put an end to Abelard's amorous advance and had him brutally castrated. Lawrence had always felt that this possessiveness verging on the barbaric was the act of a father and not an uncle. That was his premise. Harry had heard the story a dozen times, how he'd developed it in his thesis which gained him his Doctorate and finally recognition as a serious historical researcher.

Digging and delving into the past was Lawrence's *raison d'être*. He never hurried his work, he liked to become totally embroiled with his characters. Fishing was the perfect activity for a man who lived in the past, for it gave him time to think himself into a period. The dress, the smells, the manners, the intrigue, the politics, the religion and the amours.

The Professor's voice changed. Harry stopped daydreaming and listened. 'Francis Bacon has had ten years of my life. Ten years in which I've put the record straight for him. I've absorbed the life and times of Elizabeth I, admired her intellect, her grasp of political issues, her hatred of Spain, her adventurous spirit, her willingness to explore the New World as long as someone else footed the bill, and above all her courage. On all these issues I go along with the mainstream of historians, but there's one subject Harry, on which they and I part company.'
  'Her virginity,' said Harry with absolute certainty.
  'Yes, yes, you're right.' Lawrence looked at Harry in amazement. 'How did you know that?'
  'You may have mentioned it before.' About ten thousand times, thought Harry.
  'Oh, have I?' But the Professor was in full flood and not to be side-tracked. 'Well that is the basis of my book, now ready for publication, which the University Press has been screaming for. I believe that Francis Bacon was the offspring of a morganatic marriage between Elizabeth and the Earl of Leicester. I promised to have the book ready by the end of

7

this semester, that's why I spent Christmas immured in this room.'

Harry hadn't spent a lifetime in the History and English Faculty for nothing. 'Does the Bacon theory mean the present Royal family in England has no right to the throne?' 'Could be, Harry, could be, but my only intention was to disprove Elizabeth's claims to virginity, and I've done that to my satisfaction. Now it seems I'm an also-ran. Professor Robert bloody Kettle has reached the winning post first.'

'You mean your friend at Cambridge? The guy in the photograph standing next to you?'

'Yes, the man who shamelessly stole my ideas, and used my research. The man who said he was fascinated by my theory, and idiot that I am, I let him read my notes. Five years ago Kettle, bloody Kettle, had never ever had a pamphlet published, let alone a book.'

'How did you find out?'

'First of all in the *London Times* on Thursday, and yesterday a huge splurge in the *New York Times*.' Harry made a move towards the paper rack.

'You can't read them, Harry, I've torn them to shreds.'

So that's why the Prof went berserk, thought Harry.

'Harry, it's an awful thing to have to admit, but I found out last night for the first time what it feels like to contemplate murder. If, yesterday, Kettle had had the temerity to walk in here, you would have found a corpse.'

Two hours later, after the two men had cleaned up, the study was both clean and tidy. The papers, the empty whisky bottle, the shattered glass, the picture frame and photograph were all in the trash-can. Lawrence had rescued his precious books and returned them to the bookcase. The telephone, still intact, was back on the desk and apart from a dark patch on the wall where the picture had hung, no one would have suspected the mayhem of the previous night.

It was Saturday and Harry's last day as a college caretaker. He'd completed thirty years, and at the age of fifty had opted for early

8

retirement. His pension would be minimal, but enough for his frugal needs. He'd already sold his flat and had planned to spend the rest of his life on his brother-in-law's ranch in Texas. They'd done up a small chalet for him so, thankfully, he wouldn't have to live on top of them. Harry was looking forward to the change. He'd never minded hard work and his sister's problems, now that her husband Tom was suffering from angina, were immense. But before getting down to the hard work he'd a promise to keep. A promise to visit a distant cousin in England. Why he'd said he'd go was beyond him, but in Harry's book a promise was a promise, and Betty, his sister, wasn't expecting him until the end of July.

Lawrence Berkeley knew it was Harry's last day, knew too that everyone in the Faculty would miss him.

'Harry,' he said suddenly, 'why don't we go off to the cabin for a week's fishing?'

Harry grinned at him. 'I was hoping you'd ask. I don't leave for London until the middle of June, and it's a journey I'm beginning to regret having said "yes" to.'

'OK. We'll go tonight after you've had your send-off from the staff. On the way you can tell me what you plan to do in London, where you're staying, and what you're going to see.'

'There's not much to tell. I'll be staying with relatives I've never even met. Could be quite boring.'

How wrong he was!

2

Detective Superintendent James Byrd switched off the engine and sat for some moments in the car wondering why Sir Charles Suckling, his Chief Constable, had sent for him. Surely it couldn't be another post mortem into how he'd conducted his last case? Unorthodox, Sir Charles had said on the 7th day, when he'd admitted to allowing his instinct to guide him because clues were thin on the ground, before congratulating him on the 11th day when he'd finally solved the Bicester kidnapping. Had Chief Superintendent Keaton been stirring it again? He knew that Keaton hated his methods, his unwillingness to communicate at each stage of an investigation, knew too that he complained bitterly about an officer who relied on his intuition, keeping his superior officers and his team in the dark. Keaton couldn't stand his 'sixth sense' and his apparent disregard for procedure, but Byrd knew deep down he had a healthy regard for the rulebook, even if his interpretation was different from Keaton's.

He unwound his 6′ 2″ and climbed out of the car. It was on him now. In five minutes he'd know whether he was being carpeted or promoted.

'Come in Superintendent'. Sir Charles gave a slight smile as Byrd entered, not in welcome but at the sight of Byrd in a suit and tie. This dark haired, bearded Superintendent looked much more at home in the jazzy shirts and designer jeans that Keaton abhored. There's something piratical about him, thought Sir Charles, a man born out of his age. Byrd saw that his Chief had company. A grey-haired man, whose face was familiar, turned to look at him.

'Am I too early, sir? Would you like me to come back?'

'No Byrd, you're bang on time, as I expected you would be. Meet Sir Elwyn Rees-Davies, the Metropolitan Police Commissioner.'

They shook hands. 'Morning, sir.'

'Good morning Superintendent.'

The niceties completed Sir Charles pointed to a chair and Byrd sat.

What the hell's going on, he wondered. What's the Met doing on our patch?

'You look slightly surprised, Superintendent, to see the Commissioner.'

Byrd laughed. 'Yes, I am, sir.'

'The Commissioner's here because the Met has been asked by the Governor of the Tower of London to mount a covert operation.'

'Covert, sir! In The Tower! But hasn't the Tower its own guards, warders, and an army presence permanently on the premises? We've always been led to believe it's the most heavily guarded of our tourist attractions. Why does it need us?'

'The Governor doesn't know why.'

James Byrd stared at his boss in astonishment. He'd never heard anything like this before. The Governor of The Tower wanted help but didn't know why!

'Elwyn', murmured Sir Charles, 'I think you'd better explain.'

'I'll try, but I think Superintendent Byrd, who I understand is given to flashes of inspiration, will understand the dilemma facing the Governor of the Tower, and his Deputy, Colonel Kilmaster. Both men, without a vestige of proof to substantiate their suspicions, are convinced that something is going on. They can't ask questions because they don't know what to ask, and even if they knew they might alert unknown malefactors who may be committing unknown crimes. What the Governor wants, Superintendent, is someone on the spot who can fade into the background and is a trained observer. Quite obviously I can't second any of my own men. Their faces are too well known in the City. Not only that, I feel someone with your qualifications would be more suitable.'

'My qualifications, sir?'

'You play a mean game of tennis, and I believe you read Modern Languages at Oxford?' Byrd nodded.

'And you are something of a musician?'

'I once played the saxophone, but I haven't touched it for some years now.'

'A little practice, maybe? I'm sure all these abilities will be put to good use, and' said Sir Elwyn glancing at Sir Charles for confirmation, 'I believe I am right in saying you have a totally unorthodox approach which often produces results. Results are what we're looking for.'

'But, if you are asking me to do the job, how would you expect me to fade into the background? Impossible, I would have thought, in a place like The Tower where security is paramount.'

'Not impossible, Superintendent, no it's not impossible. Despite the fact that within The Tower precincts there is a closely-knit community of a hundred and fifty people all living on site, there is a way. The Governor himself, who is an imaginative man, has found the answer.'

'Major General Featherstone-Bonner, and his Deputy, Colonel Kilmaster, always vet the intake of Yeoman Warders. They are drawn from the Army, the Marines and the Royal Air Force. The full complement is 42, but at the moment, fortunately, there is a vacancy. All these men finished their careers as warrant officers and have served for at least 22 years.' Sir Elwyn looked at the Chief Constable.

'I think, Charles, you'd better take it from here.'

'We're hoping, Byrd, that you'll agree to becoming a Yeoman Warder. The easiest way to hide is to become totally visible.'

Byrd couldn't believe what he was hearing.

'But I'm at least ten years younger than most of them, and I've never been in the army. I'm bound to be asked where I've served. It's impossible. They'd smell me out at once.'

'The Governor thinks not,' said Sir Elwyn. 'To begin with you are bearded, which makes you look older, and we can give you excellent cover.'

'What sort of cover?'

'Two of the warders are former SAS men, and of all the warders they are the most secretive. Unlike some former officers of M.I.5, they take signing the Secrets Act seriously. Not only that, they've served all over the world in places where normal army personnel are never drafted. If you go in as a warrant officer with the SAS you wouldn't have to explain where you'd served. "Special Operations Asia", would be your answer, then you'd shut up like a clam. Strangely enough the SAS boys are fitter than the majority of Yeomen which makes them look younger. You'd pass. Take it from me.'

Sir Charles picked up the phone. 'We'll have coffee now, Janet.' As he replaced it he gave Byrd a quizzical look. 'Think about it, Superintendent. Think about it.'

'When do you want an answer?'

'No hurry. By the time you've finished your coffee.'

Byrd gave him the shadow of a smile, and shook his head.

The door opened and an attractive redhead entered carrying the coffee. Her tight fitting crimson calf length dress showed every contour of a shapely body, and her rich perfume, which imperfectly disguised her permanent aura of stale sweat, filled the room. 'Do you want me to pour, sir?'

'No thank you, Janet. I'll do it.'

She grinned at Byrd as she left, closing the door quietly behind her.

'Elwyn? Milk and sugar?'

'Neither.'

'Superintendent?'

'Just milk, sir.'

Byrd rose and handed the black coffee to Sir Elwyn and picked up his own. He sipped it as he walked over to the window.

There was silence. Byrd thought about his marriage, which had reached a watershed. Like so many policemen, he saw too little of his wife and daughter. Stephanie, he knew only too well, had made allowances, found outside interests, painting, music appreciation, spending two mornings a week showing tourists round Oxford, but she was always back in the house by the time Kate arrived home from school. How would she view this new assignment? He didn't have to accept, but Sir Charles, knowing his predeliction for unusual cases, was presenting him with a gift. A gift it would be hard to refuse.

Sir Charles thought the decision would prove difficult, but they desperately needed the maverick Superintendent, for there was no one else who really fitted the bill. Byrd realised his marriage was much more stable than he deserved, but he would be chancing his arm if he accepted. On the other hand he was set on becoming an assistant chief constable by the time he was forty. He sat down and continued sipping his coffee. He knew he wasn't being totally honest with himself.

'We are aware of your problems, Superintendent. The Governor feels a month might see it through, but it could go on and on, as I'm sure you realise. You'll be wanting to see your family but as Warders only get one day off every fourteen days, and a long weekend once every six weeks, Colonel Kilmaster will rearrange 'the wait' – that's the old name for the duty roster, making it possible for you to take every Saturday evening and Sunday off.'

'That's not on, sir,' said Byrd sharply. 'If I'm to be part of the scenery then I must be treated exactly like my fellow warders.'

Sir Elwyn and Sir Charles exchanged satisfied glances. They had landed their fish.

'Elwyn, you'd better try and explain what this nebulous problem is all about.' Sir Elwyn nodded.

'First of all, Superintendent, thank you. I take it you've now accepted secondment to the Met.?'

'Yes, sir.'

'Good. You'll find The Tower a fascinating place, Byrd, every stone tells a story, none stranger than the dare-devil robbery

14

which took place in the seventeenth century. Who's to say equally audacious attempts aren't being planned today right under the noses of the Governor and his Deputy?'

'Robbery, sir?'

'You've heard of Colonel Blood.'

'Only vaguely.'

Sir Elwin laughed, 'You really must visit The Tower, Superintendent. Blood, disguised as a clergyman, was shown the Crown Jewels, after which he was invited to sit at the Keeper's table. Their friendship developed, until one day Blood admired the Keeper's pistols and made him an offer. The foolish man parted with them, leaving himself unarmed, which gave Blood and his confederates their opportunity. They left Edwards senseless on the floor and made off with the Jewels. The Keeper's son raised the alarm. One rogue was caught in The Tower wharf, another, escaping on horseback, was unseated, and Blood, having flattened the Crown with a mallet, was also apprehended.'

'What happened to them?'

'Nothing, strangely enough. Blood refused to speak with anyone other than the King, and Charles II was amused by the whole episode and pardoned him. Not only that, he employed him, and gave him a pension.'

'Unbelievable!'

'John Evelyn, the eminent diarist, also found it odd until he discovered that Blood was a spy in the King's service.'

Byrd mulled over that strange story.

'Are you saying, sir, that the Governor thinks the Crown Jewels, the most heavily guarded treasures in the Kingdom, may be in jeopardy?'

'It is one of the possibilities. Both Sir Charles and I have inspected, in great depth, the precautions taken, and as far as we're concerned there's no way the Jewels could be lifted. However, the Governor's taking no chances; he's doubled the surveillance.

'If it's not the Crown Jewels, then it could be buried treasure. Rumours have been rife since the time of King John, and searches were made as recently as 1958. Buried treasure, to my way of

15

thinking, is the more credible theory. Take a look, Byrd. I don't need to tell you how to do your job, but it will take time. It's an enormous fortress, twenty towers in all, plenty of spaces in which to salt away treasure. And, of course, the possibility of tunnels. If you talk to the Yeomen you'll find the majority of them view all these rumours with a great deal of scepticism, but the Colonel tells me there are one or two who are totally sold on the idea. I wouldn't mind being a young man in your situation, Superintendent. Historical research has always appealed to me.'

'Elwyn' said Sir Charles, 'I think we'd better get Detective Sergeant Mayhew in here to explain the *modus operandi*. At the moment, Byrd, only the Governor, Colonel Kilmaster, Sergeant Mayhew, you and I know about this operation.

'You will, of course, have to let your wife know where you are. We'll be relying on her cooperation.' Sir Charles pressed a buzzer and within seconds an attractive brunette in a well-cut denim suit appeared carrying a small file of papers and a pile of books. Byrd had seen Mayhew a few times when she was still a constable dealing with traffic problems, knew of her promotion and transfer to the C.I.D, but had never worked with her. She settled herself at the side of Sir Charles's desk and opened the file.

'Take us through it, Sergeant.' Sir Charles leaned back in his chair highly satisfied with the outcome. Now only the nuts and bolts.

Detective Sergeant Mayhew, whose colleagues called her Georgie, spoke softly. Scarcely the aura of a policewoman, thought Byrd. A tall brunette, whose face reminded him of Jacquie Kennedy, and whose figure would have done justice to the cover of *Cosmopolitan*. Much more like a highly successful model then a policewoman.

'Superintendent, you'll be living in the Casemates. Number forty three. A lodging big enough to accommodate four people comfortably. There is a modicum of furniture. A bed, table and chairs, enough cutlery, china etc. for your needs. Your story is simple. Your wife's mother is seriously ill, and your wife and daughter will be joining you when the old lady has recovered. This avoids moving in a van load of furniture. It's essential to have a wife in the picture because it's a requisite for the job. There are no single Yeomen Warders.

'We've acquired a new car for you. It's a small car, a Metro, but it's a souped-up job, just in case! A classier car might attract too much attention. We've organised a mobile phone, a closed line, so that you can reach me here or at my home. Never use The Tower phones on business, but it would be unnatural if there weren't calls from your wife, so tell her to ring on The Tower line, but talk only of domestic matters. Any messages for Sir Elwyn or Sir Charles I'll relay immediately. Your name – less complicated to stick to the truth – will remain the same, the Colonel will refer to you as James or Jim Byrd. The Yeomen have recently put a jazz band together so don't leave your saxophone behind.'

A good idea, thought Byrd, I'll be able to socialise without having to talk much.

'This pile of books here, all on The Tower, will provide some bedtime reading for the next week. And that's it,' said Georgina, 'for the moment.'

'When do you want me to start?' asked Byrd looking at Sir Charles.

Sir Charles had it all mapped out. 'You're expected on the 8th, a week today. That will give you time to clear your desk, and when you return to DHQ, tell them I'm seconding you to another force on a highly secret enquiry. They'll immediately think of Ireland or this recent affair in Cyprus. No explanations, not even to Chief Superintendent Keaton. The Warders' duties commence at 8.30 in the morning and finish at 6.30, which means you'll be able to get home occasionally for a few hours in the evening without being missed. Now Superintendent, off you go, and enjoy yourself.'

Sir Charles's eyes twinkled. He knew his man.

3

Harry's retirement party was hardly a riotous success. Most of the teaching staff had already left too eager to get away, leaving only a handful of research scholars, a few cleaners, the Bursar and Lawrence Berkeley.

A wrist watch, one of the new quartz models was inscribed for Harry. *To Harry Johnson from your colleagues 1960–1990*. Harry wondered why he thought about death when he looked at the dates. Pity they hadn't checked with him. He now had five watches and all of them going. A clock would have been more acceptable.

The party didn't last long. Harry and Lawrence were thankful to get away. They threw their grips and fishing tackle into the trunk and drove off to cheers from the cleaners.

'That's the end of an era, Harry.'

'It certainly is, Professor. I should have had the nerve to do it before, and tried my hand at something different.'

'Like what?'

'Oh, I don't know. Working for a Private Eye, perhaps. I'm quite observant. Or maybe a forestry warden.'

'You really enjoy the outdoor life.'

'Yes, I most certainly do.'

'Well you lean back, Harry, and enjoy the drive. It's amazing how one can unwind and arrive at the cabin feeling and actually being a different person. All the pressures, the traumas, the problems are dispersed somewhere in the atmosphere between Princeton and Upstate New York.'

'So I've noticed. That's why you slow down when you reach the mountains. That's why you didn't finish your book sooner, Professor.'

'Less of the Professor, Harry.'

'We're two fishermen on a week's holiday. Larry and Harry, remember?'

'Sounds like the terrible twins.'

'Do you remember what you called me when we were lads? A name my grandfather thought quite apposite because at the time I couldn't even catch a tiddler.'

'Yes, yes I remember,' laughed Harry, 'but it wouldn't do to call you a jerk now because you have caught the odd fish.'

They drove in silence from Perth Amboy along the Tarden State Parkway, both men thinking about the idyllic summer holidays of their youth, when it never rained. Holidays which in retrospect grew brighter every year. Shortly they joined the thruway at Spring Valley.

'Not bad, not bad,' said the Professor, 'We've covered the worst part of the journey in just an hour and a half. We'll stop at Harrimans for a cup of coffee and a burger.'

It was a hot airless night, too hot to remain inside so they sat outside gazing at the night sky.

'Tell me Harry, what are you going to be doing in London?'

'Sight-seeing mostly.'

'And where will you be staying?'

'With a distant cousin I've never met. My great grandfather emigrated, leaving two brothers behind in England. He never made any effort to keep in touch. I don't even know whether he could write, so naturally the families lost touch. I'd never given it any thought until four years ago when I received, out of the blue, a Christmas card from Steve and Brenda Johnson with an open invitation to visit them at any time.'

19

'And you replied?'

'Of course, but I've really no desire to see England. I'm an American and there's a lot to see on this side of the pond.'

'But you are going?'

'Yes. After the Christmas card came letters every month pressuring me to return to the land of my fathers, and now I've caved in, and I'm actually going.'

'What's he like, this cousin of yours?'

'From his photo, he looks very much like the rest of them.'

'The rest of who?'

'The Yeomen Warders.'

'Good God! Are you saying that he's a Yeoman Warder at The Tower of London?'

'Yes, all bearded and looking like a Tudor doll. Just wind him up and he'll march.'

'Where does he live?'

'At The Tower of London.'

'And where will you be staying?'

'With them. They've got plenty of room.'

'What an opportunity!'

'For what, Larry?' That wasn't easy to say, thought Harry. I'll have to call him the Prof whether he likes it or not.

'An opportunity for research, man. Something I've been contemplating for decades.'

Harry looked amazed. Only yesterday the Prof had vowed never again to waste his precious life, or what was left of it, doing research or even thinking about it.

'But yesterday you said . . .'

'Yes, I know what I said yesterday, but this is today. There are so many stories originating in The Tower which don't add up. In fact the whole of English history could be changed if one examined, in depth, the stories, myths and legends that abound.'

Harry laughed. 'You sound like your old self, Professor, and don't look at me like that, I'll never get used to the "Larry" bit. After all these years, I've got out of the habit.'

The two men climbed back into the car. It was past midnight and the roads were blissfully clear. They left the thruway at Albany and took Interstate 87 as far as Warrensburg and then route

28, passing quickly through Wevertown and North Creek, and finally at 3 a.m. crawled up the steep hill in bottom gear to the cabin above Indian Lake. The car headlights illuminated a name board nailed on to the cabin door. Now scarcely legible, the weather having done its worst, the name board read 'U op a'.

'I'll repaint the sign tomorrow,' said Harry. 'Why Utopia?'

'It's symbolic,' said Lawrence quietly, 'and if my Utopia vanishes, then it's sadness indeed. Did you know Harry, that the saintly and courageous Thomas More wrote a book entitled *Utopia*? I wonder what he thought about while he was kept a close prisoner in The Tower of London, the Bell Tower to be exact, among the rats and mice, isolated, lacking warm clothes, insufficient food.'

'He was pretty philosophical, you know.'

'How on earth do you know that Harry?'

'I'm not completely dumb, Prof. Besides, I've seen *A Man For All Seasons*.'

'More was deprived of pen and ink, you know, after they caught him passing notes to John Fisher, who was imprisoned on the floor above.'

'That's barbaric.'

'Of course it was, but More used his native wit, and continued writing the notes, but in charcoal. What guts, Harry, those two men possessed. What courage in refusing to acknowledge Henry VIII as Head of the Church.'

'And what a ghastly *end*,' said Harry, hoping the Professor would change the subject.

'Yes. Executed on Tower Hill. With the axe.'

Despite the warm night Harry shivered. 'I've a bottle of Bourbon in my grip. Let's go inside and have a drink. I've had enough of The Tower of London.'

The day's fishing had been productive.

Harry sprinkled pepper and salt on the bass before placing it carefully on the hot coals and burning oak in the barbecue.

'There's enough here for six men.'

'I feel like six men, Harry. Haven't felt so ravenous for months. In fact I feel so good that I have no desire to return to civilisation.'

'Neither have I', said Harry.

It was peaceful. The two men washed the bass down with an excellent Californian Chablis, followed by strong coffee.

As they gazed down on the lake Lawrence said casually, 'You don't have to go to London. You could stay here. Why don't you write and cancel the whole thing, or even ring them from North Creek?'

Harry gave it some thought. 'Wish I could, but it's a promise, not only that, I've already started genning up on The Tower of London. Steve said it would make it much more interesting. Now there's no need for me to read any more. You can fill me in, Professor.'

'Yes, Harry, I can do that. Who's meeting you?'

'Steve says that he and Brenda will both be at London Airport.'

'You've sent them photographs, I suppose?'

'No. They don't need one. They know I'm 6' tall, grey haired, blue eyed, broad shouldered, broad in the beam and I'll be wearing a stetson. I mentioned the stetson as a joke, but Steve wrote and said he'd always fancied the real thing so that's what he's getting.'

'Good on you,' laughed Lawrence.

They sat silently as the shadows fell leaving only the outline of the mountains visible and a dull glow from the dying embers of the barbecue.

4

Yeoman Warder Steve Johnson polished the brass knocker and number plate of 5 Tower Green. Brenda, his wife, never did the job properly. It needed the pressure of his fifteen stone to make the brass shine like gold. Steve stepped back to admire his work. Just one more rub with a clean duster and it would do. The scent from the lavender in front of the window was overpowering and the hum of the bees strangely comforting. He was going to miss this place. Only two more years to his retirement and he'd be out. He'd never find anywhere like this. 5 Tower Green was special, extra-special. None of the other Yeomen were lodged in accommodation like this. Some were in the Casemates, and others in Legge's Mount, once a gun emplacement, or in the Waterloo Building. Number 5, Tower Green was exceptional. It was much larger than all the rest, five levels in all. A cellar, three floors and a vast attic in which the television aerial was housed. Steve had recently discovered features of the building which he'd never divulge, not even to Brenda. If he opened his mouth he knew he'd be out and the archeologists in.

Steve loved the life. He was part of a royal tradition, part of a body of men whose origins dated back to Henry VII. He liked being on show, there was something of the actor in him, he liked being photographed arm in arm with the Americans, the Japanese, the French or the Germans. His likeness could be seen on posters displayed on the Underground, inviting the public to visit the finest medieval fort in Britain. A peacock and Steve had a lot in common. They both liked their finery and they both like to strut. In two years all that would end, but there were ways of continuing the image. Americans loved illustrated lecture tours, and his slides of the world's most famous Royal Fortress were excellent, quite professionally produced. At least that was Steve's opinion. It all depended now on an unknown factor, his American cousin.

For five years he'd been planning his tour of America. If the Tower historians could travel and tell the story, so could he. His stories wouldn't be so factual, he would embellish them, not be pernickety about detail, add a bit of mystery and mythology. Toronto first, for a few days to visit a mate, then down to Princeton. He'd start from the University before travelling west, taking in Washington, Pittsburgh, Chicago, Omaha, Denver and San Francisco.

Steve had lived and breathed this tour for five years without mentioning it to anyone. Too many of the lads might want to steal his thunder, but he was one step ahead. His cousin was in the right place. He might be only a lowly caretaker but he knew all the right people, and where better to start than in a University? Not only that, Harry was actually employed in the History Faculty, and over the years had developed, according to his letters, an interest in the past. A cousin who was also an amateur historian was a bonus.

Steve heard the phone ringing in his sitting room on the upper floor.

Brenda shoved her head through the window.

'Steve! Steve!'

'Yes, dear?'

'Barney's not well. He's being taken off duty. Could you get over to the Wakefield straight away?'

'Yes, tell the Duty Officer I'll get changed and be there in five minutes, and tell him it's about time Barney had a proper check-up. This is happening too often.'

'You know Barney won't go to the Doc. He doesn't want to be invalided out.'

Five minutes later Steve was on duty in the Wakefield Tower. Barney had been on duty for half an hour which meant Steve had less than half an hour to go before changing with his colleague in the Bloody Tower. One hour stints were the order of the day, and the Warders changed around. In some spots the hour passed unbelievably quickly because tourists asked so many questions, but in other situations time passed slowly, but didn't lessen the necessity for keeping an eagle eye on the visitors, and the Royal Treasures. The changes helped to keep them alert. Of the twenty towers in the Tower of London complex, the Wakefield, built by Henry III, was Steve's favourite.

Henry had given private audiences in the very chamber where Steve was on duty. Steve enjoyed explaining to a group of Japanese visitors how the Kings of France and Norway and the Holy Roman Emperor had given Henry gifts of animals. The first elephant to be seen in England, a polar bear who fished for his supper in the Thames, and three leopards to represent the three heraldic lions on Henry's coat of arms. Steve's duty finished on the hour which left him no time to explain how the animals were the beginnings of The Tower Zoo. After his stint in the Bloody Tower, he returned to his lodging for a snack lunch where he waited until he was called out for an unusual duty. He'd been deputed to welcome a new Yeoman Warder who was expected during the afternoon.

Superintendent James Byrd, in his dark blue Metro, drove up to the gates of the Tower. A prominent *No Entry* sign prevented him from going any further. A Yeoman Warder on duty, in an unusually commodious sentry box, strolled over to him.

'Yes?'

'I'm a new boy. I'm expected, and I'm early.'

The Duty Warder grinned. 'Your name?'

'James Byrd'

'Have you any identification with you?'

Byrd handed him well worn army papers containing an almost unrecognisable photograph. Armed with these, the Yeoman quickly returned to his box, picked up the phone, and spoke for a few seconds before returning to the car.

'They're expecting you, Mr Byrd. Drive down towards the river, and then along the wharf until you reach the west drawbridge adjacent to the Cradle Tower where you'll see another box. Steve Johnson is waiting to show you to your quarters.'

Byrd drove slowly along the wharf. Tower Bridge looked magnificent, totally dominating the river. One thing the planners couldn't spoil because it stood alone. Several cannons faced the river, a reminder of The Tower's defensive capability through the ages. He looked at a more modern picture; workmen, dressed in jeans and T-shirts, removing scaffolding from the base of St Thomas's Tower. From his quickly assimilated bedtime reading he knew that beneath the St Thomas's Tower, with access to the river, was the most infamous gate in English history, Traitors' Gate. As he approached the drawbridge which once straddled the moat, he saw Steve Johnson waving at him.

'Welcome, Mr Byrd, we've been expecting you. Would you care to leave the car on the wharf for the moment? There is an entrance for vehicles adjacent to the Cradle Tower, but as there are thousands of people milling around you'll find it easier to walk.'

Byrd found a space on the wharf and did as instructed.

Steve Johnson seemed quite apologetic.

'Sorry about that, but you'll be able to bring the car in as soon as the tourists have left.'

'Don't apologise. I'll be glad of the walk.' Steve couldn't quite put his finger on it, but he'd met this man somewhere before. The shape of the head, the beard hiding a strong chin, the dark piercing eyes. Strange too that this man didn't seem to care too much about appearances. It was the first time he'd seen a new Yeoman arrive in an open-necked shirt and jeans, but he had to admit the SAS were a law unto themselves.

'Let's get going,' said Byrd. 'You can give me a history lesson on the way. I haven't been in this place since I was a boy.'

'Oh', said Steve puzzled 'didn't you come for an interview then?'

Byrd wanted to bite his tongue. His first mistake. He thought quickly.

'The interview took place at the War Office, when the Governor was there for a meeting. Tell me,' said Byrd quickly changing the subject, 'what are these red brick buildings on our right?'

'A part of the Royal Armouries, the hospital block, and the Royal Fusiliers Museum.'

'Hospital block! Is it used these days?'

'Yes, not as a hospital, but we do have a doctor on site with a small surgery.'

As they walked across the square, north of the White Tower, Byrd was surprised to see a Gurkha soldier on duty outside another massive 19th century edifice.

'A Gurkha!'

'Oh, we have lots of different regiments taking turns at guarding The Tower. Gurkhas, Irish, Scottish and Coldstream Guards, the R.A.F. the Royal Green Jackets, and even regiments from Australia.'

'And what's the building?'

'The building is the Waterloo Barracks. It stands on the site of the Grand Storehouse which was completely gutted by fire in 1841. Wellington was the Constable of the Tower when it happened, and wasted no time in having barracks built to house a thousand men.'

As they walked behind the barracks they came face to face with a slowly moving queue.

'What are they queueing for?' asked Byrd amazed at their patience.

'They want to see the nasties.'

'The what!'

'The instruments of torture. Until recently they were exhibited in the small Bowyer Tower, which created chaos, but now they're all safely re-housed in the Martin Tower and queueing is less of a problem. The scold's bridles, the scavenger's daughter, the rack, you'll be able to see them all at your leisure.'

'The human race does have some gruesome tastes,' murmured Byrd.

'You can say that again. We had a party of Japanese in yesterday and one of them wanted to be a victim on the rack while his pal operated the mechanism. Masochists, that's what they are.'

Byrd noticed a party of children leaving a building on his left. 'What's that?'

'It's the Education Centre, where the Kiddies do their homework, see models and diagrams, but it has another function in the evenings. It's where the jazz group and drama club rehearse, and where they put on their plays.'

Nobody told me about that, thought Byrd.

'And do you allow outsiders to take part?'

'Oh no, it's a community pastime, for residents only. Can you act, Mr Byrd?'

The new Yeoman Warder laughed. 'I've no talent in that direction.'

'Oh, that's a pity. You don't by any chance play the piano, do you? We're thinking of doing *Salad Days*'.

'No, not that either, but despite being hopelessly out of practice, I've brought my sax, but it hasn't been played for three or four years.'

'You sound just the right chap. A few of the lads have just managed to get a jazz band going, which is great because they also double as a dance band.'

'Dances here?'

'Yes. We normally use canned music, but it's sterile and provides little or no atmosphere. A live band, even if it's nothing special, is much more fun. The dances are only small affairs, but we enjoy them. Keeps the ladies happy!'

Byrd weaved his way round another large party, this time queuing to see the Crown Jewels.

'Come on', said Steve, 'we can take a short cut through the Flint Tower.'

It was quiet in the Casemates. No tourists. A few cars were

parked on the left of the inner curtain wall, and on the right were the lodgings of the Yeomen, all part of the outer fortifications. Most of the houses had tiny gardens at the front, and on the left he noticed a small vegetable garden with fair sized onions and carrots.

Steve unlocked the door of number forty three. 'You'll be able to park your car over there alongside Jock's vegetable garden, and if you need any help unloading, just give me a buzz.'

'I haven't much to unload. All our goods and chattels will arrive with my wife and daughter, but that may be sometime yet, because she's nursing her mother.'

'Colonel Kilmaster did mention something about it, said we'll give you any help you need, but,' Steve winked at Byrd, 'I can't imagine anyone in the SAS needing a helping hand. You're self-sufficent buggers.'

Byrd laughed, but said nothing.

'The rooms on the ground floor are empty. The last tenants never used them at all.' Steve led the way upstairs. 'This room on the left was their sitting room. We've fixed you up with an easy chair, a table, a couple of chairs and a bed. We even managed to find an old rug, better than floor boards under your feet.'

Steve led the way into the kitchen. Byrd made a mental note that both rooms overlooked Mint Lane. 'Is there a back door?'

'No.'

He looked out of the window. If anyone called it would be a simple matter to put his head through the upstairs window to see who was there.

'And where do you live, Mr Johnson?'

'At 5 Tower Green.'

'Is that one of those Tudor houses so often illustrated in magazines?'

'It is.' Steve thought about his enormous house and was thankful he'd successfully kept authority at bay. Visitors were always shown into the ground floor sitting room, never allowed to see the kitchen-diner. He had also managed to scotch, despite Brenda's visions, all those tales about Lady Jane Grey being imprisoned there and scratching her name on the panelling.

29

Nobody knew for certain where she'd been kept and he wasn't having the archaeologists and historians rampaging through his home. What they did after he'd retired was another matter.

'When do you suggest I bring the car in?'

'Any time after half past six.'

'How do I get it here?' Byrd knew the answer, but he thought it politic to ask.

'You can drive through the arches under the Middle and Byward Towers which are on the western approaches, and then left immediately into Mint Street. Then you can park the car alongside Jock's market garden.'

'I'll need to eat out tonight, so what time does The Tower shut down?'

'The wharf is closed at dusk to builders, cleaners and anyone who's been working on the site, but residents have access up until midnight and can leave their cars on the wharf. You wouldn't be allowed to bring the car in after the gates are locked. The Ceremony of the Keys takes place at 9.45 and finishes at 10 as the clock strikes the hour.'

'Thank you, Mr Johnson, you've been enormously helpful.' Steve acknowledged the compliment with a smirk.

'One thing I've forgotten to mention, Mr Byrd. Colonel Kilmaster is expecting to see you in his office at 4 o'clock sharp. After that you'll be measured for your uniforms. The everyday dress should be readily available but you may have to wait some time for your dress uniform.'

Steve made his way downstairs. At the bottom he turned and shouted. 'You'll be all right then, Mr Byrd?'

'Yes thanks.'

'If you want a noggin later on, drop into the Yeomen Warders' Club near the Cradle Tower, that's near where your car is parked at the moment.'

'I'll do that Mr Johnson, I'll do that.'

5

'Come in, Mr Byrd, come in, take a seat.' Colonel Kilmaster opened the door for his visitor and before closing it told his P.A. to intercept all phone calls.

Colonel Kilmaster sat down at his desk, his bifocals teetering on the end of his nose. He peered at Byrd over the top of them and liked what he saw. Byrd's attention was caught by kestrels swooping round one of the turrets of the White Tower.

'An excellent view, is it not, Superintendent, from where you're sitting?'

'It is. Unusual to see kestrels in the metropolis.'

'Yes. Wonderful, isn't it? Their second year.'

As he spoke a red-coated soldier marched past the window. How Kate would love this, thought Byrd. He could also see the Ravenmaster keeping an eye on the ravens while a party of Japanese with Minoltas in hand recorded this unlikely sight, a bird of prey sitting on his master's hand. Byrd then turned his attention to the Deputy Governor. Not at all the sort of man he'd expected. Colonel Kilmaster was relaxed, laid-back, nonchalant, elegantly dressed in a light grey suit, sporting not a regimental tie, but a bright pink one with diagonal grey stripes.

31

Byrd wasn't fooled, he knew that behind the facade lay an astute mind. Colonel Kilmaster was not a man to be trifled with.

'This assignment, Superintendent, must be the strangest one you've ever been asked to cover in your entire career. Now it's up to me to put you in the picture, but do stop me if. . . .'

Byrd interrupted, 'I'll stop you now, sir, before you go any further. It would be advisable not to address me as Superintendent.'

'Yes, yes of course you're right. Mr Byrd it will be from now on. First of all I'm going to explain why I, *by the pricking of my thumbs*, believe that all is not well within the Tower. The Governor also shares the same feeling, but we don't as yet have enough confidence to discuss such a nebulous matter with the personnel on the ground; the Yeomen, Armoury Guards, Army, and civil servants.'

'Civil servants!'

'Yes, the historians, keepers, librarians, secretaries etc. There may come a time when we have to enlist the help of our Chief Yeoman, or Pierre Gambon, our senior historian, but I'll take advice on that point.'

'I would have thought the Chief Yeoman Warder would have had some inkling that all is not well?'

'He may, but I doubt it. He's a feet-on-the-ground chap, a splendid disciplinarian, but quite wisely distances himself from the younger warders. He could never do the job and be a hail-fellow-well-met. No-one sitting in a top job can expect to be loved, but he is treated with respect and I'm sure that's all he'd ask. He's observant, never misses anything that happens on site during the day, and his verbal reports are masterful. No, what we need is someone who's virtually clairaudient, an invisible man who can pick up the vibes and listen to the gossip, a trained observer like yourself who can melt into the background and suss things out. We're relying on you, Mr Byrd.'

'Perhaps, sir, you could give me some idea what's at the back of your mind?'

The Colonel lit his pipe and puffed away for a few seconds. 'OK, but first of all let me say there are several avenues to pursue, some outlandish and some feasible. For starters there are

King John's Crown Jewels which, supposedly, were lost in The Wash, secondly the Barkstead Treasure, thirdly the possibility of finding Crown Jewels which may not have been destroyed during the Commonwealth, although we know of a great many that were; fourthly documents, which may possibly be Tower archives, turning up at recent auctions in Geneva, and New York, but lastly something a little more tangible, which I'm not quite sure how to deal with. Have a look at this photograph. It's a polaroid taken by one of the Royal Armoury Guards, as this man descended the steps on the north side of the White Tower.'

Byrd examined the photograph which had caught the faintly amused expression on the face of a fair haired man, who looking to his left, was totally unaware of the camera.

'Who is he?'

'A regular caller who has visited the White Tower on at least five occasions over the past three weeks.'

'Is that unusual? I would have expected interested members of the public to return again and again.'

'True, we do have our aficionados, like the young schoolmaster who is so fascinated with our exhibition of oriental armour in the Waterloo Building that he returns every holiday. He also enjoys an ongoing correspondence with Pierre Gambon, but the man you can see on this snapshot fades into the background, never even passing the time of day with the guards. We've no idea how long these visits have been going on, and to what end! He could be out of work, because he arrives at all hours of the day. Sometimes when the gates open and as late as 4.30, only two hours before we close. One can't escape the conclusion that he is casing the joint.'

'Not a face to stick in the memory,' mused Byrd as he took another look at the photograph. 'Looks quite ordinary.'

'So did Crippen, Mr Byrd, and think what he did.'

'May I keep this snap for a couple of days? I'll get it checked against our records.'

'Of course.'

'Tell me, Colonel, where exactly does he go, what does he look at, and who keeps tabs on him?'

'All his time is spent in the White Tower, and on the ramparts. He spends hours gazing at the armour-clad figures, before

33

turning his attention to the sixteenth and seventeenth century weapons. If he is being paid by a gang to look at our security, they're wasting their time, because this place is as secure as Fort Knox.'

'I wouldn't be quite so sure, Colonel. One only has to remember the *Great Train Robbery*.'

'You forget, Mr Byrd, we are the custodians of the largest most comprehensive collection of armoury in the world. Our defences, I can assure you, are impregnable.'

Byrd laughed. 'You haven't told me yet who keeps tabs on him.'

'I have asked Pierre Gambon, who is responsible for the Collection, to take a look at the man, and the guards have orders to contact me when he's on the premises. I don't want him to feel he's being watched or hounded, so this business has gone no further than the staff in the White Tower. Equally, I have not mentioned the more fanciful ideas which have crossed my mind to anyone on the staff.

'That makes sense. Now what were you saying about documents?'

'It's probably all in my mind, which is why I don't want to raise it at this stage. Documents, which relate to personages who have lived in The Tower, princes and so forth, have turned up at auctions in Geneva and New York during the past six months. Needless to say they fetched astronomical prices.'

'Forgeries?'

'I don't know. So far we've not heard or read about the transactions until after the sales, which means we've seen neither the documents nor the provenance.'

'And after the sale?'

'After the sale they were whipped away by American Museums and none of them, as yet, has seen the light of day. However, this time we've had a bit of luck. One of the auctioneers at Christie's rang to let me know that a letter, which may be of interest, is up for auction in their branch in Geneva.'

'Do you know anything about it?'

'We only know it was penned in Amsterdam, in 1625, to Charles I.'

'So where has this letter come from?'

'That's the sixty four dollar question. We'll only know by having sight of the provenance. A catalogue is on its way, and if you agree I'll pass it on to Pierre Gambon, just to get his reaction to the sale, without revealing my disquiet.'

'What's going through your mind, Colonel?'

'Is it possible that here in Her Majesty's Royal Fortress there is a cache of hitherto undiscovered archives?'

The Colonel was puffing away at a dead pipe. He had another go at lighting it. There were now, Byrd noticed, nine matches in the ashtray.

'Colonel, where do you keep the Tower documents?'

'We don't. They're catalogued and stored in the Public Record Office at Kew. At one time the Wakefield Tower, and St John's Chapel, were full of paper from floor to ceiling. Safety regulations these days wouldn't allow such a state of affairs, but the majority of papers were moved to the Public Record Office in the Chancery in the 1850's and eventually to Kew. There's one remote possibility the Governor has aired. During the Second World War a building standing alongside the White Tower which once housed armaments was demolished by the Luftwaffe. In it were all the archives covering the years 1912 to 1945, which means that we now have a gap during a period in which so much happened. The Governor's premise is this. Suppose there were still chests in that building relating to previous centuries which had inadvertently been overlooked during the reorganisation of documents, and suppose a member of a bomb disposal squad, or an A.R.P. warden, or a knowledgeable guard, had recognised their value and lifted them forty years ago? Would someone be prepared to sit on them for forty years?'

'Doubtful,' said Byrd, 'I've never heard of criminals exercising such patience.'

There was a knock at the door.

'If it's coffee you're bringing,' shouted the Colonel, 'you can come in.'

Yeoman Shaw grinned as he placed a tray on the desk and made his exit without saying a word. While the Colonel poured, Byrd went on with the matter in hand.

'These other possibilities you mentioned earlier, what about

35

them?'

'There is a tale about King John's Jewels which has been bandied about for centuries. He did, after all, live here in the White Tower, and no one can prove whether he lost the Crown Jewels in The Wash or whether they were mislaid in The Tower, or even hidden at his behest. To believe any part of the story we'd have to know why.'

There was a comfortable silence between them while each man tried to stretch his mind to accept the picture of a King mislaying his regalia. The Colonel smiled at Byrd. 'There's another possibility, much more feasible, which concerns the Barkstead treasure. This is a story recorded by Samuel Pepys. You should read it up Mr Byrd. It's not in the *Shorter Pepys*, you'll need to pop over to the Guildhall Library, they'll have the complete works, but let me try to put it in a nutshell. Colonel John Barkstead, Governor of the Tower during the Commonwealth, had amassed a fortune, mostly by extortion from prisoners. Barkstead was one of the judges who voted for the execution of Charles I, and not surprisingly had to flee the country when Charles II came to the throne.'

'Lord Sandwich heard rumours of the whereabouts of the £7,000 fortune and called upon Samuel Pepys to make a search. Of the treasure trove, £3,000 was earmarked for the King, £2,000 for Lord Sandwich and £2,000 for the discoverers. In 1662 Pepys – particularly short of the wherewithal – leapt at the chance. He completed three digs with a party of willing workers, but they came away empty handed. The myth, if it is a myth, of the Barkstead fortune has never died. The last official search took place in 1958, but I have a feeling that pursuing this line could be quite productive.'

Byrd couldn't wait to get cracking. Solving crimes committed in 1990 was rewarding but to solve a 200-year-old mystery would be fantastic, or as Kate would say, 'Magic, Daddy, magic.'

'My Byrd, there are many other possibilities which I'd like to discuss, but in five minutes I have a meeting with the Governor which means they'll have to wait. We'd both like to be kept informed of progress but if you come into this office too many times during daylight hours there's bound to be speculation, so I suggest we meet here in this office every two or three days, after the Ceremony of the Keys.'

'Sounds OK to me, sir. My uniform, I gather, won't be ready for a few days.'

'That's good. You'll not be able to go on duty until you're wearing it. That'll give you freedom enough to wander amongst the tourists and learn something about the place before you become officially available. In fact when your uniform arrives make sure it doesn't fit, and send it back. That'll give you a few more days grace.'

'You've an ingenious mind, sir.'

'I wasn't in Intelligence for nothing. We're birds of a feather, Byrd, birds of a feather.'

6

Steve and Brenda Johnson arrived at Heathrow only to discover Harry's plane was ninety minutes behind schedule. Not only was it an hour late leaving Kennedy but it was hampered by easterly gale force winds as it crossed the Atlantic. Neither of them minded the long wait. Steve became as engrossed as an eleven year old, and spent the time plane spotting.

Brenda wandered round looking and listening to the travellers, envying them their journeys to exotic places she'd never see.

Steve had been stationed in Germany which made it easy for them to take their holidays in Europe. It had been cheap and easy to throw everything into the car and go where the mood took them, but the mood had always taken them to Italy, which they adored. Brenda sighed as she read the place names on the departure board. Bali, Singapore, Sri Lanka, what were they really like?

By 12.30 they were ready for a meal.

'What about Harry,' asked Brenda, 'won't he want to eat?'

'No, of course not. They feed them like turkey cocks on planes, all airlines do.' Steve had never seen the boxes of plastic food

38

which were all that most airlines could come up with. Brenda didn't argue. She was hungry. Steve waited until they were at the coffee stage before tackling Brenda about the guest room. He had to discuss it otherwise she might ruin all his plans.

'What bugging you, Steve?' asked Brenda, as she watched him drumming his fingers on the table.

'Nothing . . . nothing that can't be solved.'

She didn't help him.

'Brenda . . . Brenda . . . I want you to promise me that you'll keep quiet about Harry's room. I don't want you shouting your mouth off about imaginary ghosts.'

'There's no point in keeping quiet,' she said sullenly. 'He'll see them for himself.'

'Don't be daft, Brenda, I've told you before it's all in your mind, and I want Harry to have a damn good holiday,'

'So what! I can read you like a crystal ball, Steve. It's another of your sprats to catch a bloody mackerel.'

'All right, so I want to visit the States, and no doubt if I hit it off with this cousin of mine . . .'

'Second cousin.'

'. . . I'll be invited over. Now I want you to promise that you'll say nothing.'

'If that's what you want.' She sniffed and put another lump of sugar in her coffee.

After lunch they joined a host of people standing in front of the arrivals board. As the news flashed on to the screen that *Flight PA062*, from New York had landed and baggage was now in the hall the crowd moved like sheep to an exit at the far end of the massive concourse.

'There's no need to rush,' said Steve, 'sometimes it takes ages for the baggage to go through customs.'

Brenda wondered how he knew, but she didn't argue. Arguing with Steve was a pastime she no longer enjoyed. The first travellers trickled through looking weary and travel-worn.

'They've come through the green channel, that's why they're first,' said Steve.

'Why is it you know so much?' asked Brenda.

Steve didn't answer. He was concentrating on a distant figure in a stetson.

'There he is, there's Harry in the cowboy hat,' shouted Steve as he waved.

The stranger, pushing a trolley, returned the greeting by waving his hat.

Steve felt elated. He'd been planning this for years. Phase I completed. He dashed to the gate, pulled Harry through it, and ushered him towards Brenda. They all shook hands and stared at each other.

'You've made it, you've made it,' said Steve, 'after all this time.'

'Yes, I've made it,' said Harry, 'after a god damn lousy flight, I'm actually here.'

In those few seconds Steve realised Harry was no push-over. He'd have to tread carefully.

'OK folks, where's the car?'

'Car! Oh, we didn't come by car. Much easier on the tube. Takes us home nearly to our front door, so to speak. Straight through Central London and no mucking about.'

'And no parking to pay,' said Brenda. Steve shut her up with a look.

'We've got your ticket,' said Steve as he produced it.

Harry looked at Brenda and wondered why she wasn't involved in Steve's fanfare of welcome.

'OK, you lead on, I'll follow.'

Steve pushed the trolley with Harry alongside him. They set off at speed.

Brenda didn't know why, but she was uneasy. This stranger, this long-lost cousin of Steve's, would be living with them for a *month*. She'd been thinking about it for days. I'll see him at breakfast, lunch and supper. We'll all be sharing one bathroom, a bit difficult when the only loo is in there. She'd tried to talk Steve into getting another one put in, but he wouldn't approach Admin. Their house was large enough to accommodate half a dozen loos, and lose them, but Steve was adamant.

'I won't have the buggers in here. They're not going to mess about with this building. In two years time when we've gone they can do what they like with the place.'

Perhaps they should have thought more deeply about their visitor? Brenda could see herself tied to the house for the next month, running after the two of them, doing Harry's washing and ironing, preparing meals, washing up, cleaning, which was difficult in their old Tudor house, and having to give up her dressmaking classes on Tuesday and Thursday afternoons. Brenda could remember her grandmother saying, 'Visitors are like fish, they go off after three days.' Steve and Harry were way ahead of her. She couldn't keep up their pace in her high heels. Should have worn my sandals, she told herself. She noticed people staring at Harry's stetson and grinning. Brenda didn't feel like grinning about anything. Wonder what we'll do with him for a month? The Tower will keep him occupied for two or three days, then what? We'll have to pack him off to Hampton Court Palace, St Paul's, Madame Tussauds and Westminster Abbey. Canterbury would be better still, far enough to get him out of my hair for a whole day.

'Come on, Brenda,' Steve was shouting, 'quickly, quickly, the train's in.' The two men stepped aboard, and by the time Brenda arrived they were comfortably seated, next to each other. She found herself a seat further up the carriage, sat down and breathed a sigh of relief. The callouses on the bottom of her feet were burning something rotten. It's my own fault, she thought, I missed my last appointment at the chiropodist. From where she was sitting she could see them talk, talk, talk. About what? Their grandfathers, and their great grandfathers, their uncles and their great uncles. Funny thing about families. A stranger arrives from out of the blue and because he happens to share the same great grandfather there has to be a bond. Blood isn't thicker than water, mused Brenda. Anyone who's lived in the Tower as long as I have knows all about blood relations. I know what brother can do to brother, sister to sister, uncle to nephew, nephew to uncle and cousin to cousin.

Harry blinked as he emerged into the bright sunlight and saw The Tower of London for the first time. It was splendid, four square and splendid. He stood by the railings gazing at the splendour of England, the place where, since the Norman Conquest, history

41

had been made. A magnificent fortress unspoilt through the centuries.

'Come on, Harry,' said Steve, 'Let's get home and dump these cases. You'll have plenty of time to stand and stare.' Harry followed his hosts through the Middle and Byward Towers, along Water Street to Traitor's Gate, under the Bloody Tower, and up a few steps. They stopped at the top while Steve undid a chain giving them access to the south side of Tower Green. A guardsman stood on duty outside a magnificent Tudor house.

'This is the Governor's residence,' said Steve as they passed Queen's House. 'Next is the Deputy Governor's Office, and this is our house.' Harry didn't have to be told; the bright shining number plate said it all.

Brenda unlocked the front door. The two men followed her in and dumped the suitcases in the sitting room.

'Make yourself at home,' said Brenda, 'I'll put the kettle on.'

Harry didn't sit down. He stood staring in astonishment at the walls and ceiling. All was perfection on the outside but the inside was horrendous! Why did they do it? Every inch of the room was panelled, but not in dark oak as he'd imagined. A barbarian had been let loose with a pot of paint, not just a pot, buckets of paint. The Tudor panels were alternately covered in garish orange and green.

'Have you the same colour scheme throughout?' he gasped.

'Yes,' said Steve, unaware of his guest's pain. 'It was far too dark and depressing when we arrived, and as the Tudors liked bright colours we decided to go to town. Not only that,' Steve whispered, keeping an eye on the kitchen door, 'one of the warders told Brenda he'd seen the ghost of Lady Jane Grey coming out of the house. He was having her on, of course. I don't believe any of that rubbish, but she insisted on brightening the place up.'

'So you exorcised the ghosts with a pot of paint!'

'Never looked at it that way, but you could be right,' laughed Steve. Harry sat down feeling winded and sea sick. Was it those awful colours or was it jet lag catching up with him?

Brenda gave them tea and left them to it. Harry concentrated on the view across the Green, and by pushing the armchair right up to the window there was no need to look at the walls.

'We'll be having supper early tonight', said Steve, 'because Brenda has a dress rehearsal.'

'Where?'

'Here in the Tower. In the Education Centre, which we'll show you tomorrow.'

'What's she doing?'

'The lighting for *Blithe Spirit*.'

'Early Coward! Isn't that a bit old fashioned?'

'She says it's very funny. Imaginary ghosts on stage don't worry her, but the house is a very different matter. She's for ever imagining things.'

'Like what?'

'Chains being dragged across the floor and voices. Always voices.'

'Don't you feel any vibes from the past, Steve?'

'No, not a thing. It's all in the mind. Come on Harry, let's take your cases upstairs.'

Harry followed him up two flights of stairs into a large room which overlooked the Green.

'The bathroom's on the floor below, and there's plenty of hot water morning and evening, but we turn it off during the day. I'm afraid there's no shower. Isn't that what you Americans prefer?'

'Mostly, but I'll enjoy a bath for a change, give me a chance to do some reading.'

'There's only one loo,' said Steve quickly, 'and it's in the bathroom.'

'Oh! OK, I've got the point. No reading.'

Harry looked up at the panelled ceiling. 'What's above?'

'Only the attic, nothing there except the television aerial, and a fair bit of junk. Take a look any time you want.'

Supper was a pleasant affair. Brenda had really made an effort. Home made carrot soup, beef goulash and peach melba washed down with a bottle of Spanish red.

'Thanks for a splendid meal, Brenda.'

'It won't always be like this, Harry, but it's special, to welcome you.' Brenda smiled at him. At last, he thought, she's relaxing.

'When you've lived on your own as long as I have it's an unbelievable pleasure to sit down and be waited on in style.'

'How long is is it, Harry, since Judy's death?'

'Ten years.'

'Oh, I thought it was only seven,' said Brenda.

Harry covered his eyes and forehead with both hands. 'Yes, yes, you're right, it just feels like ten, and I haven't got used to talking about it, yet.'

'Oh, I'm sorry, Harry, I didn't mean to upset you. It was stupid of me to mention it.' Brenda didn't know what else to say, but she couldn't understand how one could go on grieving for seven years? Even her mother had come to terms with her father's death after a couple of years.

'Have some coffee, Harry, before I go, it'll help to settle you.'

'Don't bother with coffee, love,' said Steve, 'I'll do the washing up and make the coffee.'

'And I'm an expert with a teacloth,' said Harry, waving his napkin in the air. That broke the tension and they all laughed.

The two men cleared up, and then sat down in the sitting room with their coffee.

'Now', said Steve, 'we'll have something a bit stronger.'

'Only a drop for me, Steve, I'm not really a drinker.'

Steve crossed, purposefully, to the oak panelling on the left of the fireplace. He pressed his thumb firmly on the centre of a rose carved in relief, and to Harry's utter amazement the door of a vast cupboard swung open. Steve had barely time to remove the whisky and glasses before Harry jumped to his feet, rushed across the room and slammed the door shut. He too put pressure on the centre of an orange rose, and again the door opened.

'That's amazing, bloody amazing! A hidden cupboard.'

'The house is full of them. Camouflaged doors, not only to cupboards but to rooms. When we've had a noggin I'll show you a thing or two.'

Harry sipped while his cousin drank. Steve was getting mellower by the minute.

'How long have you lived here, Steve?'

'Nearly twenty years.'

'And did the previous tenants know about these cupboards?'

'Oh yes. They knew about some of them, the one in this room, and the ones in the bedrooms on the first floor which are so big they serve as wardrobes, but you come into the kitchen-diner and I'll show you something no other living person, apart from me, has ever seen.'

Steve pushed the table and chairs to one side. 'You see this armoire? Well, I'm positive it's been here since Tudor times without being moved, and the only reason I shifted it was to paint the panels behind, not all of them mark you, only the ones that show.'

Harry gave Steve a hand and as they eased the armoire into the room he could see the painted edges bordering the magnificent oak panelling untouched since the sixteenth century.

'All this,' said Steve, 'was disgusting, it was no wonder we were plagued with spiders. The panelling and back of the cupboard were covered in centuries of cobwebs, not to mention dust. I lost no time in hoovering the lot before washing it down prior to painting. As I cleaned the bottom panel there was an ominous click, but I was too late to save myself. I had exerted so much pressure in cleaning the panel that I fell headlong into the darkness beyond. I'll swear the shock caused my heart to stop for a second. As it was I lay winded and petrified until I came to my senses and realised my good fortune. There were three things to be done, and quickly. First of all I polished the floor beneath the armoire to make it relatively easy to move, then I hurriedly painted the panels which showed before dashing round to the car to find a torch. Fortunately Brenda was out at her amateur dramatics which gave me all the time I needed.'

Steve opened the armoire, took out a hefty torch, then slid his hand down to the bottom of the oak panelling. There was a slight click as the door opened.

'Christ!' said Harry as he peered into the abyss. 'There are some steps there.'

'Do you want to take a look?'

'Of course.'

45

'Bolt the front door, then no one can surprise us.'

'But it's on a yale.'

'What I mean is, Brenda mustn't see this, frighten her to death.'

'You mean, she doesn't know?'

'No, she'd have the screaming habdabs and go telling everybody. I don't want the historians and the architects and the archeologists rampaging through my house. In any case I'm carrying out some research. Haven't been wasting my time either.'

'But why are you telling me?'

'Because I need help to decipher one or two things, and you said in your letters that you've developed an interest in history. Not only that, I thought, perhaps, you could ask that Professor chap you go fishing with to translate an odd thing or two.'

Despite the warmth of the June night Harry could feel cold air emanating from the tunnel. He followed Steve down stone steps until they were standing on a paved floor. The tunnel was wider than he'd expected, about fifteen feet across, not much height but high enough, thought Harry, for the Tudors and their forebears. He felt uneasy, the stillness, the unaccustomed total silence, was unnerving. They were alone and yet he felt the presence of others. If he stretched out he could touch them. Touch those who'd worked and lived and, maybe, died down here. Slowly he followed the light of Steve's torch which illuminated unexpected cavities, and arrow slits long since covered by an outside wall providing no visibility whatsoever. Steve stopped and pointed to the left. 'All that area is under Queen's House but there doesn't appear to be any access from the house itself. I've had a good look round on the rare occasions when I've done a stint in the Colonel's Office.'

To the right he spotlighted two small Norman arches. 'One is filled in with stone, but you can just about get through the other one on all fours. It's about four foot wide and three foot high. Can't for the life of me think what its function was.'

'Can we go through?'

'Yes. Are you game, Harry?'

'Of course.'

There was a strange musty smell as well as a stronger, more pungent aroma which Harry couldn't identify.

'The floor's uneven so careful how you go. Just follow me,' said Steve.

As Harry crawled through he felt something run across his hand.

'Christ! There are spiders here, Steve, the size of crabs.'

'Don't worry, Harry, you'll get used to them.'

They walked a few yards in silence before Steve stopped.

'Take a look at that.' He shone the torch on a large pile of peculiarly shaped iron tools which were all stacked on a large iron slab.

'Do you know what they are, Harry?'

'Haven't the faintest, at a guess I'd say they're medieval potato mashers.'

'Not a bad guess. They are dies, blank discs were inserted between them and coins hammered out, that's how the coinage of the realm was produced until the middle of the seventeenth century.'

'Good God man, they must be worth a fortune.'

'Might be.' Steve was offhand. 'But something far more important, Harry; you are actually standing on the site of the Royal Mint.'

Harry shivered, not with fear, but with excitement. He was standing where the Tudors had stood. At six o'clock that morning he'd boarded the plane at Kennedy, and now only twelve hours later he was standing beneath the most famous fortress in the world, in a tunnel which only two living men had ever seen. Harry thought again about the presses. Steve's attitude worried him. He had got it all wrong. Didn't he know those artefacts were valuable, and should be preserved?

'Steve, those dies should be in a museum.'

'Not yet, Harry, not yet. There's time enough for that. I've found something much more valuable. I've struck gold.'

'What! Gold? You mean gold coins?'

'Yes, only a few so far, but I'm winning.'

Steve bent down and from behind a large stone picked up his new toy.

'See this, Harry, it's a metal detector. Worth its weight in gold. I've got a lot more digging to do, but it's making life easier for me. I must show you the few coins I've found when we get back. It's the wording round the edges I want translating.'

Steve totally unaware of Harry's mixed emotions moved into the depths of the tunnel.

'We're now directly under the padre's house. Nice chap. He lives right by the chapel. No excuse for him being late for work.' Steve laughed at his own little joke.

'Steve, you can't keep those coins. Don't they belong to the Queen?'

'Yes, of course they do, but in this country anyone who unearths hidden treasure is entitled to a handsome share-out. I must make sure I do the digging and find the coins before any of those knowledgeable buggers poke their noses in and dirty their paws. There'd be no percentage for me if they do the work and come up with the goods. You see that, don't you Harry?'

Steve's American cousin didn't answer.

'It's history, Harry. This was the only mint in the country allowed to strike gold coins.'

'When did the mint close down?'

'It has never closed down, just moved a couple of times. First to a new building on Tower Hill in 1811, and more recently a more permanent home in South Wales.'

Harry caught a glimpse of something fairly solid in the half light.

'What's that over there?'

'Chests, just old chests.'

'What's in them?'

'One is empty and the other's full of papers. Haven't had time to go through it yet.'

'Well let's do it now, man.'

'No, Harry, it'll take too long.'

'But I must look.'

'Tomorrow, Harry, tomorrow. We'd better get back, leave everything shipshape and tidy ourselves.'

When Brenda arrived home she found the two men arguing about the merits of the Duke of Monmouth.

'He was like his father, only worse,' said Steve. 'All that womanising, gambling, horse racing, mad on sport and lavish to the point of stupidity with his money—'

'Generous', interrupted Harry, 'and good looking too, even better looking than his father, so no wonder women fell for him and men were ready to die for him.'

Brenda looked surprised. 'I didn't know you were a historian, Harry.'

'It's my hobby and I do know a little about Monmouth because the Professor's recently taken it into his head to do some research on the guy. An article about the rebellion got him going, so any gem I can pick up will be useful to him. He has this idea, you see, that James, Duke of Monmouth, was the rightful heir to the throne.'

'That's nonsense,' said Steve getting irritated. 'He was the eldest of Charles II's thirteen illegitimate children. You tell me how a bastard can be heir to the throne.'

'The Professor believes Charles married a Lucy Walters somewhere in Belgium, which would make Monmouth the legitimate heir.'

'So prove it,' said Steve.

'That's what he intends to do.'

Steve laughed, 'We get an awful lot of nutters here trying to prove all sorts of things, all writing theses on this or that, producing books or pamphlets, all sitting in their studies dreaming up impossible theories, it's a regular cottage industry. Take it from me, Monmouth was a bastard, born the wrong side of the blanket, but you'd better talk to Pierre Gambon, our senior historian, he'll soon put you right.

'Steve,' said Harry placidly, 'maybe I will.'

Brenda sighed. She was ready for bed.

'How did the rehearsal go, love?'

'Thought you were never going to ask. Not bad, not bad, I suppose, but it would have been a great deal better if Ruth didn't know in the first act she was going to be a ghost in the second.'

'But she doesn't know,' said Harry. 'She's not the clairvoyant.'

'I know,' said Brenda, 'so does everyone else in the cast, but Barney's wife Sylvia is playing Ruth and she always makes a meal of everything, a real exhibitionist. She signals the fact, and she'll have the audience believing she foresees the car accident which kills her. Spoils the play for me it does.'

Harry yawned, he couldn't help himself.

'Oh, am I boring you?' asked Brenda.

'No, of course you're not, do forgive me, but I'm afraid it was the early start this morning and jet lag catching up with me. I'd better get to bed if you'll excuse me?'

'You do that,' said Steve, 'see you in the morning.'

Brenda waited until the door was closed.

'They must be better educated in America. Fancy a caretaker being interested in history.'

'I'm not surprised, love. He said in his letters history was his hobby, after all something must have rubbed off after thirty years in a University.'

'Well, you historians will have to dine on steak and kidney pies out of the freezer tomorrow night, because I'm busy tomorrow. Chiropodist and shopping in the morning, dressmaking classes in the afternoon, and a second dress rehearsal in the evening.'

'All right, that's no skin off my nose.'

'That makes a change. You usually complain.'

'Having a guest makes a lot of extra work, and I don't want you to stop doing the things you are doing. Harry and I'll cope. Don't forget he's lived on his own for a long time.'

'Seven years,' said Brenda, 'which feels like ten. Odd that!'

7

The Superintendent was up early, too early. He'd have to do something about covering the windows. Getting up at 4.30 a.m. was no good to man or beast. He needed to be alert all through the day and knew only too well how bad tempered he'd be with less than his six hours sleep.

For once his day had no pattern, he was free to go where the mood took him. See the Crown Jewels, talk to Pierre Gambon, visit the Chaplain, join one of the conducted tours, sit for a blessed few minutes in the quiet of St Peter's Ad Vincula, take a look at any work being carried out on the fabric of the building, and become acclimatised to the location in the shortest possible time. The problem, thought Byrd, is my abysmal ignorance, which a week's reading has highlighted only too clearly. The Tower of London is a subject for life and yet here I am hoping to see this operation through in a month. Impossible, unless I get some sleep. A word with Steve Johnson about the lack of curtains might help. He looked in the box of groceries they'd left for him. A few eggs, but he never ate a cooked breakfast. A small loaf of bread, some butter, Oxford Marmalade, but no cereal. Well, toast it had to be, two pieces and a mug of powdered coffee. It was terrible stuff, he'd stick to tea in future.

Byrd sauntered down Mint Street towards the Byward Tower, and stood under the murder holes from where he could see the vast queue stretching back along the rails on the far side of the moat. As the clock struck 9.30 the gates opened and in they streamed giving up their tickets to the Yeoman Warder on duty at the Middle Tower, and then stopping at a table where the guards examined their bags and cameras. In less than half an hour there were several hundred tourists within the most famous medieval fortress in the world. The Japanese stuck together in small groups, all with their cameras at the ready, the orderly Germans hanging on to every word their guide uttered, and a group of French schoolchildren, far more interested in the building than in what their poor teacher was saying, rushed off in all directions. The Americans, like the Japanese, were taking enough photographs to fill a library of scrap albums.

5 Tower Green was the Superintendent's next objective. He rang the bell three times and was about to give up when he heard movement. The bolt was drawn back, the mortise turned and the door opened, but not by Steve Johnson. A tall stranger stood there, a man nearly his own height, puffing slightly and looking slightly disconcerted.

'Hallo there', said Byrd, 'you look surprised to see me.'

'I wasn't expecting anyone, that's why.'

'I was hoping to have a few words with Mr Johnson.'

'I'm Mr Johnson', said the stranger with a distinct American accent, 'but not the one you want. Why don't you come in for a moment, give me time to find a bit of paper, and I'll leave a message for my cousin?'

'That'll be most helpful.' Byrd was inside and in the sitting room before the American had had time to draw breath. The expression on Byrd's face made Harry roar with laughter.

'It's the decor, isn't it? Taken you by surprise hasn't it? All it does for me is make me feel sea-sick.'

Byrd stood for a moment, bereft of words. He looked at the panels, he looked at the ceiling.

'They can't treat an ancient building in this manner. It's desecration.' Harry felt an explanation was needed.

'Brenda, my cousin's wife, who is shit scared of ghosts, found the dark oak Tudor beams too dismal and depressing, so my cousin, who has no taste whatsoever, enlivened the place with this less than imaginative decor.'

'How could anyone do it?'

'Don't ask me, I've only been here a day, and I know my time won't be spent in this room. Forgive my uncousinly remark Mr. . . .'

'Byrd, James Byrd.'

'Well Mr Byrd, now you've got over the shock, what's your message?'

'I'm a fledgling Yeoman Warder, so new that I'm still waiting for my uniform, but your cousin said, if there were any problems, to get in touch with him. I do have one slight problem, which he or his wife may be able to solve. I'm lodged in one of the casemates and until my wife and daughter join me I'm pigging it in a most basic manner, which doesn't worry me unduly, except for one thing, a window with neither shutters nor curtains which is why I woke this morning at the ungodly hour of 4.30. All I need is something to drape across the window.'

'4.30 a.m. is the best time in the day,' said Harry, 'the time to go fishing.'

'You're an early morning fisherman then?

'Yes, when I get the chance.'

'And you fish somewhere in the States, I guess?'

'Yes from my, at least, from my prof's cabin in the Adirondak Mountains.'

'Never heard of them. Where are they?'

'Upstate New York, almost in Canada.'

'You said, "your prof". I take it you work in a college.'

'Yes, Princeton University. I'm a janitor, I mean I was a janitor in the History Faculty. Just retired, as a matter of fact, taking a few weeks holiday here and then back to the States to help out on my brother-in-law's ranch. However, Mr Byrd, my life's history's not helping you with your problem. I'll leave a note for Brenda, she's out shopping right now.'

'Thanks for your help.' The two men shook hands.

'Be seeing you around,' said Harry.

Byrd made his way down to the Byward Tower to join a sightseeing party, but couldn't put Harry Johnson out of his mind. There was something wrong. The man didn't look like a caretaker, sound like a caretaker, or behave like one. On the other hand it was a much more open society in the States. There weren't the divisions. Johnson who hadn't mentioned a wife, had the appearance of a bachelor and the attitude of a man who was self-sufficient. Then Byrd mentally kicked himself. They'd shaken hands. The American had large capable hands, but they were soft, too well-cared-for, for someone used to hard manual graft. The Superintendent changed his mind and returned to the Green. He stood by the site of the scaffold, the place where seven people, two men and five women had been beheaded. Of the women, three had been young Queens. First Anne Boleyn, three years a Queen, followed six years later by her cousin Catherine Howard, and then Lady Jane Grey, thrust into a position of power by her scheming father-in-law. It was all fresh in the Superintendent's mind. His bedtime reading for the past week. Anne Boleyn, accused of adultery by a husband who had tired of her, and who desperately craved a son, and Catherine Howard – more foolish than sinful – who'd committed improprieties before and maybe after marriage. The rapacious Henry's final atrocity was the horrific execution of the seventy-year-old Countess Salisbury, last of the Plantagenets. The old lady was commanded to lay her head on the block. She adamantly refused saying she was no traitor and remained standing, turning her head this way and that, and telling the executioner he could have her head, if he could get it off. The poor blundering fellow carried out his orders and in the process hacked her head and shoulders to pieces. Round this unhappy place, thought Byrd, there will always be a crowd.

He stood amidst the throng, not gazing at the plaque, but keeping an eye on 5 Tower Green waiting for Harry Johnson to emerge.

The crowd around him changed, the Yeoman on duty keeping an eye on The Green changed, the ravens changed, and so too

54

did the guards. The crowds gathering round The Green to see the Changing of the Guard prevented him from having a clear view of number 5. Byrd quickly found a new vantage point at the top of the steps leading down to the Beauchamp Tower. The Coldstream Guards marched past him and stood to attention immediately outside Steve Johnson's house.

The American locked his cases, put them back in the capacious wardrobe and pocketed the keys. He'd enjoyed the morning, as much as he'd enjoyed anything for years. As he did so he heard a bugle call and from his bedroom window saw a platoon of Guards on the opposite side of The Green, standing at ease waiting to take over duties from another platoon standing immediately beneath the window. It was evocative, a happening he'd never expected to see. It brought back vivid memories of the box of Coldstream Guards he'd been given for Christmas as a boy. He remembered too how he'd refused to let his cousins touch them or assemble them for battle. It was going to be difficult to drag himself away from the place, difficult to explain, but he'd work something out. Two or three days would be enough.

He'd hire a car and go north. But where? Somewhere in the recesses of his mind he remembered reading about an ancient town, somewhere in Shropshire, built by Alfred the Great's daughter, a name like bridge . . . bridge . . . Bridgnorth, yes that was it. They'd never find him there. He'd think of an excuse, but first of all he needed a car. Hertz would do, they accepted American Express. Easy enough to hire a car over the phone, but not wise to make the reservation over an internal line.

He tidied the bedroom. More bugle calls as the guards marched off. Downstairs to tidy up the kitchen and dining room. Unbolt the front door, unlock the mortise, make sure he'd got the spare key Brenda had given him and his visitor's pass. As he opened the door the heat of a relentless sun blazed down on him, too hot without a hat, he'd have to borrow the stetson he'd given Steve. A cousin's prerogative.

Byrd saw him cross The Green and descend the steps near the Bloody Tower. The Superintendent moved quickly, for he had twice the ground to cover. Down the steps, through the arch under the Bloody Tower, and right into Water Street. It was easy. The stetson was as prominent as a beacon. Under the Byward and Middle Towers and out through the gates. The tall American joined the queue outside the telephone box. Byrd took evasive action by slipping into the souvenir shop. The first thing he noticed were teddy bears dressed as yeomen warders. He'd buy one for Kate, but not until he'd finished the job. The martial music reverberating round the shop was the accompaniment to a video film of The Tower on display at the far end. Just the sort of thing for Stephanie, background for all those historical romances she read.

Through the glass door he saw Harry Johnson enter the box, pick up the phone, and feed his coins into the slot. That was quick, thought Byrd, for someone who's only been in England a day and hasn't used a call-box before. No hesitation and the right coins! Wonder who he's ringing? Pity he didn't know the number of the box otherwise he could have buzzed Georgina and asked her to run a trace on it. There was a shrill scream as a small boy who'd evaded his mother's clutches ran towards the entrance and fell flat on his face. A tourist bent down to pick up the child, a man whose face was familiar, a man whose purpose was unclear, an man who spent hours and hours in the Royal Armouries seemingly gazing at armour. The mother dashed up and grabbed the child, thanked the stranger who waved away her thanks and walked purposefully towards the entrance where he surrendered his ticket, and was through the security check in seconds. There was no point in following him, he knew where to find him. First things first. Harry Johnson finished his call, held open the door for the next caller, strolled back through the gates, past the souvenir shop and straight down to the wharf. Byrd followed him.

'Thinking of taking a conducted tour, Mr Johnson?'

'Not yet awhile. There's too much to see in The Tower first.'

They both gazed at a large ship berthed on the south side of the Thames.

'What sort of vessel is she?' asked Harry.

'A town class cruiser, HMS Belfast, used during the last war.

So, you're taking a constitutional along the wharf before you find your bearings in The Tower?'

'Yes, and no,' laughed Harry. 'Came out to make a phone call. Don't like to take advantage of my cousin's hospitality.'

'That's a gentlemanly attitude', said Byrd thinking he'd made a right ass of himself. How could an American visitor possibly be involved in any skulduggery at The Tower?

'Have you been to England before?'

'This is my first visit to The Tower. Steve and I are only distantly related, second cousins, and we're attempting to catch up on our family history. Steve has been urging me to come over for the past two years, but to tell you the truth there's so much to see in The States that I wouldn't have come except for Steve's continued pressure. Letters practically every month, hard to ignore.'

'And now you're here?'

'Should have done it before. There's nothing like the real thing. Reading about it isn't the same. 1500 years of history here in this fantastic concentric fortress.'

'1500! But the Normans didn't arrive until 1066.'

'Yes, Mr Byrd, everyone knows that, but the Romans were here first and on this site. Witness the Roman walls still standing on the south and east of the White Tower.'

'You put me to shame Mr Johnson. You should be doing my job. Yeomen are expected to know everything there is to know about The Tower, and I have a long way to go.'

They walked slowly along the wharf past the cannons towards the entrance over the drawbridge near St Thomas's Tower. They bypassed the queue and produced their passes, but were prevented from going any further by a group of German students who stood laughing and gazing down into the waterless moat at a small grave.

'Es ist ein . . . Grabe,' yelled one.

'Natürlich. Es ist für die Raben,' shrieked another.

'Kannst du die Namen lesen, Helmut?'

It was a long time since the Superintendent had last spoken German, in fact not since his days as a student at Lampeter. He had no difficulty, with his 20.20 vision, in deciphering and pronouncing the names of the deceased ravens, which he did slowly and clearly. The students cheered him and with many dankes let the two men pass.

'You're a man of many parts, Mr Byrd,' said Harry Johnson. 'I can see you'll be an asset here for the German visitors.' Byrd forebore to mention that his French was even better, he spoke it like a native.

They parted company at the Wardrobe Tower, now only a ruin, Harry to the Martin Tower and Byrd to take a look at the White Tower. It was conveniently full of people who weren't in the business of being rushed. They took their time in St John's Chapel which, Byrd later discovered, is the oldest Norman ecclesiastical building in London. Manoeuvring his way through a party of Japanese, who were gazing in awe at the Tudor and Stuart royal armours, proved to be something of an obstacle course, especially through a battery of clicking, flashing cameras. As soon as he had the fair haired man in his sights he realised the Japanese were too short to hide him from view. A tall, broad-shouldered, bearded man looking like a brigand is unforgettable, so Stephanie kept telling him, but there was no need for evasive action, his quarry was engrossed in the immaculately designed and made-to-measure armour.

The Superintendent stood watching for some time and was about to move away when the young man, who he reckoned could be no more than twenty six or seven, eased a notebook and pencil out of his pocket. Here we go, thought Byrd, now he's making a note of the exits, the number of guards and the volume of people. He's clever too, making it look as though he's drawing Henry VIII's armour. One of the guards had also observed the scribe who appeared to be making a close study of a horse caparisoned in armour which matched that of his royal rider. The guard, turning his back on the milling crowd, spoke quietly into his hand set. Beautifully done, thought Byrd. Now the Colonel knows, and the situation's under control, I can get on with my next ploy.

Taking the short cut through the Flint Tower, he walked past his own lodging in the Casemates and stopped outside 2A, where restoration was being carried out. Four workmen had stopped for lunch and were sitting on the ground alongside their Transit van eating sandwiches and imbibing whatever was in their thermos flasks. They seemed totally occupied, which gave him a chance to sneak inside. The walls badly needed repointing and most of the centuries-old floorboards had been taken up. Many of the joists were rotten, but it was impossible to guess at the depth beneath the joists without using a torch. There were a lot of cables around and no doubt one of them carried a lamp to enable the men to see what they were doing. And what were they doing? Making it habitable for another yeoman, or was it to be used as additional storage space? He must see the Colonel tonight and find out what was going on.

Byrd stepped back carefully as he opened the door. Through the unglazed window the men's raucous laughter and their comments as they passed round a copy of *The Sun* were clearly audible.

'Wish my old woman had a mouth like that.'

'It's her tits I like,' said another.

'I wouldn't say no to a weekend in Paris with 'er.'

The Superintendent quietly turned the handle and opened the door. That was as far as he got.

'What the hell do you think you're doing in there, matey?'

Byrd stared down at a fair-haired man no more than 5'6" tall, whose attentions were anything but friendly.

'Taking a look, just taking a look. I'm interested in restoration.'

'Tell that to your grandmother.' The newcomer pushed Byrd dangerously close to one of the rotten joists.

'You're not allowed in here, matey. This 'ere is private. No tourists, no sightseers, no nothing, but you're a snooper ain't yer?'

The Superintendent shoved the belligerent fair-haired man out through the open door. 'Keep your hands off me. I'm doing what I've been told to do by the Colonel.'

'Oh, and what's that?'

'I'm a new yeoman, and while I'm waiting for my uniform I've been told to utilise my time by looking at everything.'

The man stood his ground. 'Where's your credentials then?'

Byrd took his pass out of his back trouser pocket and handed it to him.

The fair haired man peered at it for some time. 'How do I know this is real?'

'What the hell are you talking about?'

'You could have forged this.'

'You're a nut case,' said Byrd, 'and you'd better give me your name, and that of your firm, and come along with me to see the Colonel.'

The bombast and the aggression evaporated.

'All right matey, sorry I got it wrong, but you can't be too careful in this place.'

The four workmen had stopped laughing, they were all on their feet in front of the Transit, all watchful and waiting. They eyed him in silence as he made his way up Mint Street back to his lodging. He could feel their eyes on him. What were they so worried about? Once inside he called Sergeant Mayhew. She answered immediately.

'Yes?'

'Get on to bossman. Tell him I'll be there at midnight.'

Georgina replaced the phone. Terse bugger, but she sensed aggravation and wondered why?

He spent the afternoon in The Tower library. The Colonel had been mistaken, there was a complete Pepys which the librarian put at his disposal. She'd also found several other articles on the Barkstead treasure, but the clearest story was the one she'd written herself. At 4 o'clock she brought him a cup of tea.

'You're certainly doing your homework, but most newcomers begin with the White Tower.' She sat down, and smiled at Byrd.

'Hidden trove has always fascinated me, ever since I read *Treasure Island* as a kid, but what I can't understand is why nothing has ever been found in The White Tower.'

'I am quite sure we know every nook and cranny, it is, of course, where we display the armoury. We know, for instance, that there were rails between the wharf and the White Tower to enable ammunition and armaments to be loaded on to ships docked in the wharf, but it's highly unlikely that treasure was hidden in such an accessible place.'

'If you were a treasure seeker, Miss Burne-Jones, where would you begin?' She mused for a few moments. 'I'd go back to the Plantagenets, think about the amazing amount of building Edward I achieved. I've often tried to put myself in his place. They were a devoutly religious people, but I have always thought that the small Chapel Royal, St Peter's Ad Vincula, would have been easy to surround, and to murder everyone inside. For the safety of my courtiers and servants who worshipped there I would have built a tunnel under the Chapel to link up with other tunnels.'

'And where would the others be situated?'

'Below the west side of the outer ward which Edward built. It took him six years to have the moat dug, plenty of time in which to build a tunnel under the casemates in Mint Street. Latterly, the tunnels would have made useful storage space for the Royal Mint.'

'Is that a strong possibility?'

She laughed. 'Let's call it an educated guess, and now, Mr Byrd, I'm going to leave you to your own devices.'

Byrd went on reading until he was booted out at 6.30. He wandered along Water Street and up Mint Street noticing a couple of cars which hadn't been there at lunchtime. Of course, the place was now closed to the public and the residents could park their cars. Byrd was blessed with a remarkable memory. He only had to look closely at a car and the number was instantly recorded in his memory. It's strange, he thought, how some areas of the country have car numbers which are easy to identify, and yet others don't make any sense. He noticed a spotlessly clean metallic silver Astra. A hired car, from Hertz. C2PDQ, pretty damn quick, he said to himself. That's easy to remember.

As he wandered back to his lodging the aggressive foreman came to mind. There was something about his speech which didn't ring true. All the Cockney vowels and intonations were there, but they failed to produce the rich, down-to-earth dialect of an East Ender.

It was too early for dinner at The Tiger Tavern. He'd give it an hour, ring Stephanie first, and then try out his saxophone, see if he could still play it. Kate answered the phone.

'Quick, Mummy, quick, it's Daddy.'

'You talk to Daddy while I dry my hands.' Byrd heard every word.

'When are you coming back, Daddy?'

'Not just yet, darling. I've only been away five days.'

'Mummy says it's like five weeks. We mark it off on the calendar every day.

'Mummy says you'll take me to the zoo, if I'm good.'

'Of course I will. I'll take Mummy too. I don't suppose she's seen an orang-utan recently. We'll go at the weekend.'

Stephanie, who'd picked up the cordless kitchen phone laughed, 'Promises, promises, as usual.'

'We'll make a firm date for the weekend.'

'Saturday, Daddy, it's got to be Saturday.'

'Why?'

'Because it's Louise's birthday on Sunday. She's nine, and she's catching me up.'

'All right, Saturday it is then. Now let me have a few words with Mummy.' There was not much they could say over the open line, but Stephanie was left with no illusions about the length of time it might take to solve the case. She was not pleased. As she replaced the phone Judith came rushing out of the kitchen. 'The zoo, the zoo, the zoo, Mummy.'

'All right, darling, we will go to the zoo, but a hundred to one we'll be on our own,' she said bitterly.

Practising was therapeutic. A blissful half hour during which Byrd concentrated on producing a melodious sound. No worrying about the lack of concrete evidence or the effect of his absence on the family. It was a pity, he thought, that he'd so little music with him, but he'd be heard, and if they were looking for a saxophonist let them come to him. God, he was rusty. *The Triumphal March* from *Aida* sounded like the death rattle of a herd of elephants. Something less ambitious was needed, something like *In the Mood*. Damn! his breathing was atrocious. Try again. That was better, much better. Now sit back, James Byrd, and wait.

News travels fast within the precincts of The Tower. In less than an hour the newest recruit found himself in the Education Centre making music as the audience arrived for the production of *Blithe Spirit*. With all the windows open, on a stultifying June night, the rousing sound of *Sophisticated Lady* reverberated round the ancient walls. I have arrived, thought the Superintendent, faster than I ever expected.

8

'Brenda, don't bother to cook,' said Harry when she arrived home from her dressmaking class. 'I'm hoping you'll let me take you out for a meal. I've booked a table at *The Tiger Tavern* for 6.45. Is that OK?'

Brenda looked pleased. 'Of course it's OK, Harry. Much more fun eating out, and I'm not needed until 7.45 so there's oodles of time.'

'Are you sure an hour's enough?'

'Oh yes, and in any case I can go when I've eaten, and leave you two boys to take all night over your coffee. Now I won't have to feel guilty about not looking after you properly. It's a sweet idea.' Brenda wondered why she'd ever thought of Harry as a drag. He was a really thoughtful man.

At 6.45 the three of them sat down in a corner by the window.

'You sit here, Harry, then you can see the river,' said Brenda, 'and we'll sit either side of you.'

At that time of day service was swift. They all started with a prawn cocktail, Brenda followed it with a lasagne and the two men both chose moussaka. Halfway through the main course,

64

Harry decided to break the news.

'You'll be a little surprised I'm sure, but I've decided to hire a car and go north for a few days, do a bit of reading, a bit of sightseeing.'

Brenda and Steve looked at him in amazement.

'But aren't you happy here?' gasped Steve. He stared at his cousin, trying to fathom why he was doing this. All his carefully laid plans were being shattered.

'Yes, Steve, of course I am, but let Brenda get her play over. It's on for three nights and having a guest to think about is one job too many. I'll be back on Sunday, and as I'd always planned to go north I may as well do it now as later. York where Constantine was crowned; Lichfield, where Dr Johnson lived. I'll go where the mood takes me.'

Brenda perked up at once. 'You are a thoughtful man, a really thoughtful man. It's funny how much you know about England, much more than we do.' Steve wished she'd shut up, putting her big feet in again and not helping his cause. Harry laughed at her but he was well aware of Steve's body language, exuding irritation and disappointment.

Brenda fairly bolted down her chocolate mousse. 'Now boys, I must leave you. See you later. No, Harry, don't get up. Thanks for a smashing meal.' She blew them a kiss and was off.

Steve hadn't seen her in such a happy-go-lucky mood for months. Harry's change of plan might suit Brenda, but if he kept popping off hither and thither it could mean disaster. Steve wanted his cousin to stay for at least a month at No 5, to be in his debt, then towards the end of the month he would ask for help with the lecture tour, and pursue the likelihood of free accommodation in the States. A sudden thought came to him. Why not go on his own, let Brenda stay with her mother, then it wouldn't cost so much?

'Another coffee, Harry, and a brandy perhaps? Brandy's on me.'

'Yes, why not?'

They sat in silence until the coffee and brandy arrived.

Harry took a sip of his Courvoisier, and glanced at Steve. He couldn't stand this tension. 'Out with it Steve, what's bothering you?'

'Quite a lot, Harry, quite a lot.'

'Why not share it then? Go on man.'

'It's difficult, Harry. Although we're cousins we don't really know each other, and it was only yesterday we shook hands for the first time. We are still virtual strangers, you understand?'

'What are you trying to say, Steve?'

'I know you're a great fellow, Harry, but you may feel it's early days and not feel like helping me.'

'Help you do what? Dig for gold coins?'

'Oh no, nothing like that.'

'Well hadn't you better explain?'

Steve had practised putting the proposition to Harry. He'd talked into the mirror in a persuasive, knowledgeable way, paused for effect, smiled at his *bons mots*, but had never imagined approaching the subject stuck in the corner of a restaurant. 'It's like this, Harry, it's all in my head, but I thought if you could get this Professor chappie interested I might be able to use the University as a jumping-off ground.'

The American hadn't a clue. What was the Englishman talking about?

'What is it you want the Professor to do?'

'Give me an introduction to the sort of organisations that might be interested in learning about The Tower first-hand. I want to give illustrated talks. My slides are very good, although I say so myself. Why don't I show them to you tonight?'

Steve stared at Harry whose expression gave nothing away. There was a long silence. Damn, damn, damn, thought Steve, I've blown it. Harry swirled his brandy round and looked into the glass as if it were a crystal ball.

'It's a good idea,' he said at last. Steve breathed out a sigh of relief.

'But there are certain snags which I'm sure could be overcome.' He chose his words carefully. 'Princeton may not be the right place. It's strictly for academics, all rather scholarly and choosy. On the other hand what you're proposing could well fit into a lecture circuit or be suitable as a short talk or Rotary lunches.'

Steve's heart sank. Rotary lunches wouldn't bring in the lolly or the kudos. 'What sort of lecture circuit are you proposing, Harry?'

'In states like Missouri, Kansas, Nebraska, the less sophisticated areas, there are plenty of opportunities. Women's clubs, men's clubs, prisons, hospitals.' Steve's heart sank. He hadn't seen it quite like that. Where did the poster he'd designed fit into all this? He'd imagined them pasted up in every town prior to his arrival, the Press notified and his hosts eager to accommodate him and Brenda, free of course. Steve's less than enthusiastic reaction to Harry's suggestions was obvious.

'What is it exactly, Steve, that you had in mind? Tell me and I'll see what can be done.'

'What you've said is food for thought, I'll sleep on it,' said the unhappy Steve. As the two men left the *Tiger Tavern*, Byrd entered. Steve, he noticed, looked morose and withdrawn, but his extrovert cousin shouted, 'Good evening, Mr Byrd, *bon appetit.*'

Harry waited until Byrd was out of earshot. 'Steve, does that new Yeoman remind you of someone?'

Yes, but I can't remember where I've met him.'

'In the Bloody Tower, of course.'

'What! What do you mean?'

'Think of that portrait of Raleigh, doesn't it strike. . . .'

'My God, you're right. It's uncanny. That's why his face is so familiar.'

'Could have been an adventurer like Raleigh, couldn't he?'

'Yes,' laughed Steve, 'But never a courtier. I can't see him spreading his finery in a puddle, because he hasn't bloody got any.'

When they arrived back at No 5 Harry asked to see Steve's slides.

'Don't you want to take another look at the tunnel while Brenda's out?'

'No thanks, Steve, next week will do.'

'But the play will be over, and she'll be in during the evenings.'

'How about when she goes to her dressmaking classes?'

'Yes, I suppose it might be possible to take a couple of hours off, though we're pushed at this time of the year.'

'Incidentally, Steve, those coins you were going to show me last night, have you got them handy?'

'Nearer than you think.'

Steve opened the drinks cupboard, moved a few bottles and pushed hard against the panelling within the cupboard itself. A small panel no more than nine inches square slid sideways and from the recess Steve took out a small tin box, once used for Quality Street toffees, which he handed to Harry.

There were fifteen coins, eleven gold and four silver.

'This is miraculous,' whispered Harry. 'It's not fool's gold. It's the real McCoy.' He handled each one gently and read the inscription round the edges.

'They've never been circulated, Steve, they're in mint condition.'

'Yes, I know. Have a guess at what they're worth, Harry.'

'I've no idea.'

'Would you believe me, if I told you that the gold coins are worth £25,000 or more, *each*? Harry shook his head. 'That's a quarter of a million, but I am definitely not stopping there. I intend to dig up a lot more before I start claiming treasure trove, but I'd love to know what the wording means. Do you think your Professor could translate it?'

'I think you could, Steve, if you put your mind to it. Here, I'll write it down for you more clearly. JESUS AUTEM TRANSIENS PER MEDIUM ILLORUM ABAT. Think about it Steve, what does transiens suggest?'

'Transiens – transiens – passing, perhaps?'

'Excellent, and how would you translate medium?'

Steve laughed. 'One who sits at a seance in the dark speaking to invisible spirits, or it could be, I suppose, something neither good nor bad, something in the middle?'

'Middle, that's exactly what it means. Translated, I think the Professor would say it reads, *But Jesus, passing through the midst of them went His way.* It's from the Bible, you know, one of the gospels, I believe.' 'What strange words,' Steve whispered, 'to stamp on a coin, and what a bit of luck you were able to translate them.'

'A little learning, Steve, can sometimes be a dangerous thing?'

'Not in your case, Harry, definitely not.'

9

The door of the Queen's House was open. Byrd shut it behind him and dropped the latch. Colonel Kilmaster was sitting in the hall reading Gerald Seymour's *Archangel*.

'Smashing book this, Mr Byrd, don't want to put it down, but I guess we'd better talk business. Come into my office and we'll have a noggin.'

The blinds were already drawn.

'Neat or with water, Mr Byrd?'

'Neat please, sir.'

'A man after my own heart.'

'Now then, how can I help you?'

'I need to see the work schedules, the costings and the contracts for all the building companies working on the site.'

'OK, I should be able to put my hands on them.'

The Colonel went into the next room and returned carrying two box files.

'These files cover the work being done on both St Thomas's Tower and 2A The Casemates. The builders on the St Thomas job are old hands. Over the past two years they've carried out any number of jobs for us. Not always the lowest tender, as you

69

will see, but on an important job they're reliable.

The Colonel handed Byrd the letters relating to St Thomas's Tower.

'Is the job really going to take two years?'

'It's not easy work, a great deal needs doing to the building below the water line, and that takes time. We intend to open the building to the public next year. You must take a look at it Mr Byrd, you'll be surprised at the standard of craftmanship.'

'I've already taken a look at 2A The Casemates and I am surprised, not by the standard of workmanship, but by the lack of interest. It all seems so lackadaisical. Are they the same builders?'

'No. We accepted the lowest tender for the Casemates. Not as prestigious as the Tower, but I must say that Cantries came up with a tender we couldn't refuse. Can't see how they can possibly make a profit, but maybe work is short and it's better to have men working than to disband your work force? But I'm sorry to say they must be losing heavily now.'

'Why do you say that?'

'They should have finished the job two weeks ago, and I can't understand why it's taken four men and a foreman so long.'

'The foreman, you mean the belligerent fair haired guy?'

'Yes, that's him.'

'You seem to be plagued with fair haired men. What's his name?'

The Colonel picked up a list of workmen who'd been issued with passes.

'William Smith.'

'Bill Smith,' muttered Byrd, 'that's fairly anonymous.'

'What are you saying?'

'I don't really know why, but I have the feeling he isn't the Cockney sparrow he pretends to be.'

'You've met him?'

'Yes, I've met him and I was lucky not to find myself shoved through rotting joists into the abyss below.'

The Colonel re-charged their glasses.

'Have you still got the tenders for the Casemates job?'

'Yes, here they are. I'll read them out. Rush and Jones £25,000, that's our usual buiider; Thomas and Richmond £23,500; Bellow and Saull £23,000; Cantries and Co. £16,500. We had no option but to use Cantries.'

'Did you take up references?'

'Yes, and they were excellent. All here if you want to read them.'

'Could you have them photo-copied for me? Safer than removing the files.'

'Let's do them now,' said the Colonel, 'and tomorrow I'll take a good look, find out what they're up to.'

While the Colonel was running off the references Byrd made up his mind not to dally any longer. Immediate action was the order of the day.

'Have you the key to 2A, sir?'

'Yes.'

'I think we should wait an hour until everyone's hit the hay, and then go in.'

'Tonight!' Suddenly Colonel Kilmaster grinned. 'It'll remind me of old times, not quite like the jungle, we'll not get sniped at, but we will be going in under cover of darkness. It will be cold down there. Have you any warmer clothes with you Byrd?'

'No.'

'OK. The answer to that little problem is simple. We'll raid the clothes store which Mr Clarkson, my senior administrator keeps in apple pie order. We have gum boots, dungarees and oilskins in case the Yeomen ever have to do a cleaning up operation.'

'Why should they?'

'The vagaries of the Thames, though it hasn't overflowed its banks since the great barrier was erected.'

At half past one they let themselves into 2A. In the torchlight some of the rotten joists were visible. Others had been covered with planks, but there was still a massive gap in the centre of the room. The old floor boards had been removed and were now stacked at the far end of the room. The Colonel splayed torchlight over the wall.

71

'Good God, they've done nothing for the past two weeks. What are they playing at?'

'Concentrating on the basement, perhaps?'

'We'd better take a look, don't you think, Mr Byrd?'

'That's what I hoped you'd say, though easier said than done because there's no sign of a ladder.'

'Hell and damnation, they must have taken it with them, and we'll not find one at this ungodly hour.'

'Hang on, sir, all is not lost. There's one, I believe, in the cellar?'

'So there is. Now how do we get down?'

'There's some rope over there? We'll tie it round one of the stouter joists then I'll slide down, put the ladder in place, and we're in business. Positive thinking, sir.'

'Don't say that Byrd, every time my wife wants a new dress, she mentions positive thinking.'

Once the rope was secure the Superintendent eased himself between two joists and slid down. After that, descent for the Colonel was an easy matter. They looked about them with interest.

'King Edward I did a great job, Byrd. He built these western walls and made sure the moat, which took years to dig out, kept the enemy at bay. These walls will last another 1,000 years if the builders do their job properly.'

'Who is responsible for checking their work?'

'Hamish Campbell, an architect from the DOE, a likeable, entertaining chap well versed in Her Majesty's historic buildings. Well, Superintendent, I mean Mr Byrd, there's nothing down here except walls and a floor which is, presumably, being prepared for the re-laying of those paving stones over there. Should have been completed days ago.'

'I wonder why Smith was so uptight when he found me in here this afternoon?'

'Can't imagine. There's nothing to hide. Could be a classic case of a small man.'

'What do you mean?'

'Small men are the most officious, that's always been my experience in the army. They have to prove something. Look at Napoleon.'

Byrd laughed. 'I thought conceit was God's gift to the small man?'

The Colonel pulled out his pipe.

'Shouldn't do that, sir,' said Byrd quickly, 'tobacco has quite a distinctive smell, could leave traces of our presence.'

'Yes, you're damned right. Should have remembered the precautions we took in the jungle. Now let's get back to the office and have a noggin.'

They put paid to half a bottle of whisky, during which time they decided Byrd should be seen in the Yeoman Warders' Club more often.

'Tomorrow night I'll try my hand at darts, listen to what's going on.'

'I find it hard to believe,' said the Colonel as he held his glass of malt up to the light and marvelled at the colour, 'that any of my Yeomen are involved in the theft of documents, but the question I keep asking myself is, where are these papers on sale in the auction houses coming from?'

'That's the 64,000 dollar question,' said Byrd, now in a mellow mood.

10

On day six Byrd was up early again. Steve still hadn't found him
any old curtains, He should have mentioned the problem to the
Colonel last night but it had slipped his mind, with a little help
from the whisky. He decided to take the evening off, go home,
see Stephanie and Kate, share their supper, and find something
to cover the windows. It was another warm, cloudless day, and
by 7 o'clock he was doing a gentle jog round the Tower precincts.
He ran towards the Martin Tower, and was about to run across
Broad Walk when he saw the silver Astra being driven out of
the precincts. Someone was up early. He continued his run
down Water Street and back up Mint Street to his lodging. He
was puffed and out of condition, but here was a heaven sent
opportunity to jog every day for a month. Unusual for him to
be able to plan anything in advance.

Two pieces of toast again, but with tea. He listened to the news,
the every-day-the-same news. More trouble in Ireland, more
trouble in Beirut, trouble in the Gulf, brain drain from Hong
Kong. The door bell rang, his first visitor. Putting his head out
of the window he saw Steve Johnson standing there, holding a

carrier bag.

'Come on up, Mr Johnson, and have a cup of tea.'

Steve looked round the room as he entered and thought nothing could be more depressing than white walls, and a white ceiling, with not a trace of colour anywhere.

'Sorry I've been so long with these old curtains, but Brenda's been busy with her play and my cousin's been staying with us.'

Byrd noticed the tense immediately.

'Been staying? Do you mean he's gone?'

'Yes, went off this morning. Bit unexpected like, but he'll only be away three days.'

'Where's he gone?'

'Don't exactly know. He hired a car so he could be anywhere. Mentioned York and Lichfield, but I think he only went because Brenda's so busy, and it'll ease the pressure for a few days.'

'Do you see a lot of each other?'

'Heavens no. This is the first time we've met. Second cousins, you know. Same great grandfather.'

'He's a caretaker in a University, isn't he?'

'Yes, but he's bright. Can't think why he hasn't done something more . . . more . . .'

'Rewarding?'

'Yes, something to do with history. He knows a lot.'

The cogs in Byrd's brain were working overtime.

'You're sure he's gone north?'

'That's what he said.'

'Funny when there's so much to see in the south; Oxford, Cambridge, Windsor, all much nearer to London, especially if you're not used to driving in this country.'

'I never gave the driving a thought, but as I say he's bright so I don't think he'll have much trouble. Must dash now Mr Byrd, thanks for the tea. You'll find giraffe wire, hooks and eyes, and a gimlet in the bag. Thought you'd need something to hang them on.'

'Thanks Mr Johnson, thanks.'

'My name's Steve. I get fed up with all this protocol.'

'All right, thanks Steve, and I'm Jim.'

Byrd waited until he heard the front door close before ringing

Sergeant Mayhew.

'Yes?'

'Get a trace on a silver Astra, C2PDQ.'

'Pretty damn quick, sir?'

'You've got it. Probably going north. Don't intercept. Have it followed and let me know its destination, and when you've done that, call Sir Elwyn. Tell him I need a pair of feet immediately, someone who can fade into the background. I'll meet whoever he sends by the ticket booth at 12 noon.'

'OK, t'will be done.'

Smart girl, thought Byrd. Gets the job done, thinks on her feet, and no questions asked.

Within half an hour Georgina Mayhew rang back.

'Good girl! You've certainly been speedy.'

The Detective Sergeant didn't much appreciate the 'good girl'.

'It's my job,' she said tartly. 'You'll find Sergeant Paxton at the booth, midday, as you suggested, but we've had no luck so far in tracing the Astra. Bossman wants you to attend an auction next week in Geneva. 10 a.m. Wednesday. Check with London Christie's for details. Your mother-in-law is worse. Take compassionate leave.'

'Understood, and thank you.'

Thank you, said Georgina to herself. That makes a change.

Byrd was thinking of Geneva, even wondering whether he could snatch three days there, take Stephanie, live it up a bit, but caution, unusual for him, prevailed. Sergeant Mayhew could arrange for him to travel out on Tuesday and back to base by Wednesday evening. There was no need to visit Christie's in the West End to pick up a catalogue, no need to draw attention to himself. His French would be more than adequate in Geneva.

Hanging the curtain was a simple matter. Now perhaps he could get his necessary six hours. St Thomas's Tower was his next objective. Look over the Tower, talk to the foreman. After that, a visit to the Librarian Angela Burne-Jones because he needed to pick her brains. There were several aspects about the Barkstead Treasure which were puzzling, especially the notes Pepys had left. Odd that a man who normally made everything crystal clear should have said so little. If he could lead Angela Burne-Jones down that avenue she might strike gold in more ways than one.

Roger Abbott, the foreman on site, greeted the Superintendent like an old friend. Within minutes Byrd knew Abbott was a happily married man with three young boys and a wife who worked as a part-time cleaner at St Thomas's Hospital.

Byrd joined in the camaraderie before being given a tour of the building. Abbot was certainly fit. He shinned up ladders, leapt across open spaces, and went round at a pace which astonished Byrd. They stopped to take a look at the oratory.

'It's small isn't it?'

'Big enough, so I'm told, for a wedding,' said Abbott.

'You're joking!'

'No, straight up guv. It's where Raleigh got married, him that put the cloak down in a puddle, but if you believe that, you'll believe anything.'

'Oh, I do, Roger, I do,' said a voice behind them. 'Raleigh had flair and a sense of the dramatic, he even made a full length drama out of his execution.'

Byrd laughed at the Scotsman's wit. 'Don't tell me,' he said, 'let me guess. You must be Mr Campbell.'

'Hamish Campbell, at your service, sir, and you are?'

'James Byrd, a rookie Yeoman still waiting for my first uniform.'

'And what was your old uniform like? Which branch of the services?'

'SAS, so my uniform could be described as camouflage.'

'Ah yes.' Hamish Campbell gave a hearty laugh which echoed round the small oratory. 'So where was this heavily camouflaged man based?'

'In South East Asia. Never two days in the same place, and all quite unpronounceable names.'

The architect grinned, 'So now you're doing your homework?'

The foreman interrupted, 'Only one more room to see, Mr Byrd, and then we're through, that's if it's OK with you, Mr Campbell?'

'Carry on, Roger.'

77

Abbott led them into the next room where new floorboards had been laid, and the stone walls cleaned.

'Take a decco at this fireplace. That's Charley Austin's work. He's done every bit himself. Smashing, ain't it?'

'Superb, Mr Abbott, superb. And when was it built?'

'Don't rightly know, I never was much good at history, but Mr Campbell will tell you. There's nothing he don't know about this place.'

'1280, Mr Byrd, give or take a year or two.'

'Who dares,' said the Superintendent, 'to say that we have no craftsmen these days.'

'Yeah, Charley's a wonderful stonemason,' agreed Abbott, 'pity we can't say the same for his brother.'

'Do you employ him as well?'

'No, not bloody likely. He's working for Cantries, the right firm for him. Can't try, see what I mean?'

'Is he also a stonemason?'

'That's what he calls himself, but I call him a lazy bugger. The only tool he can use is a pickaxe.'

'Thanks for the guided tour. I can't wait to see the finished job.'

'You're welcome, captain, come again, any time.'

Byrd nodded to both men, picked his way round a variety of obstacles and made his way over to the library.

Angela Burne-Jones gave him a dazzling smile. 'Just in time for coffee, Mr Byrd. Come and join me.'

He followed her upstairs to her office. Byrd sat down and looked around him. There was another entire library here, but as far as he could see all the books were on weaponry.

'Now Mr Byrd what are you reading up on today?'

'Back to square one, I'm afraid. Queries about the Barkstead Treasure, if you've time to listen to them? About what Pepys didn't write, about what he wasn't saying. Have you ever tried reading between the lines, Miss Burne-Jones?'

'No, not really. I've always taken Pepys at face value, never had a moment's doubt because his reports are so accurate.'

'He gave up the search, didn't he, after only three attempts? Why give in so easily? Did he suspect it had already been found and appropriated? £7000 in coin must have been a hefty weight. Unless it was removed gradually.'

'Are you suggesting,' said Angela Burne-Jones thoughtfully, 'that someone in the Tower knew where it was hidden and removed it bit by bit?

'Could be.'

'If that's your theory then Pepys may have been right when he intimated that Barkstead himself had managed to get the treasure out of The Tower.

'Perhaps he took it with him when he fled to Germany? After all, he needed money abroad, money enough to become a burger of a small town near Frankfurt.'

'But if that was the case he would have had sufficient funds to buy off his kidnappers, before they brought him back to England to face execution.'

'Doesn't that suggest two possibilities, either Sir George Downing, our Ambassador, who arranged the kidnapping, couldn't be bought, or the money was still in this country.'

'Supposing you'd been Barkstead having to flee at a moment's notice, where would you have hidden the loot, Miss Burne-Jones?'

'In a cellar or tunnel under my house which is where Pepys looked. The tunnels at one time may have run from the Bell Tower under the Queen's House and possibly all the way along Mint Street finishing at Legge's Mount.' Angela smiled at him. 'Now, Mr Byrd, that's given you food for thought. I've deliberated hard and long over this problem and have never been able to come up with an answer.'

Byrd recognised his gracious dismissal. 'One question more before I leave. Are you a descendent of the painter?'

'No, not even distantly, and with no talent at all for painting.'

Sergeant Paxton, looking more like a punk than a policeman, stood quietly by the booth. He nodded slightly as Byrd approached and without a word being spoken followed the Superintendent across the main road to a quieter spot in a small open green space. Byrd stood for a moment reading a plaque which told him he was standing on the site of the old scaffold where so many of The Tower's prisoners, innocent and guilty alike, had met their end. In his mind he could see the scaffold, the executioner, the soldiery, and the vast crowd assembling for a day's entertainment. He heard the street cries and the deafening roar of the spectators as they saw the victim appear. Only the children seemed unaware of the drama and continued playing their simple games. Suddenly there was silence as the prisoner ascended the scaffold and the axeman hidden behind his mask of anonymity gave his victim a hand up the steps knowing, that within minutes, the same hand would strike the man down – maybe not the first stroke, or the second, or the third, but the central figure of the drama would certainly be despatched.

'Five strokes weren't enough, Paxton.'

'What, sir?'

'Five strokes of the axe weren't enough to kill Monmouth. The axeman had to finish him off with his knife, and then, I believe, they stitched his head back on again.'

'Barbarians, sir.' The sergeant turned pale.

'Yes, yes indeed. How is it, Paxton, that a scene never experienced can come alive so vividly in one's mind?'

'I don't know, sir. Perhaps you were meant to be a writer, not a policeman.'

'That's an interesting observation,' Byrd grinned at the newly promoted detective sergeant. 'And you perhaps should have been a psychologist! Now Paxton, let's get down to earth. Take a look at the man in this photograph, and when he emerges from The Tower I want you to follow him. Find out his name, where he lives, what he does for a living, and whether he has a family, but be discreet, and ring Sergeant Mayhew when you've finished. No more contact with me at all.'

'Understood, sir.'

'And good hunting, Sergeant.'

As Byrd returned to The Tower there was the faintest of bleeps. There were too many yeomen, and tourists milling around, and so to his lodging.

He pressed the receive button. 'Yes?'

'We have traced the Astra. It's now parked in the grounds of Parlour's Hall, a hotel in Bridgnorth. Occupant has booked for three nights.'

80

Byrd thought quickly.

'If our boss can spare you, get up there, stay a night and report back.'

'You mean stay there tonight?'

'Yes, Sergeant, that's exactly what I mean, there's no time like the present. I'll wait in for an answer.'

While Byrd waited, he tried fitting the characters he had into a workable scenario. A foreman with a suspect accent; a constant visitor to the White Tower; an American cousin; a moody Steve Johnson; Roger Abbott, an effusive foreman who told him more than he wanted to know, and the apparently lackadaisical work at 2A. Both he and the Colonel must have missed something. But what?

Bleep!

'Yes?'

'I'm booked in for tonight.'

'Excellent. Keep awake, and don't overeat.' What's the matter with him, wondered Georgina? He's nearly human. She pocketed her electronic toy before ringing her husband on another line to tell him she'd not be home. Pete would be hopping mad as usual.

What had they missed? Dammit! thought Byrd, I need a breather. Oxford, in his souped-up Metro would take two hours. An hour there to relax with Stephanie and Kate, and then back to The Tower by midnight. *Rigoletto*, broadcast live from Covent Garden, kept him entertained all the way from London to Oxford. For once the traffic on the M40 wasn't too bad. He tore through Oxford, past the Randolph, past the University Theatre, straight through three lots of lights, past the skating rink, turned right opposite Christ's, and a couple of minutes later parked in Western Road. He was still trying to weave together disparate threads, but they were too short, the wrong colours, and the frame too large.

Kate was standing in the window staring at the cheeky blue Metro which had dared to park in their own licensed space. She was even more amazed to see her father unwind and clamber out of this strange car. She screamed with joy and ran to the front door.

'Eureka,' yelled Byrd, as he stepped inside.

'That's a funny word, Daddy.'

'Eureka, means success.'

'Like what, Daddy. Like finding the last piece in my jigsaw?'

'No, my darling, the first piece.'

Stephanie, sitting at her dressing table drying her hair heard her husband shout 'eureka' and the shrieks of delight from Kate. Damn! Damn! Damn! Why didn't he let me know he'd be here this evening. Lean cuisine, that's all we've got in the house until I shop tomorrow. Dammit, he might have told me. Must finish my hair, can't go to the interview tomorrow with it looking like this. Byrd walked into the bedroom.

'Don't say it,' he said softly. 'Finish what you're doing, and we'll go out for a meal.' He looked into the mirror and stared into her expressionless eyes. 'Why today? You usually wash your hair on Sunday mornings.'

'I have an interview tomorrow, for a full-time job.'

'What! So what happens to Kate?'

'No problem. I will be taking Kate and Rosy to school in the mornings, and Jean will collect them in the afternoons and look after Kate until I get home.'

'What's the job?'

'Full-time guide round the colleges.'

'Isn't part-time enough?'

'No. I get the jobs the full-timers don't want.'

They stared at each other for some minutes weighing up their unspoken thoughts.

She shook her head. 'No it's not the money. I am just sick to death of feeling like a widow.'

That wasn't a road he wanted to travel. He came to a halt, turned off the ignition and waited.

'We'll eat out. Chinese.' she said.

He nodded. 'We'll talk later.'

11

Georgina Mayhew's husky voice drowned out the Hallelujah Chorus trumpeting from her car stereo. The driver of a Jaguar passing in the outer lane looked at her in surprise. She shook her head at him, no she wasn't in the least bit mad. She sang because she was out of the office, she sang because she was free for twenty four hours, free of the three men in her life. Her boss, her husband, and the new Yeoman Warder. Her boss was demanding; her husband was becoming insufferably jealous, not of another man, but of her job, and that big-headed, bearded Yeoman Warder, Dickybird, as they'd nicknamed him in his own parish, was a patronising autocrat of the first order. Never mind, she could cope with the lot of them.

The traffic on the M6 was solid and she was thankful when she reached junction 10, the turn-off to Wolverhampton. It was only another fourteen miles to Bridgnorth. She'd made a non-stop journey, no snacks on the way to mar her appetite. She was going to enjoy her dinner, her freedom, and, perhaps not so strangely, her job.

Sergeant Mayhew parked her Fiesta alongside the silver Astra. So far, so good. The hotel garden was at its best and the trees, though thick, didn't obscure an extraordinary view. Bridgnorth, she'd discovered, had a double identity, low town, and high town. Parlour's Hall Hotel was in low town, deriving its name from a vast outcrop of red sandstone known as Queen's Parlour, which towered above the place. Georgina wanted to see everything, its leaning castle, more leaning than the Tower of Pisa, and its ancient buildings, but she was no longer master of her fate. She was now at the whim of yet another man, an American, and she had to do what he wanted to do.

She reported to reception, was shown to her room, and went down to the dining room immediately. It was 7.30 and dinner was already being served. The head waiter led her to the only available table, not in a bad position, she noted, from which to view the rest of the guests. Any meal would have been acceptable because she didn't have to cook it, but Parlour's Hall, she soon learnt, was special.

'And is Madam ready to choose?'

'Yes, please. First avocado, then poached salmon with mixed vegetables and a half bottle of Chablis.'

'Very well, Madam. Your room number, please?'

'Fourteen.'

Georgina gazed quite openly at the occupants of every table, displaying the sort of curiosity expected of a lone diner. There were two men dining *toute seule*. The one in the corner could never in a thousand years be a caretaker, much more likely to be a rep, and the other one, in his 70s, was too old. Dickybird had described the American as tall, broad, blue eyed, and greying, but there was no one in the room who answered to that description. She was halfway through her avocado when Harry Johnson entered. He looked in her direction and seemed slightly disconcerted. Georgina realised she'd taken over his territory. She gave him a slight smile, but there was no reaction. The head waiter scurried across to Harry Johnson, she could hear him apologising, then he scurried in her direction.

'Would you mind sharing a table, Madam? The gentleman

usually sits here, but he'd forgotten to reserve a table for this evening.'

Sergeant Mayhew nodded, 'Of course I don't mind sharing.'

'Thank you, Madam, thank you.'

Harry Johnson sat down, not failing to notice the ring on her finger.

'Sorry about all this fuss Mrs . . .?'

'Georgina Mayhew.'

'Pleased to meet you Mrs Mayhew. I'm Harry Johnson. All this is my own fault. Took it for granted this table would be available every evening.'

'Please don't apologise.' Georgina took her heaven-sent chance. 'Something tells me you're from the other side of the Atlantic.'

'You mean my accent betrays me.'

'Yes, as mine does.'

'Let me guess! North of the border?'

'Edinburgh. Are you sightseeing?'

'Yes, and no. I came for a bit of quiet to do some reading, but this ancient town has so much to offer I'm being tempted away from my books. And you, Mrs Mayhew, what are you doing here?'

'For me it's a one night stand. I've been visiting relatives in Cumbria, but Oxford's a hell of a drive so I decided to break the journey.'

'Oxford! Are you a professor?'

'No, nothing so high-falutin', merely a secretary.'

'I don't think professors are anything out of the ordinary. What was the avocado like?'

'Perfect, and the vinaigrette's a great deal better than my efforts.'

The waiter brought the poached salmon and stood while Georgina helped herself to vegetables. Harry decided to have the same, even to the half bottle of Chablis.

'Are you taking a long holiday, Mr Johnson?'

'Probably three or four weeks.'

'Just driving around are you, or have you a base?'

'I'm staying with a cousin in London, but a friend in the States had mentioned this splendid old town to me so I've snatched three days.'

'You mean you're not going to Canterbury, Durham or York?'

'I'll do the cathedrals another year.'

'What's your job, Mr Johnson?'

'I work in a University.'

Harry Johnson's intonation left Georgina in no doubt he didn't wish to be questioned further. His salmon hadn't arrived.

'Please excuse me, Mr Johnson, I was up until the early hours, and I need some shut-eye. Have a lovely trip.'

Harry stood up and they shook hands. Georgina left without looking behind her. She went straight to reception, and picked up a pen. The receptionist was quick.

'Thought you'd signed, Madam?'

'Yes, I did, but I forgot to put my postal code.' She turned back the pages and found what she wanted. Harry Johnson was in room 10.

'Can't find my name. Where did I sign?'

'Last, Madam, you're the last one.' The receptionist spoke slowly as though she were an idiot child.

There was no one about on the first floor. Sergeant Mayhew dived into her bag to find a credit card. At the third attempt the door opened. She stepped inside quickly and closed the door. Nothing in the dressing table drawers, nothing other than clothes in the wardrobe, two cases both stowed on top of the wardrobe. Two cases for three days seemed excessive. She pulled them down. The smaller one was empty, and the other one much heavier and locked with a combination mechanism. Bedroom doors were easy, but she was no good at anything more complicated. After struggling for five minutes she shoved the cases back on top of the wardrobe, and before leaving leafed quickly through several books on the bedside table, all on James, Duke of Monmouth. Erudite reading for a caretaker.

She opened the door a few inches, listened, and then peered out to make sure the coast was clear before going to her own room on the same floor.

The following morning Georgina had breakfast in her room. She didn't intend the American to know she was still in the hotel. After breakfast she donned a pair of old jeans, and a loose jacket. She pinned her hair up on the top of her head and put on a peaked cap. She looked, as she hoped she'd look, like any slightly way-out supporter of hopeless causes. From her window she had a view of the carpark and could clearly see anyone entering or leaving the hotel. For three hours she sat immobile watching the tits nibbling away at nuts hanging from a bird table, but she was bored. Bored! If freedom meant boredom she'd nearly had enough. What on earth was he doing in his room? Reading on a lovely morning like this? And if so, reading what? The books beside the bed? Suddenly she caught a glimpse of the the tall American leaving the hotel on foot. She shot down the stairs, out of the front door, and was in time to see him disappearing round a corner. Georgina hadn't been a sprinter for nothing.

He was a man who walked with a purpose. Across the bridge which spanned the Severn. No time to stop, not even to take a closer look at the albino swallows soaring high into the air before swooping under the arches. He crossed the road, and stopped momentarily, as if looking for a sign, then swiftly on up a narrow alleyway which lead, so the legend read, to *Stoneway Steps, and The Cliff Railway.* The steps would mean an exhausting climb from Low Town to High Town, but to Georgina's relief Harry climbed aboard the waiting lift. Dared she risk it? If she didn't she'd have no idea where he was going. Pulling her hat even further over her face she slipped quietly into the back seat. Harry, seated at the front, seemed totally unaware of her presence.

The lift creaked and rattled its way up the cliff face. It reached the top and groaned as though the strain had been too much. Georgina made no effort to move until she'd seen Harry pay his fare, go through the turnstile, and make his way along Castle Walk. Harry was no longer in a hurry, neither was she. The view across the valley to the distant hills and Welsh mountains beyond was breathtakingly beautiful, so beautiful she nearly lost him. While she gazed down at fishermen on the river bank Harry dashed up some steps leading to a magnificent white classical building which rose naturally out of the ground dominating the eastern corner of Castle Walk. Strange to see a church where she'd expected a castle.

She saw Harry Johnson enter the building. What on earth was there? What secrets did the church hold for an American? For half an hour she sat on the steps making no attempt to enter the church. She desperately wanted to see what he was doing but she'd be too obvious. Slowly she walked round the church and to her delight found an impressive ruin. Of course! This was the castle, the leaning castle, or what was left of it. Quite frightening to walk beneath it, she wouldn't try.

Suddenly she heard voices, the young happy voices of a party of children accompanied by two teachers. They were making for the church, providing a chance not to be missed. She tacked on behind them and closed the west door quietly behind her. Now where was the American? That was funny, she hadn't seen him leave. As they walked down the centre aisle she caught a glimpse of him, in the transport, on his knees, not praying, but reading the words on a tablet imbedded in the floor. As he rose he gave a brief look in their direction and then continued to read further tablets on the walls. Ten minutes later he dropped a coin in the donations box and left.

All that, thought Georgina looks innocent enough, and now I'd better get my skates on otherwise dickybird will want to know what's kept me.

12

'Coffee, sir?' Byrd looked up into the eyes of a smiling air hostess. 'Yes please, I think I will.' The coffee was good and the breakfast of hot croissants, butter and strawberry jam, real strawberry jam, had gone down a treat. Much better than the hugger mugger breakfasts he was managing to scrape together in The Tower.

The captain informed his passengers over the intercom that they would be landing in twenty minutes. The weather was perfect in Geneva, clear sunny skies, and temperature in the lower seventies. Everything about the trip had been perfect, and with the plane only half full, Byrd had no one alongside to disturb him. It gave him thinking time.

As Cointrin, Geneva's airport, is only 4 miles north west of the city, Byrd eschewed the courtesy bus and took a taxi straight to Christie's in the Place de Laconnerie. He settled down to enjoy the short journey, and within minutes they'd reached the crossroad at Wendt, straight over and into heavy traffic on the Rue de Servette. It took another fifteen minutes to reach the

Pont du Mont Blanc. Byrd, feeling totally relaxed, looked to his left, catching sight of Lac Leman, and the *Jet d'Eau*, a mighty gush of water soaring up to a height of 476 feet. Once over the crowded bridge they drove through the Jardin Anglais and into the old town, whereupon the taxi driver immediately said in excellent English,

'Straight ahead, monsieur, the Cathedral of St Pierre. You must not leave Geneva without climbing to the top of the north tower. There is an excellent view, and inside the cathedral you must see Calvin's seat.' Byrd knew there'd be precious little time for sightseeing but he'd make sure he climbed the north tower. The taxi stopped.

'Here you are, monsieur, Christie's.'

Byrd stood for some minutes in the Place de Laconnerie, savouring the atmosphere. Like everything else in Switzerland it was immaculate; no cigarette ends, no debris, and blessedly pure air. He debated whether to speak French or stick to English, act out the part of a philistine Englishman. Might learn more that way!

The commissionaire on duty nodded to him as he went through the doors carrying his small overnight bag containing his shaving gear, a pair of pyjamas and Rowse's book on *The Tower of London*. It was a strange feeling, leaving a bright sunny day behind him and entering into what to all intents and purposes looked and felt like a museum. Almost imperceptible smells of the past emanating from pictures, furniture and manuscripts too, which although normally kept under lock and key in glass cases, were being taken out and shown to would-be buyers. He didn't hurry. His attention was drawn to three men standing in front of a wonderfully painted pastel of a woman dressed in eastern costume. They looked and then they talked, then they looked again, showing no inclination to move on. Byrd glanced down at his catalogue. *No. 31. Jean Etienne LIOTARD (18th century Genevese.) Portrait of Lady Mary Somerville*. They were nattering in French. He listened more closely. Curators, he gathered, from a local museum. Didn't want the picture to return to England, where it was painted.

Gradually he eased his way towards the manuscripts and asked to see No 53. An assistant, taking inordinate care, removed a letter from the case, and laid it on top.

'Please do not handle, Monsieur.'

The letter, a long letter, addressed to His Most Gracious Majesty, Charles I, from his humble servant the Duke of Buckingham, stated that the forty articles of gold plate and the 105 jewels herein described were to be given into the custody of the writer, who would be responsible for the safe delivery from England to Amsterdam. Superintendent James Byrd felt himself transported back in time, and grateful for the job which had been thrust on him. In 1625 the monarchy had been faced with insuperable financial problems. The jewels, and gold plate had belonged to the realm for untold generations and, impecunious or no, it had been unforgiveable to dispose of them. Poor autocratic Charles. He never got it right.

'Shall I put them away, sir?'

'Yes, yes of course, and now I'd like to see the provenance.'

'Jacques, donnez moi la provenance, numero cinquante trois, pour le monsieur ici, s'il vous plaît.'

Jacques who was sitting at a desk behind the glass cases took out a file and handed the details to his colleague who glanced through a short letter. Byrd, an experienced upside down reader had time to memorise the name and address. *Kees Van Den Hoorn, Het Bosch, Zeist, Near Utrecht*. The letter was then detached from the provenance which he handed to Byrd.

'Monsieur, the owner does not wish to be identified. As you will see in your catalogue, the letter is the property of a gentleman.'

The letter, Byrd learned, had changed hands many times, finally being sold in 1893 by a Pieter Mooeyman to the present owner's grandfather. Looks impressive, looks correct too. A wild goose chase, perhaps?

Detective Sergeant Mayhew had made a reservation for him at the Beau Rivage in the Quai du Mont Blanc, a hotel on the north side of the lake, only twenty minutes walk from Christies. Before partaking of a snack lunch at the Lion d'Or which Mayhew had recommended, Byrd decided to climb the north tower of St

Pierre, get a bird's eye view of his surroundings, see if it made him feel as philosophic and poetic as Rousseau, who'd held court in Geneva during the 18th century.

The view was spectacularly beautiful, and from the postcard he'd purchased in the Cathedral shop he was able to identify Mont Blanc with its summit in the clouds, the Jura range to the north west, and Mont Salève to the south. The lake, fed by two rivers, the Rhône and the Arve, stretched on for ever. The Superintendent felt strangely heady and for the second time that day blessed Sir Charles Suckling.

After lunch he made for the hotel which wasn't quite what he was expecting. Mayhew had done him proud. It was luxurious and expensive, not, thought Byrd, the sort of place police officers usually frequented. As he signed the register he heard one of the receptionists calling to a guest who'd dropped his key on the desk as he dashed out.

'Mr Van Den Hoorn, there's a letter here for you.'

Byrd didn't turn his head, but managed to get a glimpse of a middle aged man, about 5'9', casually dressed, wearing dark glasses, and balding at the temples. The stranger returned to the desk and took the letter with a curt 'Thank you.' Byrd was intrigued. Why was someone who'd taken the precaution of entering a valuable document in an auction as *the property of a gentleman* here at all? What purpose could it serve?

The receptionist handed him his room key. 'Second floor, Mr Byrd.'

'Thank you.' He smiled at her. 'I've done it again.'

'Done what, sir?'

'Arrived as Mr Van Den Hoorn leaves. I'll never catch him now.'

'You're not too late, sir. He'll be here for another two days. In fact, he has a private dinner party here this evening.'

'Ah, what a blessing.'

'You here for the sale, sir?

'Yes, here today, and gone tomorrow.'

'Good luck, sir.'

She smiled to herself as he made his way to the lift. She'd never be able to understand why some people had this mad passion for collecting, and why they flew in from all over the world to buy old china, old furniture, and old pictures. She liked everything new herself.

After a leisurely shower the Superintendent found his way to the lounge where he read for a couple of hours. A strange way to read. He opened and closed the book at page 48. During those two hours he'd memorised every face. Who were Van Den Hoorn's guests, and where was the man himself?

Dinner was a solitary affair. He wished Stephanie could have been with him. She would have enjoyed a brief excursion into this sumptuous alien world, but most of all she would have marvelled at the jewellery and clothes sported by fashionable women. Not thirty pounds off the peg at C & A's, but two or three hundred pounds expended without a second's thought. A few days in Geneva would also give them time for each other, time to talk, which they so rarely did, now. Stephanie had been so vivacious, such great fun; where had all that sparkle gone? Was it his fault? Of course, it's your own damn fault, he told himself. Do something about it before it's too late.

The wine waiter opened the Chateauneuf du Pape and poured a soupçon for Byrd to taste.

'That's good, very very good.'

'1982, sir. It should be.'

By the time Byrd reached the cheese, an excellent Roquefort, he had become aware that another solitary diner was also taking his time and, all too often, looking in his direction. There was no mistake. The solitary diner was also a policeman. Why was it policemen could never be mistaken for bank managers, solicitors, or captains of industry? Byrd raised his glass, and the lone policeman returned the salute.

Over coffee and brandy Inspector Laquerry from Interpol and Superintendent Byrd from Oxfordshire furthered their introduction. Neither learnt what had brought his foreign colleague to Geneva, neither exchanged any information of importance, and neither of the two men missed any of the action in the lounge. The private rooms were off the main dining room which meant departing guests had to pass through the lounge. Byrd waited hoping he'd see some reaction on the part of his colleague if Van Den Hoorn appeared.

They sat it out until midnight.

No Van Den Hoorn.

At 9.30 the next morning the sale room was already filling up. Most of the interest was focused on the pictures. Byrd positioned himself at the end of the back row and to all intents and purposes appeared more interested in his catalogue than in the clientele, but he missed nothing. The three curators were huddled together on the third row, still talking.

The auctioneer sat down at his high stool and the chat subsided. He switched on the electronic currency converter showing Swiss Francs, Sterling, Dollars, and Yen. The pictures fetched extraordinary prices and in seconds soared from hundreds to thousands. Several pictures were knocked down to Japanese dealers, many more to Americans, and Agnews of London acquired two English pictures both by Lord Leighton. The trio of curators sat up when it came to the Liotard, their spokesman bidding against an American. Up, up, up and then the American shook his head. Their joy, their relief was apparent to all. Even the auctioneer allowed himself a satisfied smile.

To begin with, the bidding for the manuscripts didn't compare with the dizzy heights reached by the pictures. Several were knocked down for under £10,000, but there was a startling metamorphosis when it came to the Caroline letter. The convertor spiralled from 5,000 Swiss francs to 40,000 in eight moves, and then on in leaps of 10,000 a shot to 80,000. Byrd could just see the head of a woman in the front row nod almost automatically, until suddenly one of the auction staff, standing alongside the right hand wall, accepted a telephone bid and joined in the fray. She turned round with a look of disbelief on her face. There was no stopping him. Byrd knew his client was neither the V and A nor any other Government Institution. The Department of the Environment wasn't that free with its cash. But who? American? Japanese?

'150,000. Going, going, gone.' Down came the gavel.

'Name?'

Without hesitation the young man answered, 'Private buyer.'

The flight home was as uneventful as the flight out. From Heathrow he rang Mayhew at her home.

'Georgina Mayhew.'

'Hallo Georgina.' She didn't answer for a moment. It was Superintendent Byrd's voice, but he'd never called her Georgina before.

'Hallo Superintendent. Good trip?'

'Yes, yes it was. Before getting down to business I must congratulate you on the choice of hotel. It was excellent. Now, will you see what you can do about this? I need some information about a Kees Van Den Hoorn. Address, Het Bosch, Zeist, Near Utrecht. If the plane leaves on time I'll be back before 6. 'Bye now.'

'Hang on, sir. Bossman wants to see you as soon as you arrive back.'

'Why?'

'There's been an accident, probably nothing to do with your operation. He'll be in the Chapel, from 7 o'clock onwards.'

Byrd didn't press for details, not over the phone. His near perfect day was over. The name of the buyer, now that would have made it perfect.

13

Byrd slipped into St Peter's Ad Vincula, unobserved, Strains of *Jesu, Joy of Man's Desiring* filled the small Tudor Chapel. Everywhere in this place one steps back in time, thought Byrd, but where was the Colonel? Surely he didn't want the organist in on their deliberations? Byrd read the inscriptions on the altar floor. Anne Boleyn, Catherine Howard, and Jane Grey all lying beside one other. Despite Macaulay finding it *the saddest place in Christendom*, the chapel had a feeling of repose. No more heartbreak for those unhappy queens, or for all the other unfortunate churchmen and nobles lying headless under the flags. The music ceased and the Colonel's voice interrupted his reverie.

'Well Mr Byrd, how was the trip?'

'Good God, sir, are you Deputy Governor and organist?'

'Oh, no.' The Colonel chuckled to himself, 'I'll never make an organist but I like to strum when no one's around. Well, tell me, how was Geneva?'

'Beautiful. I'll return one day, with the family, but I'll not be staying at the *Beau Rivage*.'

Robin Kilmaster smiled, 'Sergeant Mayhew said she'd done her research, so there was method in her madness. Most foreign buyers stay either at *The Hilton* or the *Beau Rivage*. She had to choose one or the other.'

'She was spot on. Foreigners galore, but not all filthy rich. There were a couple of impecunious policemen residing there at their Government's expense.'

'And who was the other one?'

'An Inspector Laguerry from Interpol.'

'What was he doing?'

'I can only guess because he wasn't forthcoming. He also attended this morning's sale, showing an overt interest in an ancient bible and three pictures, but I am certain he was far more interested in the provenance of two lots of French manuscripts which didn't fetch out of the way prices.'

'No interest in the Caroline letter?'

'None. However, I have made a little progress. Despite the fact that the letter was sold as *the property of a gentleman*, I have established the identity of the vendor. The owner of the letter is, or was, a Kees Van Den Hoorn, living near Utrecht and the buyer, only an educated guess I'm afraid, could be an American University.'

'Did you get sight of the provenance?'

'Yes. The letter to Charles was written by the Duke of Buckingham who was staying with our Ambassador in Amsterdam. It changed hands two or three times before a Pieter Mooeyman finally sold it to the Van Den Hoorn family in 1893.'

'Sounds impeccable, but why was the letter in Holland?'

'Perhaps it was never sent? Buckingham may have changed his mind, sent the message by word of mouth, using one of his aides.'

'What was in the letter?'

'It related to the sale of a considerable amount of jewellery, and gold plate.'

'Was England so impoverished?'

'The monarchy was.'

The Colonel thought about it for some minutes. We've lost so much of our inheritance, either by fire, theft, destruction by Cromwell's Army, auction and private sale. Thank God our present monarch is bent on preserving our heritage. 'His wife escaped, you know.'

Byrd didn't follow him. 'Whose wife, sir?'

'Charles I's. She left by ship from Falmouth, slipped away quietly, found sanctuary in France; a silly spoilt woman. What was the date of the letter?'

'October 1625.'

'Early in his reign! Well, James, what's your next step?'

'Home, I think, for two or three hours. Haven't seen my wife and daughter for over a week.'

Yes, that's hard, thought the Colonel, remembering what Sir Charles Suckling had told him about the Superintendent's marriage. Byrd, an attractive swashbuckling type, not a darling of the establishment, had nevertheless been in constant demand. Even Sir Charles's daughter had thrown her cap at him, but the unpredictable policeman, who had high hopes of advancement, had chosen to share his life with Stephanie Delo, who'd graced Greenham Common with her presence for weeks on end. All that was in the past, but that act, Sir Charles had said regretfully, might well put paid to any hope of Byrd becoming a Chief Superintendent, let alone an Assistant Chief Constable.

'I wouldn't care,' said the Colonel aloud, 'to be cut off from my family knowing they were only two hours drive away. It was different in the jungle, one accepted privation.'

'And now, sir, this accident Mayhew mentioned, what's it all about?'

'At lunchtime today one of the workmen employed by Cantries lost his footing, fell between the joists crashing to the floor below. Had he fallen on to the level floor all might have been well, but he landed on a pile of old bricks.'

'Bricks! When we investigated there was nothing there.'

'I know, but at long last, they must have got round to paving the floor, and maybe the bricks will be used as hard core.'

'So where is he?'

'In intensive care in the East End Hospital.'

'Have you seen him?'

'Yes, immediately after the accident. Chief, who was in the area at the time, called me down. He noticed workmen carrying the injured man to the Transit van. When he asked what they were doing, they said they were taking one of their chaps to hospital.

Our Chief Yeoman would have none of it. An ambulance was called and the poor blighter was taken away in comfort, if you can talk about comfort after an accident like that.'

'How bad were his injuries?'

'Pretty gruesome, looked as if he'd been in a prize fight. Face badly bruised, and blood streaming from several cuts. He was out for the count. The foreman went with him in the ambulance, said he'd stay until he recovered.'

'What's the guy's name?'

'Austin, Jimmy Austin.'

'It doesn't make sense,' said Byrd sharply.

'What do you mean?'

'He has a brother working on the site.'

'What! That's news to me.'

'Charley Austin's a stone mason, did the carving on the fireplace in St Thomas's Tower.'

'Charley Austin! Why didn't they fetch him?'

'The grapevine tells me the two brothers didn't hit it off. Couldn't bear the sight of each other.'

'Even at a time like this! What a pity.'

'We'd better get down to the hospital straight away.'

'But, I thought you were going home?'

'That,' said his companion ruefully, 'will have to wait.'

Byrd had it planned. They'd have a word with the doctor in charge. The Colonel would ask to see the foreman in a private room and once the meeting was in progress, he would, unknown to Bill Smith, see Jimmy Austin. However, before they left for the hospital Byrd decided to do a Harry Johnson, use the telephone outside the Tower, and talk to his wife and daughter. Explain that things weren't moving. Difficult to spend a whole day at the zoo when there was still a lot of groundwork to do.

Stephanie didn't sound at all pleased.

'You said you'd get back every three or four days. Jim, do you realise you've been on this job now for eight days, and we've seen you for a couple of hours, briefly. Even your telephone calls have been few and far between. And now you're cancelling Kate's special treat.'

99

'Not cancelling it, deferring it.' He could hear Kate shouting in the background.

'I want to speak to him, I want to speak to him, Mummy.'

'All right, all right in a moment.'

Then Stephanie again, her voice softer this time. 'Kate is missing you as well, you know.'

The word 'missing' immediately conjured up his most recent case. The Bicester kidnapping had been particularly horrific. Sheer hell for the parents of the American child whose father was a lieutenant colonel with the American Airforce and based at Upper Heyford. The kidnappers had done their homework. The parents weren't rich but the child's grandfather was. He was a billionaire with fingers in many of America's fruitiest pies. First came the anonymous phone calls, and then small parcels posted in Northampton, Oxford, and Milton Keynes. A lock of hair, then the child's shoes, and then the child's dress. The mother was kept tranquillised otherwise she'd have gone out of her mind. Communication with the kidnappers had been difficult. He'd taken on the role as a friend of the family, and one of the phone boxes he'd been instructed to use was out of action. It rang, but when he answered they couldn't hear him. It was touch and go, but five days later he heard a jet taking off as they were giving him further instructions. The kidnappers had gone to earth somewhere near the base. 24 hours later he found them, and rescued the child unhurt.

'I'm missing you too,' he said at last, 'but not for much longer, we'll get away this Summer, a long long way away.'

'You mean the job's finished, you're coming home?' There was joy in her voice.

'No, not just yet, but after the case is over we'll live it up. For starters we'll all spend a weekend in a large hotel quite close to The Tower with magnificent views of Tower Bridge.'

'You mean we'll actually see something of you!'

'Every minute of the day, I promise.'

'I hope so. Now you'd better talk to Kate.'

'Daddy, Daddy, I've had my photograph taken.'

'You have! Where?'

'At school. A man came to school and took us all, everyone in the class.'

100

'Did you smile?'

'I laughed.'

'Good, so I'll be able to see the lucky gap in your teeth?'

'Yes.'

'That's good. Now darling, promise me you'll look after Mummy.'

'Yes, I promise.'

'There's a good girl, now hand me back to Mummy.'

'Bye, Daddy, bye.'

'Stephanie, I'll definitely be back for a few hours at the weekend.'

'Promises, promises, now I know. . . .' her voice hardened.

'Know what?'

'Oh, nothing, nothing.' She replaced the receiver before he could say another word.

Byrd left the kiosk wondering what Stephanie had been going to say. He didn't want to put it into words, but he could guess. She really was uptight, and feeling the strain of this operation which was moving far too slowly. He couldn't see any way to kick it along any faster. Now they must get over to the hospital. As he backed out of the kiosk a voice behind him said, 'Want some company?'

He swung round to find a young woman in jeans and a bright blue T-shirt grinning at him.

'Georgina!'

'I have an address for you, and I thought you might like to hear the news first hand?'

'Will it take long?' he asked brusquely.

'What a greeting, Superintendent!'

'Sorry, Georgina, the Colonel and I are just off to the East End Hospital.'

'To visit the victim of this morning's accident? Why don't I join you?'

'Yes, why not? You can give us a report when we reach the hospital. After that we may be able to see Jimmy Austin while the Colonel keeps the foreman occupied.'

Colonel Kilmaster parked the car behind the hospital, turned the ignition off and looked at Georgina. 'Well, Sergeant, let's be having it. What's new?'

101

'Your constant visitor, who must have improved the takings at The Tower no end, is a Trevor Rogerson who lives with his wife Maureen at 15, Victoria Road, Stockwell. Only a stone's throw from the Oval Station. He doesn't feature in our Rogues' Gallery, and Paxton couldn't find out what he does because he works from home. His wife is a supply teacher, and always in demand.'

'Well done Paxton,' breathed Byrd.

'I've also heard from the Dutch Police. They were most helpful, their English is excellent and they've given me some background on this chap Van Den Hoorn.' She handed them both a copy.

Kees Van Den Hoorn,

Het Bosch,

Zeist,

Near Utrecht.

Date of birth. 3.9.41. Rotterdam.

Family home undamaged during the war. It's thought his father collaborated with the Germans and gave them information leading to the whereabouts of valuable pictures. Never proved.

Both parents now dead. Kees carries on his father's business as a bookseller of antique books, and first editions.

Often seen at auctions in Rotterdam, Amsterdam, Brussels, London and Geneva.

His mistress, Jackie Weyden, lives it up. Expensive clothes, fast cars, younger than Van Den Hoorn, belongs to the jet set.

They have a holiday home on the island of Curaçao, a yacht and a permanent strong arm man and housekeeper on the premises.

With regard to the Caroline letters it is known that his grandfather bought a trunkload of papers in 1893. From time to time Van Den Hoorn sells rare and expensive manuscripts always giving his grandfather's acquisition as the source. Several applications have been made to the Swiss to divulge the banks and accounts used. So far no headway has been made.

Police in Holland and Interpol would welcome any information London can give them on this subject. Message ends.

'Our first break, Mr Byrd,' murmured the Colonel. 'The Governor will love this.'

'A crack, sir, not a break, it may lead nowhere. All we have is a Dutchman who's adept at covering his tracks, and who, possibly, may be on the level when it comes to the Caroline letter.'

'Oh, I hope not,' breathed Georgina.

Byrd knew how the Colonel felt. He too had often been euphoric at finding evidence which eventually proved to be useless.

'Well chaps, we're over the first hurdle,' said the Colonel, refusing to admit the possibility of defeat, 'So let's get into the hospital. I'll draw the foreman's fire while you take rearguard action.'

The two police officers exchanged glances. Bossman's exuberance was infectious but they both knew the weeks, months and sometimes years it took to produce infallible evidence. Tracing art fraud was far from easy because the criminals involved were knowledgeable, often highly educated people who took their time. Every move carefully planned. Byrd was afraid the Governor and Sir Elwyn might call in the recently formed Art Squad. He didn't want that. It was his case, and anyway he had a useful contact up at the Yard, hadn't seen Frank Pollard for years, but he was pretty sure he'd come up trumps. All he could do was pray for an illuminating flash, and a bit of luck.

Doctor Reader, in charge of the Intensive Care Unit, was occupied, but Sister Maloney, the sister-in-charge, proved immensely helpful and communicative. The Colonel explained that because the accident had happened on his territory he was concerned for the workman. Sister Maloney let her hair down. She'd had a trying day, not with the patient, who'd barely stirred, but with an uncouth and ill-behaved foreman who adamantly refused to leave, and who kept saying, 'He's my responsibility, my responsibility.'

'He feels guilty,' confided Sister, 'but there's nothing he can do except sit there with his head between his hands listening to Mr Austin's breathing, but he's driving us mad, watching every move we make. We booted him out while Doctor Reader treated the patient, and did what he could to staunch the bleeding. We also gave him a blood transfusion and put him on a drip.'

'What's the diagnosis, Sister, and what can you do?' asked Byrd.

'He's been badly knocked about, has lost a great deal of blood and is badly bruised. He's regained consciousness once, but only for a few seconds, and to give the foreman his due, he told him to relax and not try to talk. Now it's up to nature to complete the healing process.'

'And your careful nursing, Sister,' said the Colonel.

'Yes, that too.'

'You could help us, Sister,' said Byrd.

'In what way?'

'We are interested in both the injured man and his foreman, and I'm sure in your business you are often faced with matters requiring the utmost discretion.' Sister nodded.

'Colonel Kilmaster is the Deputy Governor of The Tower where the incident occurred, I'm James Byrd, a Yeoman Warder, and this is Detective Sergeant Mayhew.'

'What is it you want me to do, Mr Byrd?'

'First of all, Sergeant Mayhew would like to use your phone. We need to contact Jimmy Austin's brother.'

'Brother! But Smith said both parents were dead and he knew of no other relatives.'

'The brothers didn't hit it off. Hated each other's guts, I believe.'

'Well, we don't choose our relatives,' said Sister Maloney, thinking of her own. 'Yes, of course you can use the phone. Now, how else can I be of assistance?'

'Colonel Kilmaster would like to ask Smith a few questions. Have you a space somewhere he could utilise?'

'No problem. Use one of the single-unit wards.'

'The Colonel will also make it clear to Smith he's *persona non grata*, let him know the next of kin is being contacted, and then send him packing.'

'Thank you for that.'

'You may not thank me, sister, when you hear I want to take his place, to sit beside the patient until he's able to talk.'

'You'll be welcome Mr Byrd, but I must leave a nurse in attendance. Now Sergeant there's the phone, make yourself at home while I show the Colonel to an empty ward.'

Georgina lost no time in making for the hospital reception desk and persuading them to part with the A to D London Telephone Directory. She returned to the office, settled herself down and began ringing the Austins. At her fifth attempt she struck gold. Charley Austin answered the phone. No number, no name, merely 'Yes?'

'Mr Austin, I'm deeply sorry to be the bearer of bad news. I'm a police officer, and at the moment I'm in the East End Hospital where your brother Jimmy Austin is seriously ill.' There was a long pause.

'Christ! Now what's he been doing?'

'He had a bad fall at work today, and is in Intensive Care.'

'Good God! Why didn't Smith ring me?'

'Smith?'

'His boss. I wasn't working at the Tower today, but he could have asked Abbott to contact me.'

'Where were you, Mr Austin?'

'On a rush job at the Hayward Gallery. I'd better get down there straight away.'

'Yes, I think you'd better.'

Colonel Kilmaster had spent a lifetime dealing with men, and five years in intelligence had sharpened his antennae. The man sitting on the other side of the bed was afraid, not of losing his job for inadequate supervision, nor was he worried, whatever he said to the contrary, about Jimmy Austin's recovery. But there was fear, an indefinable fear. Byrd was right, the Cockney dialect sat uneasily on the man's tongue. The phrases, the vowel sounds, the rhyming slang and the glottal stops were all there, but the foreman sounded like an actor not getting it quite right.

'It's been a long day for you Mr Smith.'

'You can say that again.'

The Colonel smiled, a cold smile which didn't reach his eyes. 'An unenviable job, Mr Smith, being responsible for workmen who disregard the most elementary precautions. It's a pity he wasn't wearing a helmet, and quite insane to have walked across rotting joists without placing a plank there first.'

'I can't be expected to 'ave eyes in the back of my 'ead.'

'No, of course not. Where did you go to school, Mr Smith?' The suddenness of the question shook the man. He tensed.

'What's that got to do with you?'

'Not a lot, except you're both East Enders, thought you might have been at school together.'

'No, we weren't. 'E was younger than me. Now if you've finished, Guv, I'll get back to Jimmy.'

'Sorry, Mr Smith, we will relieve you of that painful task. There's no need for you to remain with Jimmy any longer. We have decided to relieve you of that painful task. His brother has been contacted and at the moment one of my staff is sitting with the patient until Charley Austin arrives.'

Bill Smith's expression said it all. He was alarmed, not panicking, thinking ahead. His jaw tightened and the Colonel knew he'd made a decision.

'All right then, if your mate can look after my mate, let 'im. Bit 'igh 'anded, aint yer, when it's my duty to look after my men?'

'Pity you didn't think about that this morning, Mr Smith.'

'Up yours,' said the foreman and made his way to the door.

Colonel Kilmaster rushed to Sister Maloney's office. 'Sergeant, I'm sure the Superintendent would want you to follow Smith. Find out where he's going and see what he does next. Here, take my car keys.'

Georgina didn't think twice. She picked up her handbag and fled, but she needn't have hurried. Bill Smith made straight for a telephone kiosk in the waiting area while she sat on a bench killing time.

Superintendent James Byrd hated hospital smells. They evoked too many memories. His mother's long lingering death from cancer and his father's more rapid death, six months later, following a heart attack. He sat brooding on their deaths while Jimmy Austin, oblivious to the upheaval his accident had caused, slept on.

At ten minutes past nine, only five minutes after Georgina had left, Sister Maloney appeared with another cup of coffee. As she

106

put it down Jimmy Austin stirred. They both moved over to the bed.

'How are you feeling, Jimmy?' asked Sister Maloney feeling for his pulse. Jimmy didn't answer. It was some seconds before the blur standing beside the bed became defined. He could see a nurse, so he must be in hospital. And the man, now becoming clearer on the other side of the bed, must be a doctor, but he didn't have a white coat on. The oddest thing of all was a bottle which appeared to be in the air. As it became clearer he noticed a tube stretching from the bottle to his chest. It was stuck to him. Why? God, how his face hurt and he had the world's worst headache, but worst of all, why was his body so painful?

Then he remembered.

The man's face came closer. 'What happened, Jimmy? You can tell me.'

Jimmy blinked. 'Jimmy how did the accident happen? Did the joists give way?'

Jimmy tried shaking his head. Mustn't do that it's too painful.

'Chest . . . chest,' he whispered, 'chest his 'ead.'

Sister Maloney intervened. 'Yes, Jimmy you have hurt your chest, but we're taking care of you.'

Jimmy's eyes turned to Byrd. 'It me,' he murmured.

'That's enough Mr Byrd. He can't take any more.' Sister Maloney had never said a truer word.

As they looked at Jimmy the rhythm of his breathing changed, and his blood pressure rose. Sister Maloney rang the emergency bell. Within seconds Doctor Reader and his staff were there to commence emergency treatment for an undiagnosed condition, but they were too late. Jimmy Austin was dead. Dead before his brother arrived. Dead having spoken seven meaningless words. Dead from a sub-arachnoid haemorrhage caused by a sudden rise in blood pressure following extensive blows to the head and body.

Dead. Taking his secrets with him.

14

Georgina Mayhew waited patiently, making sure she kept out of Smith's line of sight. He was ages on the phone and whatever he was saying was being said emphatically. He's worried, she thought. Perhaps he feels responsible for Jimmy Austin's accident? It suddenly struck her that Smith had arrived at the hospital in an ambulance. Better be quick, move the car and get into a position where I can see all arrivals and departures. She half expected a taxi to spirit Smith away, and was surprised to see him emerge when a blue Transit drew up outside the main doors. He was in it and away. An easy vehicle to follow.

Georgina kept close to the van. In this traffic the driver would be concerned with what was in front and to the side of him. They drove in convoy towards the West End, down the Strand, into Whitehall, passing Big Ben as it struck 9.30. Right at the north end of Lambeth Bridge into Horseferry Road, and left at the traffic lights into Marsham Street. The van went round on amber and the intrepid sergeant followed on red hoping none of her colleagues were around. In less than a quarter of a mile the van slowed down and finally came to a standstill outside a block of flats. Georgina quickly pulled into the kerb and stopped, much to the annoyance of the motorist behind her, who hooted and gave her two fingers as he passed.

Smith jumped out of the Transit, waved the driver away, and sauntered at a leisurely pace towards the flats. Georgina gave him ten minutes before driving the car into the forecourt. Victoria Court looked more tasteful and solid than the hencoops of today. She walked through a stylish arch, up some steps, and into a small foyer containing two lifts and a desk. The janitor stared at her. Ah yes, thought Georgina, it's these jeans and the T-shirt. Not the usual sort of attire for visitors to Victoria Court. She waved her identity card in front of him and smiled. I wonder whether you can help me, Mr . . .?'

'Thomas, Mick Thomas, but just call me Mick. I'll help you if I can, miss.'

'Do you, by any chance, know the short fair-haired man who arrived a few minutes ago? A fair-haired man with a Cockney accent.'

'Yes, that's Mr Anstey-Lloyd, but he don't have no accent. Top drawer, you know.'

'Does he live here?'

'He's lived here for years and his old man before him.'

Anstey-Lloyd, the name rang a bell. 'Wasn't he an M.P. and Minister for the Arts at one time?'

'Yes, that's him. Nice man, always so polite. Been dead these three years.'

'What does his son do?'

'No idea. Keeps himself to himself. Never talks, not even to my wife, and she cleans for him twice a week. Pernickety, you know, but generous with his lolly, just like his father.'

'What's the number of his flat?'

'62, right at the top. Wonderful views.'

'Does he ever have visitors?'

'Yes, the Missus is always washing and changing bedclothes. They're mostly foreigners, and they don't talk to her either.'

Better and better, thought Georgina. 'Do you have a telephone number for Mr Anstey-Lloyd?'

From under the desk, Mick extracted a large, well-thumbed address book.

'834–9991.'

'Thank you, thank you a lot, you've been most helpful, and please don't mention my visit to anyone.'

'You don't want to go up and see him then.'

'Not today.'

Georgina left Victoria Court on a high. This would cheer the Superintendent no end. She knew he'd been getting more and more uptight at not being able to put his finger on anything tangible. Now he had a solid piece of concrete evidence. The Super had been right about Smith, about his name and his accent. She sat in the car wondering whether to call Byrd on their hot line. A short burst would do. If it was inconvenient he wouldn't answer, but he could be sitting for hours and hours with Jimmy Austin wondering what she was doing. The truth of the matter was she couldn't wait. Ping, ping, ping, she pressed three digits.

'Yes?'

'Convenient to talk?'

'Yes, we're back at base.'

'What!'

'Subject dead.'

'Oh, I'm sorry.'

'So am I,' said Byrd, 'seven hopelessly unhelpful words.'

'You'll like this,' said Georgina. 'I followed X to a block of luxury flats.'

Georgina heard his sigh of relief. At least something was going right.

'Don't talk now. Come straight here.'

'OK boss.'

By the time Georgina arrived the Ceremony of the Keys was over the fortress virtually closed down, but the guards were expecting her. They told her she could park in Mint Street and from there directed her to Queen's House. She drove through the Middle and Byward Towers, parked the car, and made her way to the Colonel's office.

110

Byrd was sipping coffee. He didn't ask Georgina whether she wanted one. She was given it willy-nilly.

'Now Georgina, tell us about this luxury flat.'

'Bill Smith, as you always suspected, sir, is a pseudonym. His real name is Jeremy Anstey-Lloyd.'

'Is he related to the M.P. who died a few years ago?'

Georgina nodded. 'His son.' Colonel Kilmaster couldn't contain himself.

'This calls for champagne, it's not just a step forward, it's a bloody great leap.'

Byrd laughed. 'It's a good job you're not in the Police, sir. Your salary wouldn't run to champagne every time you made a break-through.'

'Come on Sergeant,' said the Colonel, 'tell us more.'

'Anstey-Lloyd lives on his own in a very expensive apartment on the top floor of Victoria Court with wonderful views of the Houses of Parliament, Lambeth Palace and the river. From time to time he has foreign visitors and Mrs Thomas, the janitor's wife, cleans for our well-heeled foreman.'

'Good, I'll do a recce tomorrow while the Colonel keeps an eye on Smith here in The Tower.'

Georgina looked at Byrd, an unspoken question in her eyes.

'Yes, he died, Georgina. Only said seven words. *Chest . . . chest, chest 'is 'ead, and it me.* His head and his chest, the places where he felt the most pain. Poor sod. Why is a policeman's life made so difficult? If only Jimmy could have told me more, another sentence or two, that's all I needed. And Charley Austin's reaction, not at all what I expected.'

While the Superintendent sat shaking his head the Colonel left the room saying he had a mission to complete.

'What's bothering you, sir?' asked Georgina softly.

'I'd like to know why Charley Austin was so perturbed, so upset over his brother's death?'

'Isn't it natural for a brother to mourn?'

'But they weren't close, they never spoke despite working on the same site. You'd think, wouldn't you, that Charley Austin, being the elder brother would have kept an eye on the younger idle, tearaway Jimmy who was no good with a chisel, but put a pick in his hand and he might cope. Charley knew instinctively that Jimmy's hurts weren't caused by an accidental fall. He wasn't surprised, it was almost as if he'd been expecting the tragedy. But why?'

'You think he was pushed?'

'More than pushed. He looked as though he'd been thrown on to that mound of bricks, not once or twice, but several times. Charley Austin's expression when he looked at his brother was inscrutable. Two minutes in the ward, the time it took to ask Doctor Reader when the postmortem would be, and then he left.'

'And when will it be?'

'Tomorrow, no hanging about, tomorrow.'

15

As Colonel Kilmaster returned triumphant, carrying a bottle of Moët et Chandon, the phone rang. 'Damnation. We can do without these everyday interruptions.' He handed the bottle to Georgina and sat down to answer the phone.

'Tower of London.'

'American Embassy here, Sir.' A resonant voice, over the loud-speaking telephone, filled the office. 'We need to get in touch with a Mr Johnson, a Mr Harry Johnson, immediately. We understand he is spending a holiday at the Tower with relations.'

Byrd sat bolt upright. 'Steve Johson's cousin,' he whispered.

'Can you tell me what the problem is?' asked the Colonel.

'We'd rather speak with Mr Johnson, if that's possible. The matter is urgent.'

'If you don't mind hanging on a moment I'll see if a member of my staff can locate him for you.' The Colonel put his hand over the mouthpiece. 'If I give them the private number we'll never know what it's all about. Could you get over there, James, and tell Harry Johnson to pick up the house phone? You'll see his reactions and we will hear what's going on.'

Byrd knocked.

'Oh, hallo Mr Byrd,' said Brenda. 'You haven't seen Steve, have you?'

'No.' She looked worried. 'Is anything the matter Mrs Johnson?' asked Byrd.

'No, not really, but for a moment, I hoped you might be Steve, he often forgets his key.'

'It's Harry Johnson I want. Is he here?'

'Yes, come in.' He followed her into the sitting room.

'Harry, a visitor for you.'

'Hi there. You're only just in time Mr Byrd, I was about to go to bed.'

'There's an urgent phone call for you on the house phone. Colonel Kilmaster will connect you to the caller.'

'Why couldn't he ring direct?' asked Brenda.

'The switchboard may be on the blink. We thought it safer to do it this way.'

Harry picked up the black house phone. The white cordless one was Steve's toy, for which he paid the rent.

'Harry Johnson here.'

'Putting you through,' said the Colonel. Georgina and the Colonel listened in the office while the Superintendent's eyes never left the American.

'John Sainsbury, here. I'm Third Secretary at the American Embassy. We have an urgent message for you, from your sister.'

'My sister!'

'Yes, your sister in Texas. I'm sorry to have to tell you this but her husband died this morning, from a heart attack. The local Mayor managed to trace the Embassy number and put your sister through from his office. She wants you to return, at once, for the funeral.'

Harry hesitated. 'Return! I don't see the point in rushing back for a funeral, he's dead and there's nothing I can do about it.'

'Your sister,' said Sainsbury rather tersely, 'sounded distraught, Sir, as though everything was too much for her. I got the lot. Problems of ordering cattle feed, the difficulty in finding

114

labour, the awfulness of having to face the funeral on her own. She does need you there, sir.'

'All right, all right, I can see the problem.' There was a long pause. 'Are you on duty all evening, Mr Sainsbury?'

'Until midnight.'

'I'll come over straight away. Grosvenor Square, aren't you?'

'Yes, but . . .'

Harry replaced the phone.

Brenda looked at him astonishment. 'Your sister, is she dead then?'

'No, my brother-in-law. My sister wants me there to endure pointless death rites, and as far as I'm concerned rushing back for a funeral doesn't make any sort of sense, but I am going to rush over to the Embassy. There's sense in that.'

'Steve could run you there, if we knew where he was.'

'No, don't worry, Brenda, I'll get a taxi.'

'You won't be able to get back in, you know, not if you arrive after midnight.'

'No problem. I'll stay in a hotel. Now if you'll excuse me I'll get moving.'

Byrd waited until he heard him mounting the stairs before asking Brenda how much longer she expected Harry to be staying.

'We're not sure. Possibly another two weeks, perhaps longer because he's gone bananas over this place.' Byrd made a move to leave.

'Mr Byrd if you see Steve tell him to hurry back. I don't like being here on my own, at night.'

'All right, Mrs Johnson, I'll take a look round.'

A resounding pop greeted Byrd as he opened the office door. The Colonel was determined to celebrate their progress.

'Did you listen in on the conversation, sir?'

'Yes, A bit cool, wasn't he?'

'Yes, but I can see his point. He'd planned to stay at least another fortnight, and in all probability it's the last long holiday he'll ever have. Once he moves to the ranch, on a permanent basis, his sister will need constant help. Farming is a demanding business. Not only that, he may never again be able to find the ready, although, he doesn't seem short at the moment, not if he's thinking of taking a taxi to the Embassy, and staying overnight in a West End hotel.'

Their glasses were full. 'To success,' they said as one man.

Byrd hardly noticed the aromatic quality of the champagne. He was asking himself whether Sir Charles or Sir Elwyn had any contacts at the American Embassy? Their help could short-circuit enquiries. What, he wondered, was Harry Johnson saying to the Third Secretary?

'Have you any contacts at the American Embassy, Robin?'

'No, none, but if you want to use the old boy network the Governor's your man. He plays golf with the Ambassador, John G Chesterton, don't ask me what the G stands for, they usually play at Woburn. You need a report on Harry Johnson, is that it?'

'Yes. It may have no bearing but . . .'

'By the pricking of your thumbs, something evil this way comes?'

'I wouldn't go as far as that, but Harry Johnson is an unfeeling brother, cool, too cool.'

'OK, James, I'll speak to the Governor first thing tomorrow.'

Brenda waved goodbye to Harry. He was right, she thought, his brother-in-law was dead, it didn't make any sense whatever to make the long journey to Texas. She realised with some misgivings she didn't want him to go. She'd got used to having him around the place. He wasn't the drag she'd expected, he was thoughtful, much more thoughtful than Steve. Made his own bed, took them out for meals, even offered to do his own washing, but that wasn't necessary, because all she did was throw his soiled clothes into the washing machine. It was strange but Steve hadn't taken to him. She thought she knew why. Hadn't Steve been making plans for years, imagining Harry would do his bidding, set up his lecture tour? Steve, always cagey, didn't tell her too much but she guessed. Secretly she was pleased it wasn't going Steve's way. She didn't want to tear across America, a different place each night, meeting people she didn't know, always tagging along behind Steve. The story of her life. Once a sergeant major, always a sergeant major, but he'd come up against an immovable object. Harry wasn't going to be bossed around, told what to do, like the Tower visitors. She had to laugh, there was no way Steve could, in his devious way, manipulate Harry, and the biggest joke of all, she giggled to herself, was that his cousin outstripped him when it came to history.

Brenda didn't want to close the front door. She didn't want to be alone. The days were now as nerve-wracking as the nights. Only yesterday when she'd changed the sheets on Harry's bed the heart-breaking sobs had started all over again. She froze, still clutching a pillow in her hand, closed her eyes and held her breath hoping it would go away, hoping it was in her mind. Suddenly the crying ceased. She hugged the pillow to herself trying to derive comfort before daring to open her eyes. No, it wasn't imagination. The young Queen, a slip of a girl in a pale blue dress embroidered with pearls was kneeling by the window praying quietly in a language Brenda didn't understand. When she'd finished she rose and stood quite still looking up The Green towards the Beauchamp Tower. Brenda shivered, the cold in the room was intense, She fought the nausea and fear which overwhelmed her. She felt faint, but gathered herself together, and fearfully, took a step towards the girl. She wanted to comfort her, but stopped in her tracks as the grief stricken Lady Jane gave a deep felt moan and clutched her throat. Brenda moved slightly and peered through the window, and was amazed to see buildings she'd never seen before, and workmen in Tudor dress standing motionless and silent as Jane's husband was escorted to the scaffold. The young girl, now quite composed, raised her hand and waved. Lord Guildford Dudley looked up briefly, seemed to shake his head, and marched on. It was too much for Brenda.

'Don't let them. Don't let them do it,' she cried.

The scene faded. She found herself alone, and The Green once again peopled with tourists. Is it possible, she wondered, that I'm beginning to live with the ghost of Lady Jane? But now I'm plagued with those new noises that I can't bear, scary frightening noises of heavy furniture and chains being dragged across a floor, and why does it always seem to come from under the house? Those noises, she knew, were forcing her out, forcing her to spend more time with Sylvia and Barney. Their quarters in the Waterloo Block didn't have ghosts oozing out of the walls. No prisoners had ever been kept in their flat. Why did Steve always have to pour scorn on the theory – suggested by some historians – that Lady Jane Grey had been kept a close prisoner in their house? She knew they were right. She talked to the shadows. She had to talk to them, it was the only way to keep sane. She didn't consider herself an imaginative woman but she knew what she felt, what she heard, and what she saw.

As Brenda closed her door, Georgina climbed into her car which she'd parked outside the Tower gates, but she had no intention of going home. There was something she wanted to see for herself, and see it she would. After Byrd had seen her off, he decided to take a stroll along the ramparts before turning in. It was a wonderful balmy evening, red skies gradually fading and the lights on Tower Bridge giving it a fairy tale quality. There was still traffic on the river and he could hear laughter from a launch going upstream. Only then did he remember his promise to Brenda. Steve was probably home by now but he'd drop into the Yeoman Warders' Club, have a beer, find out whether Steve had been there during the evening, and test the strength of another thought which had just occurred to him.

The Club was full of Yeomen, hardly recognisable, in their off duty gear.

As Byrd perched on a stool at the bar Paul Hanson, the Chief Yeoman Warder came and stood alongside him.

'Good evening, *stranger*.' All the emphasis on stranger, hardly a good beginning, thought Byrd.

'Good evening Chief, what are you drinking?'

'A lager.'

'Make that two,' said Byrd to the barman.

'Mr Byrd,' said Hanson in his gravelly voice, 'when do you think you'll be in a position to fulfil your duties? And why are you being so bloody minded over the fittings for your uniform? I've never had this problem before. Rookie Yeomen normally can't wait to get cracking.'

'That's a long speech, if I may say so.'

'You've been a long time doing nothing, and the Colonel's excuses are wearing thin. And another thing, why have you been sitting at the bedside of an injured workman?'

Byrd sat bolt upright. 'How did you know that?'

'Yeoman Baker's wife is a nurse. She recognised you.'

There was only one way to satisfy the Chief Yeoman. He would have to be told. Another pair of eyes wouldn't come amiss. The Colonel himself had said the Chief never missed anything which occurred on site during the day. It was that remark which had triggered off his present thoughts about what a unbeatable combination the Deputy and his Chief could prove to be.

The two bearded men, one greying and the other younger, dark haired, sat silently looking at each other in the bar mirror. Despite the hubbub in the bar their silence, more unbridgeable by the minute, became a chasm. Byrd took the plunge.

'Have you, by any chance, seen Steve Johnson this evening?'

'No, don't expect to, it's his day off. Why do you ask?'

'His wife is worried. He didn't join them for supper.'

'Them!' Paul Hanson gave a guffaw which stopped the potter about to make a master stroke at bar billiards, and disturbed the Yeoman who'd been aiming at treble twenty. Everyone in the bar was silent. They listened to the conversation and nodded knowingly.

'You mean the American cousin of his who thinks he knows more about The Tower's history than all the rest of us put together. Do you know what I think, Mr Byrd? I think Steve's had a basinful of his distant American cousin, and I think he's gone out for the day, probably racing at Kempton with two of the lads.'

'Racing? But wouldn't he have told his wife?'

'Yes, he would normally, but Brenda seems taken with this guy, perhaps it's got up his nose.'

119

'Do you feel like taking a walk round The Green?' asked Byrd quietly, 'There are a few things you should know.'

Paul Hanson took a long look at the man beside him. The man who'd arrived for his new job in jeans and a shirt he himself wouldn't be seen dead in. He couldn't get this guy's measure, but there was no telling what an SAS man would do next. He gave a slight nod and left the club. Byrd followed him. As they passed No 5, Paul Hanson noticed a bit of paper in the letter box, addressed to Steve. He removed it. *Am round at Barney's, ring me when you arrive, Brenda.*

'Why on earth didn't she leave it inside the house?'

'Perhaps Steve is a practised loser of keys?'

The big man laughed. 'Bet he's not in my league. The only ones I've never managed to lose are the massive ones we use for the Ceremony. More than my life's worth to misplace them. Now, Mr Byrd, you didn't bring me out here to talk about keys. What's going on?'

'Let's sit on the wall over there. It's a long story.'

They crossed The Green and sat facing No.5. It was nearly dark but the lights Brenda had left burning beamed across The Green.

Byrd left nothing out, and Paul Hanson was too flabbergasted to interrupt. The story he was hearing could have come straight out of the pages of an Anthony Price or a Deighton thriller, but he found it hard to believe such disparate facts really had anything to do with the Tower. Much too far fetched. An American cousin, a Dutchman, an accident to a workman on site, a foreman, and lastly the inexplicable visits of a Trevor Rogerson to the White Tower. How could all these factors become inextricably entwined to produce a sinister scenario affecting the Tower? The shock waves emanating from the Chief said it all. He was certainly above suspicion, so too was the Deputy Governor, no collusion there.

'Thank you Mr Byrd for filling me in. I must say it's stranger than any of the fiction I read. However, I can quite see you have a job to do, and I'll ease your path. You may not realise it but you are a most unpopular man, not pulling your weight, you know.'

'Yes, the vibes have petered through.'

'Take my advice, join in the bowls matches, play a bit of tennis, do a bit more with the jazz group. I'll think up an excuse for not including you on the duty roster. I know', he said triumphantly, 'you may be called back on a special mission to the Far East, so what with that and the illness of your mother-in-law it's best not to put you on permanent duties.'

The sound of raucous laughter reached them.

'It's Nobby Clarke and Little Tich, back from the races. Hang on, Mr Byrd, I'll see if Steve's been with them.'

Paul Hanson, for all his weight, moved fast. 'Nobby', he shouted.

Nobby stopped in his tracks. 'Now what have I done, Chief? The place is still standing, isn't it?'

'We're looking for Steve Johnson. Not been with you, has he?'

'No. Have you got it in for him?' Both men laughed.

'Not this time. He's been missing all day. Brenda's worried.'

'Living it up at long last, is he? Good old Steve,' roared Little Tich.

'Did you win, or have you been drowning your sorrows?' asked Byrd.

'We won one, and we lost one or two.'

'You should have more sense,' growled the Chief.

'Come on Mr Byrd, we'll go over to Barney's place, those silly blighters have been no help at all. We'll have a word with Brenda.'

They let themselves into the Waterloo Block and then up in a slow creaking lift until they reached the second floor. Byrd noticed that all the rooms near the lift were allocated as office space, but beyond the offices there were flats for the Yeomen and their families. Paul Hanson fairly hammered on the door, but with the T.V. going full blast, his efforts were in vain. 'Bloody noise,' he muttered, as he opened the door and yelled in a well trained sergeant major's voice, 'Anyone at home?'

Sylvia Barnes rushed to the door. 'Oh, hallo Paul, come in, and you too Mr Byrd. She grinned at the Superintendent. She'd heard a lot about him from Barney. She'd been hoping to meet

121

him. 'We've not met officially but I've heard you playing with the group. We're all in a huddle at the moment trying to keep Brenda amused. There's a quiz programme on, only another five minutes to go, but we can turn it off if you want to talk to her.'

'We'll wait until it's finished, love,' said the Chief.

Once Brenda started talking there was no stopping her. Steve never went off for the day without telling her where he was going, and he had not taken his overnight case. Yes, his electric razor was still in the bathroom. Yes, both his uniforms were hanging in the wardrobe. No, there was nothing wrong with his heart. He had a check-up six weeks ago. Yes, he could have gone to the Guildhall Library, but he was never late back.

Never.

16

It was a long long night for Brenda. She slept fitfully on Sylvia's uncomfortable sofa, waking all too often to wonder what had got into Steve. He'd never behaved like this before, but she had noticed a change in him over the last five or six months. A willingness to help a bit more, a suggestion now and again that she should take up new interests. He'd always expected to be waited on, had never thought of doing the dishes, not until recently, it was almost as though he wanted her out of the house.

Harry, on the other hand, did himself proud. He stayed at the luxurious Mayfair Hotel, slept like the proverbial log, had breakfast served in his room and at the same time devoured *The Times*, and *The Guardian*. He neither worried about Steve's absence, nor the departure of his brother-in-law from this mortal coil.

Superintendent James Byrd did without his six-hour sleep. Instead he drank cup after cup of strong tea enabling the cogs of his inventive mind to keep turning over. He desperately, through instinct and intuition, attempted to make connections between Jimmy Austin's death and Steve's absence, but the pattern didn't fit. There was no thread, it seemed, to tack them together.

Colonel Kilmaster didn't lose any sleep. A workman had died, carelessness on the part of the foreman. A post mortem first and then, perhaps, an inquest. It was up to the coroner to apportion blame. And as for Steve Johnson, his absence must be intentional. In his book Steve had always been singularly uncommunicative, an odd man out. Very few visitors, very few friends, kept himself to himself. Probably gone off with another woman. Why else did a man vanish?

Georgina rang Byrd at 6.50 as he was preparing for his early morning jog.

'What's the matter, can't you sleep?'

'I took a look last night, sir, at Trevor Rogerson's place. There's something odd about it. They have a car which they park on the hard standing outside a garage which is heavily padlocked. There was a hell of a lot of banging going on inside the garage which didn't seem to perturb the neighbours or his wife, Maureen, who was watching TV with the curtains wide open. The room is quite tastefully furnished, a few pictures on the walls, and a couple of sculptures. Doesn't look much like the home of a small London gangster.'

'Neither did Anstey-Lloyd's flat look like the home of a well-heeled criminal.'

'Touché! But I thought you'd rather know than not know!' she said crisply.

'Thanks, Sergeant, that's what I call devotion to duty.'

More Brownie points, she muttered to herself as she replaced the phone.

As Byrd jogged round the precinct of Her Majesty's concentric fortress, he began to feel increasingly uneasy about the padlocked garage in Stockwell which was being used for anything but the purpose for which it was intended. He thought about Maureen Rogerson, Maureen who could be Irish, and Paul Rogerson, possibly living under an assumed name, who might also be Irish. What was he manufacturing

124

in his makeshift workshop that could damage The Tower? As he pondered the problem he saw Brenda leaving the Waterloo Block. An opportunity here to test one of his theories. As she reached her front door, so too did Byrd. He stopped in his tracks, puffing quite considerably, and asked if she'd heard from Steve. Brenda's red eyes and swollen lips told the whole story.

'Why don't you make a cup of tea, Mrs Johnson, and I'll join you, that is, if you don't mind.'

She unlocked the front door and Byrd followed her into a kitchen. The panels, Byrd noticed, were painted, like those of the sitting room, in a bilious orange and green. Everything was modern with the exception of a large dark oak armoire.

'That's a magnificent piece of furniture, Mrs Johnson.'

'If you like that sort of thing, Mr Byrd, but I don't. It's too dark, too large and too old.'

'It looks like a late 16th century piece,' said Byrd. 'Has it always been here?'

'Steve thinks so. He's crazy about it and won't have it moved.'

Byrd ran his hands over it lovingly thinking how well it would look in a Georgian house he coveted in Enstone.

'You can open it, take a look, if you want.'

Byrd turned the key and opened the immaculately carved door. It was superb. Shelves down one side, drawers down the other, and hanging space in the centre. He noticed two large torches on the bottom shelf and an assortment of tools, quite odd tools for a man who spent his life in London. He closed the doors, thoughtfully.

'Mr Byrd, have you had breakfast?'

'No, not yet.'

'Would you like a piece of toast with your tea?'

'What a good idea.'

Brenda gave him a watery smile. 'You must be tired of living here on your own.'

Byrd didn't want to continue that theme. 'It won't be for much longer, I hope. Tell me, Mrs Johnson what . . .'

'Oh, do call me Brenda, everyone else does.'

'All right then. Tell me, Brenda, what are Steve's interests? What does he do with his time?'

'He's not a great mixer but he does like his bowls. His real interest, though, is the Tower. It's his life, you know, doesn't want to retire, even hates taking holidays.'

'Don't you ever manage to escape?

'"Escape" is the right word. Yes, we escape, but not far enough. We have a cottage in Cropredy, next door to my sister's place. We go there a lot but you can hardly call it a holiday, a change, maybe, no more than that. It's all very dull after holidaying in Italy.'

'Italy!'

'When Steve was stationed in Germany, we spent a lot of time in Europe, particularly Italy. Sun and pasta in the right doses. It was great.'

'Cropredy, isn't that near Banbury?'

'Yes.'

'So, now you never go far afield?'

'Never. Steve's saving up for an American tour, wants to give lectures about the Tower, but he's keeping it close to his chest. Harry, his American cousin knows, of course.'

'And when you stay in your cottage, what does he do with his time?'

'He walks a lot, we both do, and he plays bowls when he can get a game.' Byrd chose his words carefully.

'Doesn't indulge in treasure hunting, I suppose?'

'No, thank God. We hear enough about lost treasure here, but if you ask me, that's all my eye!' Tears poured down Brenda's face. She could see Steve's reaction when she'd poured scorn on all the latest theories he dreamed up of buried treasure. If he were with her now, she'd still be scornful, and he'd smile his tight smile, and say *you'll never know, Brenda, you'll never know.*

'Mr Byrd, something's happened to Steve, I know it has. Barney and Sylvia think I'm making a mountain, but I'm not. He's had an accident, he's been knocked down. Steve's always saying that the mad drivers who drive round Tower Hill as if they were at Brands Hatch should be put inside, but the traffic passing the London Museum is even worse. That's where it could have happened because he's always traipsing over there to read up on stuff. I don't know why he bothers because he has enough books here on the Tower to fill a suitcase.'

Brenda was choked. She put her head down on the table and sobbed her heart out.

Byrd felt totally inadequate, whatever he said would make matters worse. There was nothing he could do except wait. Brenda lifted her head. 'I'm sorry Mr Byrd, I'm sorry to inflict this on you.'

He took her hand. 'Brenda, if you like I'll let both Colonel Kilmaster and the Chief know what's happening, but before leaving may I have a look round the house, make sure everything's as it should be? You never know, something might strike me!'

Brenda thought about this for some moments. Steve didn't like strangers in the house, but he couldn't object to her receiving a helping hand could he? 'Yes, please have a look round.'

The Superintendent, adopting his usual method of search, started from the top. The massive attic, supported by beams roughly hewn from elm trees, housed an aerial, a couple of trunks, chairs, and an old record player. Everything was covered in years of dust. No clues there.

On the floor below were two enormous bedrooms. One each side of the vast staircase which split the house in two. The bedroom on the right was empty, but the one on the left was in use. The American's gear was strewn all over the floor. There were books on the Tudors, books on the Stuarts, books on The Tower, and on the bedside table two books on James Scott, Duke of Monmouth interlaced with several bits of newspaper to mark any points of interest. Under them an A4 notepad which Byrd read with increasing interest. All the notes related to Monmouth. 'Wonderful', he shouted to the empty air. He sat on the bed knowing his instinct had not led him astray. All he needed was confirmation from the American Embassy.

On the floor were two large suitcases, the larger of which was secured by a combination lock. This was the case Georgina had described to him, the one she'd been unable to open. What wouldn't he give for Sergeant Quinney's presence. Quinney, his right hand man on so many occasions could open anything. Time was running out. He had to move fast before Harry Johnson returned, and before Brenda wondered why he was taking so long. Georgina, she was the key. He tapped out her number.

'Yes?' She never wasted words.

'Remember that combination lock you couldn't open?'

'Yes.'

'Ring Sergeant Quinney at Kidlington. Describe it to him. I want to know how to open it in the next five minutes.'

'Say abracadabra, and hey presto, three times.' He heard a slight giggle and then she was gone.

In the small case he found more notebooks containing innumerable illegible, or nearly illegible scrawlings about The Tower. Under the heading *St Peter's Ad Vincula* there was a list of nobles who were executed on Tower Hill and buried in the Chapel. A shorter list giving details of the seven men and women who were beheaded in private on Tower Green. With every additional note his hypothesis became more tenable.

Beep, beep, beep.

'Yes?'

'Try first of all using the owner's name. Assume A=1, B=2, and so on. Use zero to separate the numbers. It's all he can suggest off the cuff.'

'OK, Thanks.'

Byrd ripped a sheet of paper out of one of the notebooks, and worked out a simple code on the basis Quinney had suggested. At his first attempt using a ball point pen to select the digits he dialled 80. 10. 180. 180. 250. 100. 150. 80. 140. 190. 140.

Nothing, absolutely nothing, sweet Fanny Adams. In the States perhaps Johnson was spelt Jonson. He tried again leaving out the 'h'. Nothing! Byrd painstakingly tried several variations, first making A=2, and then 3, but the code remained unbreakable. He was getting desperate. Any minute now Harry Johnson would be back. One last shot. Why not dial the place name first? 160=P, 180=R, 90=I, 140=N, 30=C, 50=E, 200=T, 150=O, 140=N. There was a click and the hasp sprang open.

The Superintendent, kneeling in front of the case, froze. He gazed in bewilderment at the assortment of handwritten papers in front of him. A strange musty smell filled the room with unspoken messages from the past. It wasn't what he'd expected. His intuition was way off beam. After he had carefully extracted a document from the middle of the pile, its seal still intact, he pressed the hasps home, and left the case as he'd found it, hoping one small document wouldn't be missed.

Byrd knew exactly what he was going to do. No waiting around for the old boy network to operate. He needed information, like now. He dashed back to his lodging to change from his trainers and shorts into a lightweight suit, making a concession to the man he was going to see by wearing a tie. First of all he must call at the Byward Tower. Luck was with him. Paul Hanson was standing in the archway holding the 'wait' in his hand.

'No, I've no duties for you today Mr Byrd.' He winked, always enjoying being part of a conspiracy. Byrd drew him away from the building.

'Can you keep an eye on the American? I imagine he'll be back any time now; I want to know where he is every minute of the day. Once he's in, don't let him out again, and make sure Brenda spends the day with Sylvia Barnes.'

'We'll let him in, Mr Byrd, but we'll not let him out. Once a fortress, always a fortress.' His attempt at humour was wasted.

Byrd was thinking, and didn't like what he was thinking. This impostor, this so-called Harry Johnson, might be responsible for two murders. Might be, might be, but his instinct told him to tread carefully. Nothing in this case was straightforward, but where, oh where was the real Harry Johnson, and where was Steve Johnson? What did the two missing cousins know?

Hanson knew he'd lost the Superintendent. The man at his side was engaged in hypothetical conjecture, it was written all over his face, so too was the fact that he was discarding theory after theory. Byrd spoke at last.

'Have a quiet word with the Colonel. Tell him I'm on my way to the American Embassy. If he wants to get in touch, ring Georgina.'

'Georgina! Who's Georgina when she's at home?'

'She's hardly ever at home, and she's my linkman,' and with that parting shot Byrd vanished, leaving his companion to dwell on another twist in the story.

The Superintendent decided to use the Underground, parking where he was going would be an impossibility. As he stood waiting he thought about the padlocked garage, a recurring thought, which remained uppermost in his mind. If the articles being manufactured in that garage were what he imagined, then it was up to him to put the matter firmly and squarely upon the shoulders of Special Branch, but it would be politic to test the waters first. Waters! That was the answer. Mayhew and Paxton could take on the role of water-rating assessors. Get into the house, look in the garden for outside taps, and with luck get themselves into the garage.

John Sainsbury, the Third Secretary at the Embassy was feeling distinctly out of countenance. On the previous day he'd been on duty until midnight, and on Saturdays he always lay in until about eleven, had a shower, followed by a leisurely breakfast with his wife. His Excellency had ruined his day by ringing him at an uncivilised hour, on a day they'd planned to spend at Wimbledon. Not only that, they had V.I.P tickets for seats on the Centre Court, with lavish hospitality laid on. His Excellency wanted to see him *tout de suite*. An urgent matter, couldn't wait until the morrow.

With exceedingly bad grace he sat down at his desk and glared at the swarthy, bearded individual who looked more like a middle-aged hippy than a police superintendent. Hadn't wasted much time either in making himself at home. The steward on duty had looked after his visitor, coffee, cream and biscuits. You'd think the man hadn't eaten for a week. Munch, munch, munch and the biscuits were gone. He looked at his watch, 9.40, the most lowering time of the day because he was never even properly awake. His Excellency had briefed him. A Detective Superintendent was waiting to interview him. All questions were to be answered, quite frankly, and assistance unstintingly given.

130

'Well, Superintendent Byrd, I've been given my orders, what is it you want to know?'

Byrd sensed the antipathy. A young man dragged out of bed on his day off to answer questions, searching questions about one of his fellow countrymen. Despite the orders issued by the Ambassador, he could see that the young man would only give him the bare outlines unless the situation could be sweetened. A fulsome apology, perhaps?

'Mr Sainsbury, forgive me for calling at this uncivilised hour.' On Byrd's clock there were no uncivilised hours. All hours were the same when running someone to ground. 'I understand you were on duty late yesterday evening, and that today you hope . . .'

No, hope was the wrong word, he quickly added, 'and intend to enjoy the ballistics at Wimbledon this afternoon. I'd hate to deprive you of a second of that so I'll come straight to the point.'

Byrd felt an almost imperceptible change, a little more *entente cordiale*.

Sainsbury leant forward and poured himself a cup of coffee,

'OK Superintendent, I'm here to help. What do you want to know?'

'Harry Johnson, is why I'm here. He rang you yesterday, Mr Sainsbury, and came to see you yesterday evening.'

'I didn't see Harry Johnson yesterday evening, and I'd like to know, Superintendent, why the Governor of the Tower telephoned my Ambassador?' One up to the Colonel, thought Byrd. He really did get off the mark. No wonder my way to the Ambassador was strewn with palm leaves.

'I'm afraid I can't divulge cause or effect, Mr Sainsbury, and that's something you don't have to worry about. All I need to know is what passed between you and an impostor posing as Harry Johnson.'

John Sainsbury's unease was patently obvious. He frowned as he clenched and unclenched his fists. His Excellency had laid down the ground rules, every question was to be answered. The

Superintendent was sitting where, on the previous evening, his old college professor had sat. What on earth had the old guy been up to?

During Lawrence Berkeley's short visit he'd been quite clear in his demands, and expected his requests to be carried out immediately. It was strange how ten years had dropped away, the student dutifully carrying out his Professor's orders. First the phone call to the police in Wevertown, virtually ordering them to go immediately to his cabin above Indiana Lake, to find Harry Johnson. If he wasn't at the cabin he'd be fishing, so scour the lake until you find him. 'When you do,' he'd said, 'tell him to contact his sister because there's been a death in the family. Tell him to fly, the Professor will pay.' What had any of this to do with the police?

'Well, Mr Sainsbury, who was the impostor?'

'My Professor, Lawrence Berkeley.'

'Your Professor?'

'Yes, I majored in history at Princeton.'

'And where is the real Harry Johnson?'

'On holiday, or he was until yesterday, at the Professor's cabin in the Adirondak Mountains.'

'I see! So they changed places. Why?'

'Harry had been pressured by his cousin, for years, to spend a holiday in The Tower. He wasn't interested. He's a quiet man, would rather spend his time fishing, the bright lights don't appeal to him.'

'OK. That makes sense. So why did Professor Lawrence Berkeley want to change places?'

'It was an idea which occurred to him during a period when he was suffering the effects of an unforgiveable literary theft. For over a decade he'd carried out research on a subject dear to his heart. He'd lived, and breathed the subject, which became as important to him as anyone's first born. His wonderfully developed, carefully researched ideas were stolen and used by an academic whom he'd met at a Cambridge symposium, some five years previously. He'd made the mistake of talking quite openly about his project to Professor Kettle, and the men became friends. Five years later Lawrence Berkeley's

132

monograph on Francis Bacon was ready for publication, but he was too late. Kettle had beaten him to it. There sat the thief at high table, awaiting the scholastic eulogies which poured in from academia worldwide. Naturally the Prof was heartbroken, angry, and suicidal. Wouldn't you be if your nearest and dearest had died? He was at a desperately low ebb, his only solace was to hide away, escape to his retreat in the mountains and spend a few weeks fishing. Harry Johnson accompanied him and it was there, I believe, that Harry told him that he was expected to spend a holiday at The Tower with relatives he didn't know, and really didn't want to know. Thus, the idea of changing places was born. The adrenalin flowed again. The Prof realised it gave him a heaven sent opportunity to revive a theory he'd held for years about the Duke of Monmouth.'

'Monmouth of the Monmouth Rebellion?'

'That's the guy.'

Byrd thought about the documents he'd removed from the case. It all fitted.

The Third Secretary couldn't understand the interest the police were taking in Lawrence Berkeley. It was hardly a crime to change places with a janitor who had willingly aided and abetted the deception. What had the Prof done? If only the Superintendent would give him an inkling. He might be able to warn the Professor, but that wasn't ethical. On the other hand he was pretty sure the Prof hadn't done anything criminal. He could still hear the Prof explaining exactly how the impersonation had arisen. No he mustn't warn him, he was jumping to conclusions, *False face might hide what the false heart doth know*.

'Relax, Mr Sainsbury.' It was as though the policeman could read his mind.

'If you've time before you dash off to Wimbledon could you check up with the Wevertown Police? Make sure they've found Harry Johnson, make sure he's still alive.'

'Oh, yes they did.' Sainsbury was eager in his affirmation. 'The Ambassador received a fax in the early hours. He was at the cabin cooking his day's catch. They drove him to the airport where, fortunately, he caught a plane with only ten minutes to spare,'

'Good. Now that I know Harry Johnson is alive and well, I'll leave you to enjoy your day off.'

'One thing before you go, Superintendent, does this complete your enquiry or do you still have an interest in Lawrence Berkeley?'

'Yes, inasmuch as he's led two unsuspecting people up the garden path. Two hospitable people who opened their home to him, two people who will be hurt by the revelation.'

'Yes, yes, there's that, sir, but the Professor told me that Steve Johnson was using Harry. Using him to set up a lecture tour throughout the States.'

'We all use each other, Mr Sainsbury, some more voraciously than others.'

'Perhaps you can tell me, Superintendent, whether there can be any rapport or affection between two men whose only point of contact is a great grandfather? It's poetic justice, isn't it? Instead of Steve using Harry, Harry through Lawrence was using Steve.'

'Very convoluted,' said Byrd drily, 'but I get your drift.'

'So what else have you got on Professor Berkeley?'

'Nothing I want to shout about at the moment, so quit worrying, Mr Sainsbury, and I'll get out of your hair.'

17

Roosevelt, statuesque and stony faced, gazed with unseeing eyes at Byrd as he left the Embassy. Before returning to The Tower he decided to make two calls in the West End. Twenty minutes later a taxi deposited him outside Victoria Court.

'Not an M.P. are you, Guv?'

'Why do you ask?'

'That block of flats is full of 'em.'

'No, nothing so exalted,' said Byrd. 'I'm flatfooted.'

The taxi driver was quick, but not that quick! 'Oh, you mean you've got dropped meta whats its?'

'Something like that.' Byrd grinned and left him pondering.

Mick Thomas, the janitor remembered Georgina, a nice polite lass. 'Will you be wanting to take a look round, sir?'

'A brief reconnaissance with your wife in attendance would be most helpful.'

Mick peered at the identity card being wafted in front of his nose. 'They haven't done you justice, sir. Your photograph makes you look more like a convict than a policeman.'

'You do understand, don't you, that I haven't had time to raise

135

a search warrant, but I'll be most circumspect.'

'That's OK sir.' Mick didn't like Anstey-Lloyd, didn't know why, could never quite put his finger on it, but he'd be secretly pleased if Anstey-Lloyd was in trouble, big trouble. It was those foreign friends of his that bothered Mick. They never said much in the foyer, nor did they talk if he took them up in the lift. He knew, in his bones, they were up to no good.

'Mr Anstey-Lloyd's going away next week, expects to be away for a few days, possibly a week. My wife's up there now ironing the shirts and bits and pieces he wants to take with him.'

'Do you know where he's going?'

'No idea, sir. Foreign parts, I expect, it usually is.'

The flat was something else! Hardly the setting for a Cockney foreman with its Louis Quinze settee, Dutch ebony chairs inlaid with mother-of-pearl, a Chippendale cabinet in his Chinese style, and an incredible collection of clocks. Byrd loved its elegance, its stupendous views and its comfort but living there would have driven him spare. Every clock was ticking away. The noise was deafening.

'Do you keep the clocks wound, Mrs Thomas?

'Oh no, I wouldn't dare. It's his hobby, you see. He buys them, always meaning to sell them, but he never does, and he don't half love to hear them tick, and you wait until they start chiming.'

'You mean all these nineteen clocks chime?'

'Yes, he won't buy them if they don't.'

What an extraordinary quirk, thought Byrd. He could understand a collector's mania for accumulating clocks, but failed to understand why they all had to tick and chime. How could anyone listen to music or watch television with an invasive sound that took over, depriving one of the ability to think?

'You get used to it, sir.' Mrs Thomas knew what he was thinking. 'The noise don't bother me no more. You take a decco while I get on with the ironing.'

Before giving the flat the once over, he called Georgina. He had to know what was going on at 15, Victoria Road, Stockwell.

'It was wonderful, sir, absolutely fabulous.'

'What was?'

'Mrs Rogerson is Welsh, not Irish, and she paints, quite well,

136

in fact, but her husband is a sculptor who works in metal. He is making the most amazing models of Henry VIII's armour, on a smaller scale, of course, as well as producing a horse caparisoned and ready for war. They are fantastic and have been commissioned by the chairman of a Belgian steel firm, who wants something spectacular in the boardroom. Trevor Rogerson's a quiet kind of guy who doesn't seem to know how clever he is. It was his wife who told me he's just invented a new method of chasing metal.'

'Chasing,' said Byrd acidly, 'is what we're supposed to be good at. Well, since that's a blind alley, find out from Bossman whether the foreman and his labourers are on site today, and also whether records have anything at all on Anstey-Lloyd. Let me know the answer, pronto!'

Georgina didn't bother to reply. She merely replaced the phone.

The 18th century walnut knee hole desk yielded no secrets. The bottom drawers were empty, and the others filled with headed notepaper, envelopes, playing cards, and a selection of board games. The notepad by the telephone on the desk was virgin, or that's what Byrd thought until he ripped off the top sheet and was able to discern faint indentations. Taking care not to fold the evidence he placed it in his wallet for later scrutiny. Nothing in any of the bedrooms spoke to him. Clothing and shoes carefully arranged. A dozen suits and as many pairs of shoes. Nothing other than underclothes in the chest of drawers. No photographs of the owner. No photographs of family or friends. No groups of rugger teams, surprising because Smith alias Anstey-Lloyd looked like the typical scrum half. No proud looking cricketers, no school trophies. Nothing. There was nothing, yet everything. Maybe there was a hidden safe, but where? He looked round the sitting room, trying to think, in spite of the ticking, where he would hide anything of importance. The pictures! Of course. He painstakingly removed and replaced each picture. As he was hanging the last picture he caught his little finger on a panel pin causing it to bleed profusely. Propping the picture up against an armchair he administered first aid with a disgustingly grubby handkerchief. Once the bleeding had eased he picked up the picture. He couldn't believe his luck. At last his labour was rewarded. The picture had never been properly framed; brown adhesive paper was peeling off and the panel pins were only lightly hammered home. He wanted to take it apart without Mrs Thomas seeing. But how, time was the essence? His bloody finger, there lay the answer. Off came the handkerchief, and with a gentle squeeze the blood started oozing again. Mrs Thomas, most obligingly, nipped down in the lift to find plasters and antiseptic cream. He waited until the indicator told him the lift had reached the ground floor then he pressed the button recalling it back to the top floor. With only one flat on the 6th floor there was no problem. He placed his shoe against the side of the lift door to prevent it closing, rushed back to the sitting room, leaving the front door open, picked up the picture, carried it to the hall table and proceeded to remove the backing. It was a simple job.

He whistled in surprise. It was not at all what he expected to find. Why had he imagined details of a Swiss account would be tucked behind a picture? What he was looking at was much more subtle. A picture behind a picture.

A small, but exquisite, still life signed by Braque. More food for thought. He heard someone trying to call the lift. He had to hurry. Back went the Braque, the panel pins were pressed home with a gadget he always carried with him, and the paper which was still sticky in places was stuck on again.

He could hear someone trying to operate the lift. They'd given up. Quickly now, retrieve the shoe, close the lift gate, shut the front door and replace the picture.

As Byrd rehung the picture he realised the hall table wasn't a table at all. It was a dough bin, a piece of furniture he'd only seen in books on antiques. It was too late to take a look. Mrs Thomas rushed in as eager as Florence Nightingale with a large blue box decorated with a red cross.

'You shouldn't have gone to so much trouble. All I need is a plaster. It's only a pin prick, Mrs Thomas.'

'It's bleeding a lot. How'd you manage to do it?'

'Stupid of me really. I straightened up one of the pictures. Caught my finger on a small tack.'

'You'd better go to Casualty and get a tetanus injection.'

'It doesn't warrant such stringent measures.'

'You won't be saying that if you get poisoned.'

Byrd laughed. 'I'll survive. Don't you worry about me, I'm sure you've got plenty to do.'

'You can say that again. Well, if you're OK, sir, I'll get on, can't stand about, you know.' She gave him a quizzical look. 'Haven't you seen enough?'

'Nearly, but I'll walk round again, get the feel of the place.'

'Mick said to tell you, in case you're interested like, that Mr Anstey-Lloyd doesn't keep any valuables here, apart from the clocks, of course. The rest of the stuff is in the bank, the Midland Bank at the end of the road.'

'Thanks, Mrs Thomas, I appreciate your help.'

The noises from the kitchen sounded reassuring. A great deal of banging, shelves being moved. Cleaning the oven, he guessed. The lid of the dough bin opened easily and came straight off. It was hewn in one piece with two enormous wooden dowels which slotted into holes in the back of the chest. The dough bin full to the brim with sheets and blankets which he hastily dumped on the floor. It looked innocent enough and yet he could have sworn the outside was deeper than the inside. There was a small hole in the bottom of the chest caused by a knot in the wood. He put his finger through the cavity and tugged. Gradually the false bottom was eased out. The musty smell which regaled his nostrils was familiar, but the cupboard was bare. The oak dough bin was old, early sixteenth century, he'd guess, which might explain the distinctive odour. A disappointed Superintendent replaced the contents, and made his way slowly down the stairs, noting the names on every flat as he passed.

What had Lawrence Berkeley, alias Harry Johnson, and Anstey-Lloyd, alias Bill Smith, in common? And what connection, if any, had both of them with Kees Van Den Hoorn?

'Any luck, sir, did you find what you were looking for?' Mick Thomas sitting behind his desk heard the slow march of footsteps

139

down the stairs. As Byrd entered the foyer he popped up like a jack-in-the-box. Byrd put a finger on his lips, and winked. Mick nodded knowingly.

'Always knew he was up to no good,' he whispered.

It took him only twenty minutes to walk from Victoria Court to New Scotland Yard. Along Horseferry Road, through the street market, across Victoria Street and into the building. Detective Inspector Frank Pollard owed him. He hated himself for having to call on old debts, but he'd be on the job for ever unless he got things moving. Frank Pollard wasn't the man to let him down. It was fourteen or fifteen years since they'd been uniformed constables called to a hold-up on a trading estate. When they arrived the Securicor van door was open. One guard lay on the ground, motionless, and the other man was struggling to his feet when one of the robbers shot him in the leg. The two constables driving down the narrow lane to the electronics factory were unarmed. There'd been precious little time to think and maybe they hadn't made the best decision. It could so easily have been curtains for them both, but they had blocked the escape route by placing the police car athwart the exit.

They leapt out of the car, Byrd having the presence of mind to remove the ignition key. He was protected by the police car but Frank Pollard found himself face to face with the gunman. A shot whistled past Frank's head. 'Now shift the bloody car,' shouted the thug, 'otherwise you'll both be butcher's meat.'

It came to Byrd in a flash that they had a chance because only one of the robbers was armed. The driver of the red Cortina, reported stolen the day before, made no move to get out of the car. Another shot, singeing the outer edge of Frank's sleeve. Byrd held the key aloft, and shouted, 'Here's the key, matey.' Somehow he had to needle the fellow.

'Well get in then, get in you bloody idiot, and move the car.'

'Don't feel like driving.' Byrd ducked as the thug, facing him across the car, took aim. That was three bullets gone. Now he had to provoke him into firing the last three by throwing the key into a flower bed alongside the factory wall. That was too much for the frustrated gunman who, in his anger, ran round the car and let off the last three rounds, this time at Byrd. At that moment they heard sirens as more police cars converged on the estate. It was a five minute episode in their lives, five minutes which bound them together for life, five minutes they'd never mentioned from that day to this. Byrd didn't enjoy the prospect of leaning on Frank, but he had to admit he was beginning to feel a little out of his depth.

Inspector Pollard knew Detective Superintendent Byrd wasn't making a social call. Byrd was here on business, private business, otherwise he would have phoned.

'Well James, if you want to talk, we'd better have coffee in the canteen where we won't be interrupted.'

They settled themselves in a far corner overlooking the road with a glimpse of St James's Park beyond.

'You're out of your parish, James. What brings you to the Great Wen?'

'I'm working in the City on a highly secret operation, can't spell it out, I'm afraid, not at the moment, but you're the man who has the expertise I need.'

Frank took a long look at the man facing him, a man who eschewed asking favours, who was uncomfortable in his mission. There was nothing he wouldn't do for this man, nothing. He vividly recalled the figure in a dark boiler suit, stocking mask, waving a revolver in front of him. Not even time for a *Hail Mary*. It could have been yesterday, but he owed Byrd fourteen years of yesterdays.

'Tell me what you want, James.'

'It's your field, Frank. You'll be able to put me right. Tell me, are all auction houses allowed to auction goods, works of art, and what have you, without ever revealing the name of the vendor?'

'Yes, both can remain anonymous, because the goods can be variously described as the property of a gentleman, or of a nobleman, or of a lady and so on.'

'Presumably you boys can demand the information?'

'Only if we suspect the article to have been stolen or faked. That's our remit.'

'And the Inland Revenue, can't the tax boys pick it up?'

'In this country, I'd say probably, yes, otherwise they'd be losing a fortune on capital gains.'

'You mean France, Germany, Switzerland could be different?'

'I'm sure the French, with all their bureaucracy, wouldn't lose out on capital gains, but the Swiss may well turn a blind eye.'

Bush stirred his coffee thoughtfully. 'If it's not putting you on the spot, could I have a sight of your catalogue of stolen pictures or manuscripts over the past five years?'

'We don't have a complete list, but there are moves in the right direction. All auction lots of over £2,500 are now checked against a master list of goods, prior to sale. The Arts Trade Liaison Committee, the IAALR, has established a central computerized register of stolen art. It should help, but at the moment thefts total £3.5 million and only about 5% is recovered. We don't, at the moment, allow access to our confidential files, and I hope we never do, because it could prove to be a political football. The computer system doesn't cover fakes, or smuggled works of art, so what exactly are you after, James?'

'A list of rare and valuable manuscripts, or documents stolen or sold over the past five years.'

'Our lists are enormous, and comprehensive.' Frank was tuned in. 'You're wanting the Interpol list, of course, which covers Europe?'

'You've got it,' smiled Byrd.

'Where shall I send it?'

'Don't send it. Why don't I wait for both lists to be photocopied?'

A whole range of emotions flickered for a moment in Frank Pollard's eyes, which changed to a less than friendly stare, something which Byrd didn't miss.

'Frank, I'll level with you. I'm on a job which isn't coming together, a job which I foolishly thought would occupy me for no more than a month. I'm not living at home, you know what discord that can create, and the sooner I make some headway the better. I'm a beggar, Frank, and I need every scrap you can give me.'

Frank relaxed. Byrd as a beggar was distinctly different from Byrd pulling rank, and he owed this man.

'It'll take some time, James. Why don't you take an early lunch here in the canteen, and I'll get cracking with the lists?'

The smell of canteen curry hanging heavy in the air reminded Byrd that all he'd eaten since he stepped off the plane at Heathrow, the day before was a piece of toast and half a dozen biscuits. His hunger was swiftly assuaged with soup, curry, and steamed jam roll. While he munched away he pondered the words of a dying man. *Chest . . . chest, chest, is ead, it me.* Seven words. Why would a dying man repeat chest? Because it was damn painful. As simple as that. If Jimmy Austin hadn't been a Cockney he might have said *Chest . . . chest, chest, his head, it me.* Lord, what an obtuse idiot I've been! *it me* Hit me, he was saying. And whose head had butted poor Jimmy Austin in the chest? Was that what he was trying to say? The post mortem should have been carried out, why not call at the hospital en route to the Tower? Perhaps, when he got back to base, those two missing once-upon-a-time cousins would have returned? He'd a lot to say to the Professor, and one most pertinent question for Steve Johnson.

Frank Pollard interrupted his reverie.

'James! You have set the cat among the pigeons.'

'And what does that well worn cliché mean?'

'I asked one of our computer operators to call up everything relating to manuscripts. There have been dozens sold privately over the past twelve months, but very few have been auctioned.'

'Where have the transactions taken place?'

'Berlin, Geneva, Tokyo, New York, Paris and Madrid.'

'Not London?'

'No.'

'So why the kerfuffle?'

'It appears, and we haven't had time to do any research in depth, that all the letters, and state documents cover events in 16th and 17th century England. What I can't understand is why this hasn't been picked up before.'

'It has been noticed, that's why I'm here.'

'But it's our job, we're the experts.'

'Of course you are, but I've assumed the colour of the people I'm working with, supposedly at the heart of the problem, but it hasn't made things any clearer.'

Frank was no fool. 'If I had to take a guess I'd say you were investigating something unsavoury at Hampton Court or possibly the Tower of London. Of the two I'd opt for Hampton Court.'

'Why?'

'Because many of the letters that have changed hands relate to passages between Henry VIII and Wolsey, Charles II and Lely, and designs for the maze.'

'Frank, you're not too far out, very nearly a hole in one, and the day the wraps come off this investigation, you'll be the first to know.'

Sister Maloney was sitting in her office writing notes when Byrd put his head round the door.

'Why, hallo there Mr Byrd. Will you sit down and have a cup of tea with me?'

'Yes, Sister, I will.'

'It'll be the post mortem you're after.' Not waiting for his answer she picked up the phone and spoke to Dr Reader. It seemed he wasn't too keen to talk, but Sister Maloney told him quite firmly that her visitor had no intention of departing without seeing the notes. After all, wasn't that the purpose of his visit?

Doctor Reader took his time. It wasn't that he had to do the things he did, but he was putting off having to explain his omission, his faulty diagnosis.

'He may still have died, Mr Byrd, even if we had diagnosed the sub-arachnoid haemorrhage in time. It's a condition he's lived with all his life. On the other hand he could have lived to be eighty if the battering he received hadn't raised his blood pressure and exacerbated the condition.'

Byrd re-read the actual words. *Death was caused by a sub-arachnoid haemorrhage brought on by extensive damage to the liver and kidneys which could only have been caused by ferocious blows of some force to the body. He was also badly concussed commensurate with blows to the head which, had he lived, may have left him brain damaged. In my opinion the injuries inflicted were not caused merely by falling.*

Byrd handed back the report. 'Thank you, Doctor, you've been most helpful. One more favour before I go. Could you

144

let Colonel Kilmaster know how Charley Austin reacts when he's given the results of the post mortem? It is quite important, and your assistance would be welcome.'

Doctor Reader expressed no interest in the whys and wherefores. He was too wound up about missing what should have been patently obvious. It's a job I wouldn't do for a king's ransom, thought Byrd. It's not like an ordinary job, where you can get away with the odd blunder. In his job a mistake can be fatal.

There was a message at the gate for Yeoman Warder Byrd to call in at the Byward Tower on his return. Paul Hanson was waiting for him.

'He's not turned up, Mr Byrd.'

Who hadn't turned up, wondered Bush; Steve or the American? He certainly didn't want him to know, at this stage, that Professor Berkeley had taken on the mantle of his servant. It was too Shakespearean for words.

'You mean Steve hasn't turned up?'

'Yes, and I'll tell you something else. We've combed the place. We've been through every tower, all twenty of them, we've been in all the basements, in the places the public don't see, down steps and up on the ramparts. He's not here, Mr Byrd, and I'm worried.'

'Has Steve ever talked about the myths of the Tower's hidden treasure?'

'No more than anybody else. From time to time we all talk about it, but take it from me, it would be easier to win a million on the pools with one line of treble chance, than to find treasure in the Tower.'

'Have you any equipment, metal detectors and so on, which might aid the process?'

'Good Lord, no. The Governor wouldn't have that. Mind you, an official search was carried out in 1958. They found damn all. I'll guarantee they were looking in the wrong place.'

'And where should they have been looking?'

'I could tell you, but then you see I'm no historian, haven't got a string of letters after my name, haven't been to the right schools or taken the right exams, don't talk the right language, see?'

145

Byrd didn't see, but he understood the lack of opportunity, the bitterness.

'Where, then, would you have looked for treasure?'

'If you really want to find it take a look at the tunnels which run from Legge's Mount to 7 and 8 The Casemates. Those tunnels, matey, connected Legge's Mount with the Royal Mint.' The Chief looked at Byrd and chortled. A bit of one-upmanship never came amiss.

'Now then, Mr Byrd, you'll be wanting to hear about Harry Johnson. He's back, spent a couple of hours sitting in the Chapel but I'll bet my last dollar he wasn't praying.'

'What was he doing?'

'Both Little Tich and Barney took parties in there. They said he hardly noticed them, just sat there thinking.'

'And where is he now?'

'Back at No.5 on his tod. Brenda's in such a terrible state that Mrs Rees-Morris, the Chaplain's wife, insisted on her staying with them. The big house, No 1, The Green, adjacent to the Chapel, plenty of room for guests. She's made up a bed for Brenda, she'll be better there being looked after. Doc's seen her, given her a sedative. So what's the next step, Mr Byrd?'

'I'll call at No 5, see Harry Johnson. He has a lot of questions to answer, and may prove unusually informative.'

'He's a bloody know-all.' The bitterness surfaced. 'Good luck with the bugger.'

18

Professor Lawrence Berkeley opened the door and stood aside for Byrd to enter.

'If it's Brenda you're looking for, she's staying with the Chaplain and his wife, but if it's me, as I suspect, then you'd better sit down.'

John Sainsbury must have warned his old tutor. Professor Berkeley, totally relaxed, not looking like a man in trouble, sat down.

'No holds barred, Superintendent. Fire away, ask your questions.'

'Did your friend at the Embassy tell you to expect me?'

'No. You forewarned me Inspector, or Superintendent, or whatever your rank is, you warned me loud and clear.'

'How's that?'

'First of all you've never been in the army. You're an individualist. Your grasp of allusions and your knowledge of both French and German tell me you're a university man. I know there was a drive both here and in the States to persuade graduates to enter the Police Forces. They wanted grey matter, and that's what you've got . . .'

'Superintendent. Detective Superintendent.'

'Ah yes. Now why were you following me, Superintendent? Why were you interested in the telephone call I made from the public phone box outside The Tower gates? And why did that Scots lass, the lovely Mrs Mayhew, follow me across the bridge in Bridgnorth, up the shortest and steepest rack and pinion railway in England, along Charles II's favourite walk, with its magnificent views over the Severn, and into St Mary's Church? Her dissimulation was admirable, but one can't disguise a walk, or the way one's head is held, or conceal an avid interest by assuming indifference.'

'We haven't made a very good job of it, have we?'

'No, but you made an excellent job of providing me with a lively and beautiful companion to share my dinner, or most of it. By the way, I doubt whether she's ever been trained in the art of searching premises. May I ask why she spent at least twenty minutes in my room, and what she was looking for?'

'It seems to me, Professor Berkeley, you have something to hide. Not only have you something to hide but you've conned these simple souls here into opening their home to you. You owe them an apology.'

'Yes, I do, and I'm deeply sorry. I planned to explain the reason for swapping identities on my second day here. Explain, as best I could, Harry's indifference to, and my fascination with The Tower. I took them out for a meal, but couldn't bring myself to the confessional. I mistakenly put off the apologia because Brenda was up to her eyes with the production of *Blithe Spirit*. You may remember the day? You came into the restaurant as we were leaving. So, Superintendent, do you intend to charge me with false representation, deception, deceit, and duplicity? What do the English courts have to say on those subjects?'

Clever, thought Byrd. Be faced with a lesser charge, if Brenda would go along with it, and walk away with impunity from the treasonous charge of lifting three hundred year old state documents.

'If it puts your mind at rest, Superintendent, I intend to make my apologies and leave as soon as Steve turns up.' Byrd said nothing. Let the man talk, he could learn more this way.

'Steve is all set to embark on a tour of the States, giving illustrated lectures on The Tower. I shall, of course, give him all the help he needs. It's the least I can do. In fact, Harry wouldn't have known where to start. If you're wondering where Harry is . . .'

'I know where he is,' interrupted Byrd.

'Good. I thought you might. Once I've apologised and craved the pardon of my hosts I have one last concern.' Byrd remained mute. 'I have borrowed a number of documents, some of which support a theory of mine. A theory which I intend to develop, but the documents must be returned and I can only do that when Steve returns.'

There was a long silence, but the air was full of clamorous thoughts.

'I don't think Steve will be returning, Professor.'

'What! Why ever not?'

'I believe he's dead.'

'Dead!' Professor Berkeley looked at the Superintendent, stupefied. He's not acting, he really is shaken, thought Byrd.

'You've proof, have you?'

'No. Instinct, intuition lead me down that path.'

'What makes you think he's dead?'

'I thought you might have an answer. In fact, I thought you might have answers to several questions. You might even know why there was a metal detector in the armoire in the kitchen.'

'Good God, you don't think Steve has electrocuted himself with some of the gear he uses for his treasure hunting?'

'It's a possible hypothesis. Maybe he struck gold, so to speak, and at the same time got in someone's way.'

Beep! Beep!

'Excuse me.' Byrd pulled his miniature switchboard out of his pocket.

'Yes?'

'Nothing on Smith. He's clean, and he's been working on site all day.'

'I know that. You're too late with the info. Get down here, in some disgusting gear, and check up on the movements of the

149

dead man's brother. Got that?'

'Understood, but afraid not possible, sir.'

'What! What are you saying?'

'I'm due back at Kidlington at 6 p.m.'

'To do what?' he barked. 'They can't just take you off the case.'

'I was never meant to be legs, sir. My orders were to remain at DHQ as a go-between.'

'So, who the hell allowed you out?'

'No one. I took leave that was owing to me, and about the message, sir, you didn't get it because your wretched bleeper . . .'

'Never mind the message. Get hold of Sir Charles, at once, NOW, and tell him I need you here. The matter is urgent.'

'Very well, sir.' Georgina grinned to herself. That would put the cat among the pigeons.

'And thanks, Georgina, thanks for your support.'

The Professor listened and wondered whether this policeman was always as aggressive? Damnation, thought Byrd, I'm getting up her nose, didn't mean to take it out on her.

He watched, in surprise, as the Professor opened the large cupboard, which to all intents and purposes looked like immovable panelling. He put his hand deep into the cupboard and pressed hard against the left hand side of the lower shelf. Another small aperture opened and from it he withdrew a box.

'Take a look, Superintendent.'

In a battered Quality Street tin lay fifteen coins, eleven gold and four silver, coins dulled with age. Byrd picked out a gold coin, *Henricus Rex VII*, 'The real thing, Mr Johnson, there's no doubt about it.' He felt elated. At last, at long last one step forward.

'They were struck here, in The Royal Mint, Superintendent, and never used from that day to this.'

'Where did he find them?'

'In the tunnel beneath the house. It's taken him nine months to locate them.'

'Tunnel! How did he get into it?'

'Through the kitchen. There's an entrance behind the

armoire.'

'Well, what are we waiting for, Professor, let's get moving!'

'Not so fast, Superintendent, there's one thing more.'

'And what's that?'

'I've borrowed a number of documents which I've now read and catalogued, but they must be replaced.'

An academic, and too clever by half, thought Byrd.

'Replaced where?'

'In the chest where they've lain for three hundred years. But they can't all be replaced until you return the letter you're holding. The one written by James, Duke of Monmouth, to Lucy Walters.'

'The letter, Professor, which is basic to your research on Monmouth's inheritance.'

'You always seem to be one step ahead, Superintendent.'

'The letter is in the hands of the Governor and that's where the rest of the purloined papers will be taken.'

'Purloined is too strong a word.' Lawrence Berkeley thought about the implications for some moments. 'Does returning them mean Brenda and Steve won't benefit from the discovery, won't get their share of the treasure trove?'

'I'm not a lawyer, Professor, I'm a policeman, but are you saying Steve has discovered State Papers?'

'You could say he did, and he didn't. He was far too keen on digging up gold coins, always expecting to find a large hoard stashed away by Barkstead, a previous Governor. The papers were secondary, but there's no doubt in my mind that if Steve hadn't found the tunnel then neither the coins nor the papers would have seen the light of day. They remain part of Steve's great discovery.'

Byrd thought differently, but as yet he had no proof. He had to plod on, hopefully.

'How did you get into the act, Professor?'

'On my first evening here Steve waited until Brenda had gone off to her play before taking me down into the tunnel. He'd been bursting to tell someone, but was afraid to precipitate the arrival of the know-all brigade, the historians, archivists, archaeologists, architects; anyone who might have deprived him of his treasure trove. On my first evening here I saw two chests, but didn't have time to examine either. Steve mentioned in passing that they contained papers, but refused to stay underground too long in case Brenda returned.'

'Are you saying Brenda doesn't know about the tunnel?'

'That's right. She was scared enough being in the house on her own. Swore Lady Jane Grey haunted the place. She'd have gone berserk if Steve had mentioned the tunnel. I waited until the next day when Steve was on duty, and Brenda had an appointment with her chiropodist. Two hours grace. It was all I needed. The armoire in the kitchen, which has been there since the time of the Tudors, pushes back fairly easily. Steve took the precaution of screwing an eighteen inch horizontal steel bar on the back of it to enable him to close it from the tunnel side. I borrowed one of Steve's double duty torches and let myself into the tunnel. It was a rare experience to travel back in time, centuries of time. Printing dies still lying where they'd been thrown when the Mint was moved to another site. It was easy to discern the pattern of Steve's dig. Nothing haphazard about it. However, I didn't waste much time on surmise, the chests were my objective. Imagine, Superintendent, what those undiscovered papers could divulge. They could change our view of history, give us a chance to understand the background of events never fully documented before. I must admit to spending sleepless nights wondering which gaps could be filled, which myths scotched for good and all. I expected to unearth the modern equivalent of the Dead Sea Scrolls, the find of a lifetime, several lifetimes. Now envisage my friend, and in your job I'm sure you can, what you would feel when you reached your objective and found the cupboard bare. The first chest was empty. I stood for minutes before daring to open the second. Didn't dare ask myself whether Steve had cleared them out, destroyed them, thinking them useless, but common sense prevailed. Steve, a man steeped in the history of The Tower could never have committed such a sacrilegious act.'

'Sacrilegious!'

'History is my religion.'

Byrd looked at a man who had lived his life with a singleness of purpose. A man who, like himself, doggedly pursued clue after clue until he'd solved the equation, reached the solution, and justified the research.

'And being such a devout historian, you dared to open the second chest?' Lawrence chose to ignore the sarcasm.

'Had I been a truly religious man I would have prayed, but prayer or not I was rewarded. The chest was half full of papers, an exultation of papers. A miracle! I stood there half crying, half laughing. For me it was more rewarding than landing on a new planet. I came to my senses and rushed back into the house, and collected the larger of my two cases. I filled it, regretfully leaving many many papers behind which remain, as yet, unread.

'Professor, let's get down there straight away.' Byrd was impatient.

'OK Superintendent, let's go, but what we find is Steve's inheritance which he'll claim because I don't believe, for one moment, that's he's dead.'

Professor Berkeley led the way into the kitchen, straight over to the armoire, and with a sudden tug pulled it away from the wall. Byrd watched, fascinated, as he ran his fingers down the centre panelling, activating a catch which caused a small 2'6"×2' door to open outwards. The Professor led the way and once both men were through Byrd pulled the court cupboard towards him masking the entrance.

Both men were broad and over six foot, but they crawled without difficulty through the cavity Steve had created.

'My God!' whispered Byrd, 'Who would have dreamt this existed.'

'Why are you whispering, Superintendent? There's no one here, other than spirits of the past, to hear what you're saying.'

'It's certainly unearthly, I'll give you that, but it's uncanny, and fantastic enough to provide the setting for a Spielberg film. Frankly it gives me the shudders. I have a feeling . . .' Byrd didn't finish. It was more than a feeling . . . it was that damned imagination of his working overtime. Or was it simpler than that? Merely the intuition which had so often led him, despite his more rational thoughts, directly to the Holy Grail? Only this time there was nothing holy about the pilgrimage . . . only a terrible foreboding . . . a feeling of evil. God alone knows what had happened in this place in the past. Grim, heinous deeds . . . leaving no trace, no smell, but an atmosphere of malevolence. He shivered. It was damned cold, colder than a mortuary. He should have brought a jacket.

The foreboding which assailed him hadn't affected the Professor, who was humming to himself as he headed confidently in the direction of the chests.

'Well, I'm damned.' He stopped suddenly.

'What's the matter?'

'Ten days ago, Superintendent, only ten days ago, there were two chests right here. Now there's only one. Steve must have moved the other one, but how on earth did he manage it on his own?'

Byrd didn't answer. He lifted the heavy oak lid. 'Is this the chest that was empty.'

'Yes.'

Both men gazed into a void. A void which produced no answers to the questions Byrd had been asking himself. He closed the lid and ran his hand lovingly over the chest. 'Another splendid artefact for the public to see. Now give me the torch, Professor, and show me exactly where the other chest stood.'

'It was here, near this arrow slit which was never used after Edward I built the moat.'

It's not a history lesson I need, thought Byrd, as he shone the torch on the paving stones. If Steve had moved the chest on his own he'd have dragged it, but there were no recent scratch marks to be seen. Leaving the Professor standing by the empty chest, Byrd peered into each shadowy alcove and found to his surprise that the tunnel narrowed and changed direction. Eventually he reached a solid stone wall bisecting the tunnel. Good God, he thought, it's not solid at all. Now we're getting somewhere. The wall had quite clearly undergone recent structural alterations. An access route a yard square had been roughly hacked through the stone, but there was no way he could get through. It was solidly blocked off by an old wooden door which he couldn't budge. 'Shit,' he said softly to himself knowing full well what was on the other side of the door. He then turned his attention to the

154

paving stones. At long last he found what he'd been looking for. Deep deep scratches, deep and distinct. He breathed a sigh of relief. And there in the corner was what he'd been hoping to find.

'Professor, come here quickly,' but the Professor was truly in the dark. Not a glimmer of light to lead him in the right direction, only a voice echoing round a cavern.

'Where are you, Mr Byrd?' The Superintendent retraced his steps.

'Here, Professor, follow me, and take a look at that.' Byrd shone the torch on a dark rectangular shape.

'My God, Superintendent, how did he get it here?'

'With difficulty,' said Byrd softly. 'Are you prepared to take a look?' Lawrence Berkeley didn't notice the caution in his companion's voice.

'Of course man, of course.' The lid didn't budge. 'Well I'm darned, it's screwed down. Why on earth did Steve do that?'

'Here, hold the torch,' said Byrd sharply, 'while I see what can be done with this little toy. From his pocket he produced a gadget looking like a penknife with several blades, but only one was sharp, the rest could be used in a variety of ways, from scraping mud off golf shoes, tamping down tobacco, uncorking bottles, or unscrewing the lid of an antique chest. The screws came out easily enough, the Superintendent popping each one into his mouth. Losing one would be disastrous. When the last screw was out, Byrd took the torch and muttered with his mouth full, 'Open it, Professor.'

Lawrence lifted the lid fully expecting to find it half full of yellowing State Papers, instead he found himself looking at an incredibly dirty dust sheet.

'Oh no,' he breathed, 'That will ruin them. Slowly, and carefully he removed the sheet. 'Christ!' he yelled. 'How did he get there? What happened?'

Both men gazed, in silence, at the corpse of Steve Johnson. His eyes were open, and his expression was anything but friendly.

'How the hell did this happen? Lawrence felt an acute pain in the pit of his stomach. He swallowed the acid bile which filled his mouth. What should have been a joyful moment turned into a sombre, and horrific experience. All he wanted to do was vomit.

155

His question to Byrd sounded like an accusation. 'How did you know he was dead?'

'Instinct told me he'd been murdered and I fully expected to be faced with a difficult case of *habeas corpus*, thinking the body may have been weighted and dropped into the Thames.'

Despite feeling sick Lawrence couldn't drag his eyes away from Steve's face. 'He's angry. He's trying to tell us something.' Lawrence shivered. This was way outside his academic experience.

'I'm fifty five, Superintendent, and this is the first time I've ever seen a dead body. Do they always look as ghastly, as though . . .'

'As though what?'

Suddenly the enormity hit Lawrence. 'He's been fighting, that's why he's in such a mess, and the look in his eyes means it was him or the other guy. I didn't realise Steve could be so determined.'

'He fought like a tiger, Professor, to protect his territory. A fight which resulted in the demise of two men.' He carefully covered the dead man with the sheet and closed the chest. 'We'll leave him here for a few more hours.'

'You can't do that.'

Byrd heard the unmistakeable tones of the Princeton Professor who, in his own little world, was cock-o-the-walk.

'It's hardly ethical. You've Brenda to consider. For the past twenty four hours she's been worrying herself sick. Wondering, worrying, waiting, and waiting is hell.' Lawrence thought of the worst hours he'd ever spent waiting for news of his parents. They'd flown from Kennedy to Vienna to see the house where his grandmother had been born and celebrate their golden wedding. On their return flight the plane blew up in mid-air. Ironic, really, because they should have returned the day before but decided to snatch another twenty four hours. The waiting had been purgatory. Rumour followed rumour until eventually he learned the truth. Another terrorist action for which no group ever claimed responsibility.

'Brenda must be told,' he said again.

'Leave my business to me, Professor,' said Byrd sharply. 'You can help by bringing your mind to bear on an immediate problem. You've been studying the topography of The Tower. Where do you reckon we're standing at this moment?'

Lawrence gave it some thought. 'I guess we're under Mint Street, midway between the Queen's House and the Casemates. Not too far, in fact, from the building in the Casemates which is being renovated.'

'Exactly my reckoning. You're going to help me Professor, help Brenda too, and atone for your sins of omission. Now let's get out of this mausoleum'

The two men pushed the armoire back into position, having made sure the panelling was firmly closed. Lawrence rushed to the kitchen sink, put his head under the tap, and swilled his face.

'You can't wash the image from your mind, Professor. Lady Macbeth had the same problem.'

Lawrence sat down at the kitchen table looking ashen, troubled and older. 'Nothing will ever wash away my stupidity. A crazy idea dreamt up in the balmy air of the Adirondaks, which at the time seemed harmless both to Harry and me. I'm only just beginning to realise what this could mean. Mrs Mayhew searched my room, but unlike you, and I'm presuming it was you, she couldn't open the combination lock, so she hasn't any idea whether I was selling State Papers for phenomenal sums or whether I was perusing them for pleasure. It seems to me, Superintendent, that you have an open and shut case. You can accuse me of theft and prove it by producing a case load of State documents, England's heritage. No one would ever believe my story. It gets thinner by the minute. As for Steve's death, you could no doubt nail me with that too. I'm probably the only person other than the murderer who knew the way into the tunnel. And the reason for his death? Any good QC could prove in a court of law that I'm a research fanatic. A heavily built man, capable of murder, masquerading as the victim's cousin. A man who would go to any lengths to get what he wanted. The achievement is yours, Superintendent, and the suspect is condemned by his own prognosis.'

Byrd didn't answer. He merely yelled, 'Got it!'

'Got what?'

'At last, at long last, Professor, the words of a dying man are crystal clear. A workman who was employed on the restoration of 2A said seven words to me before he was expunged. Seven words which haven't made sense until now. Jimmy Austin was a true Cockney, which meant his aitches were few and far between. He actually said "chest . . . chest . . . chest is ead," and "it me." *Chest*, I interpreted as *his chest*, because he'd taken some damaging punches. *Is ead* I took to mean *his head*, and *it me* as *hit me*. So I came up with the theory that an unknown attacker had butted him in the chest with his head causing a bad fall on to a pile of bricks. But, Professor,' and Byrd in his excitement began speaking more rapidly. '*Chest* equals *the chest* we have just discovered. *Is ead* is not *his head*, but *he's dead*, and *it me*, as I have discovered means *hit me*. Jimmy Austin was trying to tell me Steve Johnson was dead, and the whereabouts of his body, hidden in the chest. He also absolved himself by telling me he didn't start the fight. *Hit me* means Steve lashed out first.'

'You mean Steve and Austin were fighting, and Steve started it. Sounds a reasonable hypothesis, except if Austin was so badly hurt how did he manage to lock Steve in the chest?'

'Find me the next piece of the jigsaw and I'll tell you.'

Lawrence breathed out a sigh of relief. 'So I'm no longer a suspect?'

'No, Professor. I've been in the business long enough to recognise shock when I see it. You'd have to be a Gielgud to act so convincingly, and even he wouldn't be the colour you are now. Relax man, relax, sit down.' Professor Lawrence Berkeley did as he was bid. He sat. The Tower of London was turning out to be more than he'd bargained for.

James Byrd left the house on The Green knowing he needed a breather, thinking time to review the case, time to delve into the recesses of his mind, to find out whether he'd missed anything crucial. He also had to set up arrangements for removal of the body. Unlikely that he'd get hold of Sir Elwyn Rees on a Sunday afternoon, which meant everything would have to be left in Georgina's capable hands. But, first things first, he had to call Stephanie, let her know he wouldn't be home as planned.

'Promises, promises,' she'd said. There was nothing he could do about it. Naturally she'd be furious, and Kate would be too upset to tell him, as she so often had, that her teddies missed him. Damn! Damn! Damn! He couldn't put it off. It had to be done before he grabbed a quick snack at the cafe at the end of the wharf, followed by a constitutional round the ramparts before his deliberations began.

The kiosk outside the souvenir shop was free. 30p should be enough. The number rang and rang, funny that, they must be in the garden. He repeated the process and again no reply. Puzzled, he replaced the receiver and walked slowly along the wharf towards the cafe. It's Sunday, so they're not in Oxford shopping. Perhaps Stephanie has taken Kate punting on the river? It was an outing the child loved, especially in the shallows when she was allowed to handle the quant. The cafe was full, bursting at the seams, definitely a no go area. Cheese and biscuits it would have to be in his lodging. He nodded at Barney who was taking tickets at the wharf entrance, and made his way up to the ramparts. Despite it being lunchtime the place was crowded and his progress slow. As he ambled round at snail's pace he glanced towards the White Tower and what he saw stopped him dead in his tracks. At the top of the wooden steps about to enter the Tower stood a diminutive pig-tailed figure in a familiar white and red sun dress. The child clutched a guide book in her left hand and held on to her mother with her right. My God, what are they doing here? Is this how Stephanie keeps a low profile? He fairly scuttled down the stone steps, across a grassy patch and into the White Tower by the same entrance as his wife and daughter.

Once inside it was impossible to hurry, which gave him time to weigh up the situation. Stephanie, he realised, was one step ahead. She'd guessed that the longer the case took the more involved he would become, and the less she'd see of him, but surely she must have realised that catching a glimpse of him in this enormous conglomeration of buildings was a remote chance? She obviously hadn't asked for him, otherwise Barney would have said. By the time Stephanie and Kate had reached the cases containing Henry VIII's magnificent armour he'd caught up with

159

them. Kate's voice carried clearly, 'Mummy why does the king's horse have armour?'

Stephanie's reply was inaudible. 'Look Mummy, it's got the same patterns,' then shrieking with delight yelled at the top of her voice, 'Look see that armour there, it would fit me.'

Stephanie again was sotto voce. 'A dwarf! Why does a dwarf go to war?' The people around laughed at the question but no one attempted to answer.

He stopped directly behind them as they stood gazing at an oil painting. This time Stephanie was audible, 'That's King Henry VIII, he's famous for having six wives.'

'All at once?'

'No, darling, one at a time,' said Byrd softly as he put his arm round Stephanie.

'James, oh James,' her voice trembled, 'we didn't really expect to see you. It's such a big place, I'd no idea it was so enormous.' Her eyes were moist, but Kate's sparkled. 'Daddy, it's like a treasure hunt finding you.'

'Wish I could get to the end of my treasure hunt, darling, then I could come home.' He lifted her up. 'How would you like to see my present home?'

'Oh yes please.'

'I haven't had lunch yet, so you'd better join me for cheese and biscuits.'

'We can do better than that,' laughed Stephanie. 'We've got sandwiches and home made fruit cake.'

While Stephanie made the tea her husband closeted himself in an empty room to make a phone call. Georgina answered immediately.

'It's Sunday, there'll be no builders on site today, but I want the police mortuary alerted. A corpse needs to be collected from The Tower during darkness tomorrow. Tell the Colonel to call an early meeting tomorrow for all concerned. He's yachting down at Burnham, doesn't know the score at the moment. Understood?'

'Yes, understood,' said Mayhew, 'and, sir, Sir Charles has seconded me full time.'

'Good girl,' he breathed, 'that's excellent.'

160

Stephanie felt a different person, all the angst had evaporated. Why had she been so stupid? Wondering where he was living, how he was living, and with whom? This sparse lodging said it all. She hummed as she made the tea. Now, she felt, we can discuss holidays. I'll tackle Jim before we leave. Kate, too, was happy. This was a really old place, like the pictures in her fairy stories, lots and lots of towers and men in funny costumes, but she couldn't tell her friends. Mummy had made her promise.

An hour passed all too quickly.

'Now girls,' said Byrd, 'we're going to pay a visit to the souvenir shop because Teddy looks lonely, and Mummy needs some background for all those historical novels she reads.' Kate screamed with delight as her father thrust a teddy bear dressed as a yeoman into her arms, and Stephanie gave him a full blooded kiss as he dropped a video cassette into her capacious handbag.

'Mummy,' whispered Kate, 'you shouldn't do that here.'

'I won't do it again,' laughed Stephanie, 'not today.'

There was another surprise in store.

'Follow me,' said Byrd, making his way to the river bus booking office.

'Good. You've only five minutes to wait.'

'Wait for what, Daddy?'

'The next boat will take you from here to Westminster, then you can see Big Ben and the Houses of Parliament.'

'That's great.' She ran without waiting for her parents down to the landing stage. 'We're going on top, Mummy, then we can see everything.'

Byrd stood waving until the figures on the boat faded into the distance. He felt relaxed, replenished, and ready to face anything that fate hurled at him.

19

At 8 a.m. on the following morning, round a table in an upper room in Queen's House, where nearly four hundred years before, Guy Fawkes had been interrogated, sat six men.

Since his appointment as Deputy Governor, Robin Kilmaster had never managed to get through a meeting round that table and in that room without thinking about the Gunpowder Plot conspirators. Fawkes had been employed for his expertise in handling explosives, but he was totally inexperienced in facing a merciless interrogation, nor could he possibly have imagined the pain and indignity of being stretched on the rack. Inevitably, he confessed. Within the next few months eleven of the seventeen named conspirators had been hanged and only a fortunate few released.

The six men sitting round the table in 20th century England were also concerned with a conspiracy. A conspiracy to defraud Her Majesty of ancient State Papers. The six included the Governor, Major General Featherstone-Bonner who chaired the meeting, his Deputy, Colonel Kilmaster, Sir Charles Suckling, Sir Elwyn Rees, Pierre Gambon the historian, now only too aware of what

162

was happening in his beloved Tower, and Superintendent James Byrd. This meeting, thought Robin Kilmaster, won't make the history books; it won't even be recorded, but it doesn't let us off the hook. We still have to solve the deaths of Steve Johnson and Jimmy Austin, retrieve the missing documents, and look after Brenda. We'll have to tread softly, we don't want the media on our doorstep. The Colonel turned his attention to the bearded Superintendent and wondered how he would have stood up to questioning if his name had been Fawkes, but his reverie was broken by the Governor who hated long meetings and intended to get down to business.

'Well, gentlemen, we have a pretty taxing situation on our hands, and I'm looking to you, Elwyn, to advise me, to lead the way out of this morass and keep recent events here as quiet as possible. I realise we can't hush up the murder, or if Mr Byrd is right, two murders, but let us solve the problem before the Press starts speculating. In the meantime I'll have a word in the Home Secretary's ear.'

'Sir Charles and I have discussed the matter of secrecy,' said Sir Elwyn.

'We can't, of course, go along with anything that obstructs justice, but we could make use of delaying tactics. We all realise the implications, but there are ways of tackling the immediate issues and I think we should leave Superintendent Byrd to explain.'

'Thank you, sir,' Byrd looked at the five men, knowing two were definitely for his proposition, two against, and the historian, Pierre Gambon, whom he knew very little about, was the odd man out. He spoke, looking at each man in turn.

'If, at this stage, gentlemen, we make any moves which alert the malefactors, we lose any chance of retrieving the stolen documents. It's fortunate that Professor Berkeley managed to remove half the papers which were stored in one of the chests before it became Steve Johnson's coffin. The rest of the documents the thieves have spirited away. It's absolutely crucial that we leave them with the thought that Steve removed those documents, which, happily, are now in Mr Gambon's care.

Pierre Gambon couldn't restrain himself. 'Beyond my wildest imaginings. Far more valuable than Barkstead's Treasure. History begins with every passing moment, but the moments covered in these documents will unravel for us so much of the past, so much we didn't know, so much we have had to guess. . . .'

The Governor cut him short. 'Thank you for your comments, Mr Gambon. We'll have a full session on them when you've had time to digest and catalogue.' Major General Featherstone-Bonner looked at Sir Elwyn. 'Now Elwyn, I know you only managed a few words with Superintendent Byrd prior to this meeting, but would you care to speak to the proposal of additional support?'

'Yes, indeed. I will make arrangements for the Superintendent to call on all the help he needs from the Art Squad, and I will make sure that Inspector Frank Pollard is seconded to the small unit we're setting up.' 'And you, Charles, are you able to spare the two detective sergeants Byrd has requested?'

'Yes, from today Sergeant Mayhew and Sergeant Quinney have both been seconded full time. Quinney has worked on many many cases with Mr Byrd.'

The Governor nodded in approval. 'Now,' he said, 'that all leaves one little matter outstanding. We need to consider Superintendent Byrd's final request. Knowing how engrossed Mr Gambon is going to be with the latest discoveries, it might not be a bad idea to take on board, as an addition to our small unit, the services of Professor Berkeley.'

The Colonel came straight out with what he was thinking, never a man to hide a truth. 'Having *borrowed* those precious papers, and we have only his word for that, I wonder whether he's a man we can trust?'

Immediately Sir Elwyn thumped the table with his fist. 'You've hit the nail on the head, Robin.'

The Governor looked at Sir Charles. 'You know your man, what is your view?' 'If the Superintendent wants to use expertise which isn't available anywhere else, then I suggest we make the most of the opportunity.' 'Perhaps, Mr Byrd, you'd explain what exactly is in your mind.?'

'Thank you, sir. Both Mr Gambon and the Professor are scholars, but when it comes to documents I think Mr Gambon,

164

by reason of his position must have the edge, and to know he's here in *situ*, when we have a problem to face, would be a bonus. Now the Professor has other qualities. First of all he's an American with a chair at a world famous university. He can blatantly appear in the auction houses of Europe and as soon as the word gets around he'll be approached by all the wide boys in the business who want to sell their ill-gotten gains, privately.'

Pierre Gambon came in quickly, 'That makes sense, sir. I'd soon be rumbled, and all I'm interested in at the moment are the documents we have to hand.'

'All right, gentlemen, it seems we have two for, and two against. My casting vote will make it three for and two against.'

Byrd breathed a sigh of relief and was astonished to see Sir Charles give him the ghost of a wink.

All right, gentlemen,' said the Governor, 'we'll not prolong this meeting, and we'll leave the unenviable task of calling on Mrs Johnson to my Deputy.'

The Governor never wasted words. The meeting was short. Byrd looked at his watch. Half an hour flat. He wished all meetings were chaired in the same manner.

The Colonel found the God-fearing Presbyterian architect waiting in his office. Hamish Campbell was an old friend and he felt uneasy at having to deceive him, but there was no way he could be more forthcoming about what was happening at 2A. He needed Hamish to go in and ask all the right questions, make all the right noises, which would give him a chance to to take a close look in the basement. Byrd had told him what to look for. There was the business too, of keeping Bill Smith occupied for at least half an hour while James Byrd and Paul Hanson did what they had to do.

The two men made their way across The Green, under the Bloody Tower and along Water Street. Surprise! Surprise! Paul Hanson was not in his day uniform. He'd put on an old track suit which made him look enormous.

'Morning, sir. Morning, Mr Campbell.'

Hamish grinned at the figure in front of him. 'Thinking of entering next year's Marathon?'

The Colonel gave him a warning look which clearly said, 'say nothing.'

'Getting into training, Mr Campbell. Have to show the Fiji Rugger side round the old place next week. Don't want to be breathless, do I?'

'You'll never be that,' said the Colonel quickly. 'Incidentally, Chief, we'll be here for the next half hour, so if you have other commitments, please carry on.'

The message came across loud and clear.

'I think you'll find, sir, there's been a little more activity in 2A. They must have heard Mr Campbell was coming, hurrah, hurrah.' He left hurriedly, smiling at his little joke.

The front door to 2A was open. They set foot in the small hall, recently re-tiled, with direct access to the downstair rooms and the stairs to the upper floor. The sound of hammering led them into the room on the left. Two men were nailing down the last few floorboards. The beams and the stone walls had been meticulously cleaned and the window frame replaced. Graham Tooley, the Tower's Marketing Officer and Accountant was right, thought the Colonel. In fact Graham was rarely wrong, and was always coming up with ideas on ways to increase The Tower's income. He looked at the room through Graham's eyes. Yes, here was another splendid space for a souvenir shop. The teddy bears and the recent film had been selling like hot cakes, but Graham had suggested that one shop should be totally devoted to nothing but models. Models of the most famous of the twenty towers, models of the Yeomen, the Gurkhas, the ravens, the Chapel, the armour, even the Crown Jewels and the kings and queens who'd lived in the place. Oh, yes, this room would be excellent.

Bill Smith hovered while Hamish Campbell examined the room with a practised eye. 'A bit of pointing needed in that corner, Mr Smith, but apart from that you've made a good job of this room.'

'Thank you, sir.'

'But it's a pity you've taken so long.'

Smith gave him an enigmatic stare before he answered. 'We don't skimp jobs, Mr Campbell, we do them right, and doing them right has its rewards.'

166

'What rewards might those be Mr Smith?' asked the Colonel.

'We get more jobs, it's as simple as that, which means my men are never out of work.'

Hamish Campbell led the way into the right hand room and looked surprised when he saw that several floorboards hadn't been secured.

'I thought these boards were finished last week, Mr Smith.'

'We've had to ease them slightly. The wood has warped, and they're squeaking something 'orrible.'

'But it's old matured wood,' said the Deputy Governor firmly. 'The movement stopped centuries ago.'

Hamish laughed, 'Robin, you're forgetting the supporting cross beams, all of new wood, new and old always fight, always present difficulties. Now,' he said changing the subject, 'let's take a look at the basement.'

He opened a trap door to reveal new wooden steps descending at a reasonable angle. Lifting the door activated the light, and the three of them descended. Much more civilised, thought the Colonel, than the last time I was here. The rounded walls and the small alcoves every few feet had all been cleaned. The ancient paving stones had all been replaced, but the Colonel saw what he expected to see. A large pile of floorboards, standing end on, were propped up against the north wall conveniently masking an entrance to the tunnel complex under Mint Street.

Concentrating his attention on the paving stones, Hamish wanted to know whether there'd been enough of the original stone to complete the job. No problem, Smith had said; they'd brought in sufficient hard core, and mixed the aggregate on the spot. To the Colonel, Smith's phoney Cockney accent was even more pronounced, now he knew the score.

'I 'ope, Mr Campbell, you won't blackball the firm because we've been an 'ell of a time on the job?'

'Not if the work is good enough, the price right, and the client not in a hurry. In fact, Bill, I've something at Hampton Court you could tender for.

'I'll get my secretary to put the details in the post to your governor.'

'Thank you, sir. I'd appreciate that.'

167

Robin Kilmaster detected relief and satisfaction in those few words. Now all he had to do was get Smith out of the building, and make sure the trap door was closed.

'Hamish, I'm wondering whether the exterior looks a little too pristine, shouldn't it look a little more antiquated and blend in with the surrounding buildings?'

'Let's take a look, Robin.'

The 'look' and the discussion which followed took at least twenty minutes. Ah, thought the Colonel, here's another diversion, as he noticed one of the labourers changing the front nearside wheel of the Transit. He wandered over. 'That's a bit unfortunate.'

'It is,' said Smith, 'especially with the load of stuff we intend to move today. Could have kept blowing it up, 'oping for the best, but changing the bloody thing is safer. At least it keeps Andy occupied for a few minutes.'

'What's your next job, after this?'

'The firm's renovating an old pub in Whitechapel, but I'll be away.'

'On a job or on holiday?'

'On holiday, thank God. I've a few days owing to me and I intend to make the most of it.'

'Off to the Caribbean?'

Smith laughed. 'You must be joking. I might get as far as France in my old jalopy, but the Caribbean's for millionaires, not for the likes of me.'

'Before you leave tonight,' said the Colonel in a jovial mood, 'I think you should celebrate. Go along to the Yeoman Warders' Club for a couple of hours. Have a noggin with the boys.'

Smith hesitated. 'Thanks, sir, for the invite, but I've got to have the Transit serviced. Promised to let the garage have it by 6. o'clock.'

'All right then, take a raincheck.'

Hamish Campbell was satisfied with the work.

'It may have taken them an unconscionable time, Robin, but it's a job well done, and cheap at that. I'll certainly use the firm again. Now if you'll excuse me, I'll get across to St Thomas's Tower and see how the experts are getting on.'

Byrd and Hanson hadn't wasted a moment. They left the Professor keeping guard in the house with instructions to push the court cupboard back into position if Brenda happened on the scene. On the first sortie they carried a lifelike dummy of a Yeoman which Pierre Gambon had dug up for them in his basement store under the Educational Block, and on the second a camera, stretcher, blanket and bag of tools. Before unscrewing the chest, Byrd took a number of shots of the passage, the chest, and the scratches made on the old paving. Byrd then unscrewed the chest, handing the screws, one by one, to the Chief for safe keeping. There was no time to mess about. When the screws were out Bush removed the lid, and took more shots from all angles. Only then did they carefully remove Steve from his resting place, and place him on the stretcher.

They'd not had time to deposit the dummy in the chest when they heard, quite distinctly, the voices of Smith, the Colonel and the rich tones of a Scotsman. They froze, switched off the torch and remained stationary and silent in the darkness. As soon as they heard the unmistakable sound of the trap in the floor of 2A being dropped back into position they recommenced operations.

The dummy was covered with the dust sheet, and the lid screwed on.

'With luck,' said Byrd, 'they'll never open the chest.'

As Paul Hanson tightened the straps around Steve's body, he thought of the bloody battle in Korea, where his mate fighting alongside him, had been killed. He'd tightened the straps round Gordon, but all the time he'd known in his heart of hearts it was a useless exercise.

'We'll take him out like this, and put the blanket over him when we're through the cavity. Be easier, that way,' whispered the Chief.

While Byrd and the Chief were wrestling with their problems, Sergeant Quinney was on his way from Oxford in a battered old Fiesta with a variety of number plates, a selection of hats and dark glasses. At the same time the Colonel made his way to the Chaplain's house.

Mrs Morris-Jones was expecting him. 'Come in, Robin. Go into

169

the sitting-room.' The Colonel knew there was no one better in the whole of The Tower complex than Catherine Morris-Jones when it came to dealing with human crises. How someone who was less than five foot tall and who'd never had children of her own came to be recognised as a 'Mother' figure was beyond his comprehension, but she never shirked a challenge, and dealt sympathetically with many of the domestic problems that arose in the Tower village. The Colonel often wondered whether she would have been different if she'd had children. He felt great affection for a lady whose face was unlined, whose hair was gradually greying and who had the ability to make anyone feel welcome, no matter what time you chose to call.

'Sit down, Robin, Brenda will be down in a minute.' He couldn't sit down. He'd been the bearer of bad news too often. Instead he walked round the room looking at the delicate 18th century water colours painted by the Daniells in India.

'They really are magnificent, Catherine. I've never asked you how you came by them.'

'My mother's ancestors settled in India about the same time as the Daniells, and occasionly one of the family would brave the appalling hazards of storm, heat and floods and accompany Thomas Daniell and his nephew William on their travels. This one here,' said Catherine, pointing to a vast fortification on a hill, 'was shown at the Royal Academy.' She looked at Robin, 'Are you going to tell me what's happened?'

'Yes, stay with me, Catherine, while I try to explain to Brenda?'

'Yes, of course. I'll call her.'

Brenda came slowly into the room. The Colonel swallowed hard, his throat was dry, and his hands sweaty.

'Good morning, Colonel.'

'Hallo Brenda.'

'You've some news for me.' It was a flat statement. She knew before he'd uttered a word. 'It's not good news, is it?'

'No, Brenda, I'm afraid not.'

'He's dead, isn't he.'

The Colonel nodded, unable to speak.

Brenda gave a wild cry like a dog in pain before falling to the ground in a dead faint.

170

'Oh Lord, Robin, she's hit her head on the fender. We'd better put her on the sofa.'

Brenda, whose colour was ashen, lay prone looking for all the world like a marble effigy.

'Robin, you ring Barry, while I find a blanket to cover her.'

Dr Barry Rose was in the Tower surgery seeing the last of the morning's patients. With little ceremony he told his patient, one of the garrison suffering from Athlete's Foot, to return the following morning.

'The Doc's coming straight over,' said the Colonel as he watched Catherine wrap a blanket round the patient.

'You'd better tell me, Robin, what's happened to Steve.'

'You'll not believe it, Catherine, it's like something out of a thriller. He had a punch up, and got killed fighting in a tunnel under Mint Street. His assailant, or accomplices of his assailant, hid his body in a chest. Hopefully, Superintendent Byrd and Paul have removed the body which, at this moment, should be resting in the house.'

'Superintendent . . . you don't mean the new man is a policeman, and not a Warder?'

'Yes.'

'Then you were expecting something like this to happen. If you were expecting it, why couldn't you stop it?' Catherine made it sound like an accusation.

'We weren't at all sure what to expect. We were working in the dark.'

'Dear God,' she whispered, 'whatever are we going to tell Brenda?'

'That's not all,' added the Colonel. 'The American staying with them isn't the cousin they were expecting. He's a Professor from Princeton University who's masquerading as Harry Johnson, a college servant.'

'Oh, dear God,' she said again, then more practically and down to earth.

'What do you want Evan and me to do?'

'Take it step by step, Catherine. Steve knows, I mean knew, about the tunnel. He'd been doing his own research, foolish man, and had dug up several gold coins. More importantly he found a

171

chest full of documents dating back to the Stuarts and possibly earlier.'

'But, Robin, that's fantastic.'

'Unfortunately he wasn't the only one ferreting away, that's where the trouble began.'

'There's a great deal . . .' They were interrupted by Dr Barry Rose who opened the front door and strode into the sitting room, taking in the situation at a glance.

'Poor lass, what caused this?' he asked as he took Brenda's pulse. 'A little slow, perhaps, but nothing to worry about.' He took a small bottle out of his case, and held it under her nose. Brenda stirred. 'That's better, my girl, that's better. She'll be out for a few more minutes yet. What happened?' he asked looking at the Colonel. 'Not bad news about Steve, I hope?'

'Yes, I'm afraid so, Barry. Steve's dead, but it's worse than that, he was possibly murdered here in the Tower.'

'Good God, sounds like Sir Thomas Overbury, all over again.'

'Not at all like Overbury,' said the Colonel drily. 'Steve wasn't poisoned. Barry, I want you to take a look at the body, immediately. Chief is waiting for you at No 5 The Green, but please don't discuss the matter with anyone. Steve's death must not be leaked. Governor's orders.'

'Oh, come on, Robin, don't ask me to get involved in a cover-up. We're not in the Middle Ages now.'

'Governor's orders, taken in consultation with two Chief Constables.'

'Good God man, what's it all about?'

'If we are to solve Steve's murder, then the criminals involved must not know they've been rumbled, so take a look at the body, will you, before the Home Office Pathologist arrives?'

'You'll never keep it quiet in this place, not on your nelly.'

Brenda stirred again

'She's coming round,' whispered Catherine. 'What are we going to do?'

'I've given her a mild sedative.'

Doctor Rose took another look at Brenda, and shook his head. 'Be best if you could keep her here, Catherine. I'll send nurse over to give you a hand. She'll be fully conscious, soon enough. Poor

172

lady', he whispered as he put another cushion under her head. 'What are you going to tell her, Robin?'

'The truth, what else! I only hope she doesn't insist on an open inquest. Could be embarrassing.'

'I hope you know what you're doing,' was Doctor Rose's parting shot.

The Colonel knew he had to come to grips with the business of secrecy, and sooner rather than later. Better for his men to hear it first hand than pluck rumours out of the air which flourished, in the Tower, more quickly than nasturtiums on a compost heap. He made up his mind to have words with Byrd and call a meeting the same evening.

Half an hour later Brenda was sitting up in bed. Catherine held her hand while the Colonel struggled to unfold the awful story, the true story of how her husband met his death.

'Yes, yes,' she said hardly above a whisper. 'Steve is a fighter. It takes a lot to rouse him, but if he's nettled he'll have a go. He boxed, you know, for the Army, a middle weight.' Catherine made no attempt to stop her. The shock was taking effect sooner than she'd expected.

'I remember once,' said Brenda, 'standing in a telephone box, we were both in it, quite a crush it was. We were on holiday, and ringing home because Mum was ill.' Brenda was smiling to herself. The Colonel and Catherine gazed at each other in astonishment. They'd both dealt with shock, but they'd never seen anything like this. Brenda was back in the past, totally rejecting the present truth.

'And what happened, Brenda?' asked Catherine.

'It took ages and ages to get through, something wrong with the lines. A man stood outside the box shouting four letter words at us, which we ignored, then he hammered on the window, called me a silly bitch and told me to get moving. Steve said nothing. He opened the door and charged. The poor sod didn't know what had hit him. When we finished the call and left the box, he was still lying on the pavement, out for the count.'

Brenda shook herself and for a few seconds stepped out of the past.

'Who was Steve fighting?'

'A labourer working on the Casemates.'

'Was he hurt, too?'

'Yes.'

'Is he all right?'

'No. He died a few days ago.'

'Silly weren't they. What were they fighting about?'

'We're not exactly sure.' The Colonel shook his head at Catherine. There was no need to go any further. Brenda was in no state to understand.

'Brenda', he said, 'I think you'd better rest now. I'll come back tomorrow and talk to you.'

Then suddenly, more rationally, came a clearly articulated question.

'Where were they fighting?'

The Colonel took a deep breath. The question hung in the air. It was a question that wouldn't go away. He'd have to answer it, sooner or later. 'Somewhere under the house.'

Brenda giggled. 'That was Steve's secret. Thought I didn't know. Those coins he kept finding, he hid from me, in the secret drawer in the cupboard, but I knew.' Brenda moaned, 'But I didn't want to know, in case he took me down there. I know what's gone on in that house, that poor girl, that poor sixteen-year-old girl, I often hear her crying for her husband, and he's only a slip of a lad. There were two coins, you know, and then three and then four. Last time I looked there were fifteen. Steve and I are going to be rich, aren't we?'

'It's possible, Brenda, it's possible,' breathed the Colonel.

Catherine rose, 'I think, Robin, you'd better leave me to look after Brenda. Evan and I will do what we can.' He breathed a sigh of relief.

'Thank you, Catherine. You're a wonderful woman, an ever-present help in trouble.'

A sad and melancholic man left the Chaplain's house and walked slowly back to his office.

20

The atmosphere in the Warders' Club was strangely low key. No one playing bar billiards, or darts, or exchanging risqué stories, no television. Little Tich, whose turn it was to be barman, served with less than his usual camaraderie. Like everyone else he feared the worst. The men talked quietly, not daring to voice their thoughts, knowing it was five years since the Colonel had last called an emergency meeting. They were all asking each other why Byrd was sitting with the three civil servants, Pierre Gambon, Graham Tooley, and Angela Burne-Jones. And who was the stranger with him? Barney, normally so voluble, sat in a far corner saying nothing. All he could see was Brenda's tearstained face, her eyes and mouth swollen from endless weeping. Thank goodness the Padre and his wife had taken over. They would cope, they always did, but where on earth was Steve, and what was he doing? If he'd had an accident surely they would have heard by now? Perhaps he was lying in hospital, suffering from concussion and loss of memory, or maybe, and it was a thought he'd never dare mention to Brenda, maybe he'd gone off with another woman? Somehow his absence caused a shadow over them all.

As the Colonel entered the low hum of conversation had a dying fall. The Yeomen looked in vain for his usual smile, and bright good evening, but all they were given was a brief nod. Robin Kilmaster glanced round the bar noted who was missing, and then stood with his back to the small counter.

'Gentlemen,' he said quietly, 'Thank you for attending this meeting at such short notice.' He paused and appeared to be examining his fingernails.

'You are, no doubt, wondering why I have called this meeting and what, in effect, has triggered it off, but before I explain what has been happening in the Tower I must emphasize, most strongly, that this meeting is highly secret. We've all served Her Majesty in one way or another and, when it comes to affairs of State, we're accustomed to keeping our council. In an army barracks it was relatively easy, but here in The Tower it will be a bit more difficult because we'll be returning to our families who, quite naturally, will ask what this meeting was all about. You'll not be able to share it with them. As Hamlet said, *The rest is silence*.

'First of all, I'll introduce you to Detective Superintendent Byrd, who is not, and never will be, a Yeoman Warder, but his cover was necessary as you will hear. You will forgive him, I'm sure, for not pulling his weight, but I can assure you he has not been idle. His was a difficult brief. None of us has enjoyed trying to fool you, but it was imperative that casual workers on the site regarded Mr Byrd as a Yeoman. One, perhaps, who was too damn curious, and who had a tendency to poke his nose in where it wasn't wanted, but that was his mission.'

Byrd felt the atmosphere change. Instead of resentment, hard stares, and the scornful looks of the past two weeks he saw curiosity, amusement, and a reaching out; a comradeship which had been missing. There was a murmur of appreciation as Byrd stood up and made a slight bow. The Colonel let it die down before continuing.

'Gentlemen, I will start at the beginning, so please bear with me. During the past twelve months the Governor and I have had our attention drawn to the sale of ancient documents at

176

auctions in Europe and New York. On several occasions lots have been withdrawn before the sale takes place, and one can only assume private transactions have taken place. To date, only four lots offered for sale have reached the open market. These documents interested us because they were directly related to events which occurred during the Tudor and Stuart periods. Now we all know our history of the Tower, we live with it daily, and I don't have to remind you where all the documents relating to the monarchy and our heritage were stored during the two periods in question.'

'Here,' murmured several voices.

'Wakefield Tower,' another voice.

'Cold Harbour,' another and, 'St John's Chapel,' another.

'Yes, all of those places, not to mention The Great Hall which was demolished.'

Robin Kilmaster stopped for a moment, to sip his whisky and soda, before continuing.

'One of the documents which changed hands last week was a letter to Charles I from a correspondent in Holland confirming an agreement on the sale and method of transporting hereditary treasure belonging to the Crown. The royal coffers, it seems, were empty. From our point of view, the sale of important artefacts is something we all regret. Maybe we'll never know what actually left our shores, but you can fairly safely assume that jewels, gold plate and many rare objects changed hands. Now where would you have expected a letter written to a King of England to turn up?' The Colonel didn't wait for an answer. 'In the Royal Archives, of course, not at a public auction in Switzerland.'

'The Governor and I had no idea how to tackle something so nebulous as the sale of a letter in Geneva which might possibly affect us here in The Tower, but we both had a strong feeling that the root of the matter originated not in the 15th and 16th centuries, but here and now. But we had no evidence, it was a gut feeling, so we decided to take advice. Mr Byrd was the answer to our prayer. As part of the scenery, he was able to observe a great deal, and latterly, with the help of the Chief, covered even more

177

ground.' The Colonel paused. There wasn't a cough, a shuffle or a sound. The men were on the edge of their seats.

'Now you know Superintendent Byrd's role in all this, I'll come to the most disturbing matter. We've spent days searching for Steve Johnson. None of us really believed he'd had a brainstorm and gone off with another woman. We've all been hoping, at the worst, that he might have had an accident and be lying in hospital suffering from temporary amnesia. I'm afraid it's much more distressing than anything we could have imagined. Steve, I'm sorry to tell you, is dead. Murdered, here in the Tower.' The men looked at each other in total disbelief. Things like that didn't happen in their safe, closed community. How could it happen? Byrd saw incredulity, horror and anger on the faces around him before the shock really hit them. The Colonel paused, took out his pipe, was about to fill it and then changed his mind, placing it on the counter before continuing.

'We believe we know why Steve was murdered and if we are to bring the criminals to justice, and salvage the State Papers, we'll need your help, and your silence. We will avenge his murder, make no mistake about that, and I believe Mr Byrd and his team will lead us to the murderer.'

The Colonel finished off his whisky, and wiped his brow. It was hot in the club, but he'd insisted on keeping the outer door bolted while the meeting was in progress. 'Would you like me to stop for a few moments while you replenish your glasses?' He looked at the bewildered faces in front of him. 'No, sir, please carry on.' The answer was the same from all corners of the room.

'Very well. It is better for me to tell you the truth, better that you should know everything. Steve, as I'm sure you all realise, didn't welcome visitors at No 5. He was a sociable chap here in the club, but not in his home. The reason, it seems, was not to keep you out, my friends, but to keep out archeologists, or historians, or anyone who might turn his home upside down, even evict him, find him new lodgings, and put paid to the treasure he has been painstakingly unearthing. For more than twenty years Steve had lived in No 5, during which time he's discovered secret cupboards, secret drawers and, more recently, a door ingeniously camouflaged in the kitchen panelling which led to a tunnel under the house.'

'Tunnel,' many of them muttered.

'Yes, a tunnel, gentlemen, on the site of the Old Mint. We all know about the tunnels leading from Legge's Mount which Mr Gambon now believes were at one time linked to the tunnel which Steve discovered. In his tunnel he'd searched, systematically, for treasure, and he'd struck gold in the shape of coins fashioned here in The Mint during Henry VII's reign. He'd also found two chests, one of which, we know for sure, was full of documents. Fortunately half these documents are now with Mr Gambon, but the rest are missing. Steve wasn't alone in his discovery. There is another entrance to the tunnel from the basement of 2A The Casemates. A workman whose boss, we believe, knew all about the chests, and their contents, may have been removing papers and was surprised by Steve. They fought in the tunnel. Both men are now dead. At this stage we don't know if they killed each other or whether both men were finished off by a third party. The workman, Jimmy Austin, died in hospital. Steve was discovered by Superintendent Byrd, and Mr Hanson in one of the chests covered in a dustsheet, and the lid of the chest firmly screwed down. Last Friday, as I'm sure you know, workmen were observed attempting to carry the injured Austin to the van used by Cantries. Chief, quite rightly, would have none of it and called an ambulance.' The Colonel paused, and took a look round the room. The men were all shaken, and quiet. He'd never known the club so quiet. He gave Byrd a nod.

'Now I'd like Superintendent Byrd to explain his modus operandi for tomorrow.' He sat down, pulled out his pipe, and concentrated on filling it, as Byrd took over.

Before embarking on his plan he introduced Detective Sergeant Robert Quinney. 'Bob joined us today, a bonus, as he will tell you himself, because his face is easily forgettable, and on top of that is totally unknown to any of the men employed by Cantries or, for that matter, any of the daily workers.' Quinney stood up, grinned at a sea of faces, and then sat down smiling broadly at Angela Burne-Jones. She disagreed. It wasn't a face she'd forget,

179

more like a corsair than a policeman. A man who could have sailed with Raleigh on his fateful voyage to discover El Dorado. A weatherbeaten face, large nose, laughter lines deeply etched round his eyes and mouth. He had a lean figure, but it was those warm brown eyes full of fun which attracted her.

Byrd had their attention. His voice, deeper than the Colonel's, carried easily to each corner of the room. 'Tomorrow, the work at 2A will be completed. The builders will remove tools, wood, cement, and all of the gash objects no longer needed. They may also remove the chest which they believe contains Steve's body. It doesn't. In it is the dummy of a Yeoman which has been lying in Mr Gambon's store for many a long day. The dummy is now covered with a dust sheet and the lid screwed back into place. They may be planning to leave the chest in situ, but my guess is they'll load it with all the building paraphernalia, but they'll not do it if any of us are in the vicinity. Now who lives in 3 The Casemates, the one with the lace curtains?'

Little Tich held up his hand. 'It's my lodging, sir.'

'And you are?'

'Gary Atkins.'

The men laughed. 'Little Tich,' they said as one man. 'That's what we call him. Look at his feet.'

Byrd laughed. 'Well, Mr Atkins, I'd like you to do your music hall act tomorrow, but first of all tell me whether there's anyone in your house during the day?'

'No, sir. My wife works.'

'Good. Once Cantries start loading, I'd like you to walk up and down Mint Street. Look as if you're keeping an eye on the crowds by the Bell Tower; look interested in the builders' departure. This will make them uneasy. I don't want anyone else patrolling this area. Now, when you feel they're rattled, have a word with them. Let it be known you're thirsty and going to make yourself a cuppa. Then enter your house and watch from behind the curtains. If you see them loading the chest and making preparations to leave, call the Colonel's Office at once. Chief will be waiting there. He'll then ring whoever's on duty at both the Cradle Tower and the outside gates. When the Yeomen on duty at the Cradle Tower see the Transit leaving the premises

180

I want them to stop it, not officiously, but with the excuse that there's a large party entering the main gates. Chat them up, keep them talking for a couple of minutes. The short hiatus will give the Yeoman on duty at the main gates time to warn Sergeant Quinney, and his partner who will be sitting outside the gates in a battered Fiesta. We don't want to use radio communication so close to the van in case it's picked up. Once the message has been relayed to Bob he'll drive the car round the block and be in a position to follow the Transit as it emerges from the Tower.

'Now for the rest of you there's another job. As you change on the hour it's essential that you all know what I'm looking for, so please indicate time and position on any notes you might make. I need a minute by minute report on the cleaners, the tour leaders who may come in several times a week and the builders renovating St Thomas's Tower. How many men; time of arrival; who goes in and out; car and van numbers. This may have no bearing on the case but it would be foolish to miss something right under our noses. That, friends, is all for the moment, but your help and observation could prove invaluable.'

'Sir,' a burly Yeoman, with the greyest of beards, looking like Old Father Time, stood up, 'what about further work on the Martin Tower?'

'What!' the Colonel shouted. 'Further work! What are you saying, Nobby?'

'Well, I thought it was the same builders, sir, the ones working on St Thomas's. I've seen a man go in and out several times with a notebook, as though he's making an estimate for more reconstruction work to be done. Looked official.'

'Well, it's not official. There's no more work scheduled for the Martin Tower. It was all done last year.'

'Could be a researcher,' said Pierre Gambon. 'There's a historian from London University writing a monograph on the 9th Duke of Northumberland.'

'Has anyone else seen this man?' asked the Colonel. A shaking of heads and murmur of 'no'. 'You're positive, Nobby?'

'Yes, sir. While my wife was ill with 'flu I was in and out of our place. That's when I saw him.'

'Where is your lodging?' asked Byrd.

'In the Waterloo Block, facing the Martin Tower.'

'What did this man look like?' asked Byrd.

'Nondescript.' Everyone laughed.

'That's no good. Try again.'

'Hair, long, mouseyish, 5'7" or 8, always wears jeans, sometimes a black T-shirt, sometimes pale blue.'

'Does this sound like your researcher, Mr Gambon?'

'Could be, could easily be. I'll give him a call in the morning, ask him how many T-shirts he's got.'

'In the meantime, Chief, could you arrange a little more surveillance in and around the Martin Tower?' Paul Hanson, nodded. 'And Mr Gambon could you spare a few minutes after this meeting to give me a history lesson, fill me in on the Martin Tower?'

Pierre Gambon smiled. 'A few minutes, Superintendent! It'll take a few hours.'

Barney stood up. 'May I ask you something, sir?', he said looking at the Colonel.

'Yes.'

'What is going to happen about Steve, and does Brenda know?'

The Colonel rose to his feet, and said quietly, 'Brenda knows, at least, she's been told, but, quite naturally, she's finding it difficult to accept. She'll stay with the Padre and Mrs Morris-Jones until she's well enough to be taken to her sister's home. Steve's body will be moved later this evening. There will eventually be an inquest, but at the moment we don't know when or where.'

'Won't there be a memorial service, sir?'

'Yes, yes there will be, once the case has been solved. It will take place in St Peter's. And now, gentlemen, we must finish. The Ceremony of the Keys is upon us.'

The Colonel, Byrd and Quinney stood silently watching the ancient ceremony. The Last Post reverberating round The Tower became Steve Johnson's farewell to a life he'd loved, in a place he'd treasured. Colonel Kilmaster remained erect, his face expressionless. This was the worst moment in his twelve years at The Tower. If only they knew who was behind this. . . .if only he'd raised the matter sooner. . . .Steve could still be alive, still polishing the brass number plate every day, which he could see, from where he stood, gleaming like gold. Gold, Steve, gold, that was your downfall.

21

Colonel Kilmaster wasn't one for letting the grass grow under his feet. Jim Byrd had asked for scene of crime facilities to be set up in The Tower as soon as possible, and in his book, as soon as possible meant immediately. He asked Graham Tooley to take the two policemen over to the Waterloo Block to look at an empty lodging adjacent to Graham's office on the second floor which might serve the purpose. A great improvement, thought Quinney, on our usual mobile unit. The small flat, once a Yeoman's lodging, consisted of a bathroom, kitchen and two rooms. One room, he decided, the one with the hatch through to the kitchen, would make an admirable control room, and the other, slightly smaller, would be comfortable as an office.

While Quinney, the Superintendent's sergeant-magician, worked through the small hours installing a fax machine, telephones, and computer, Byrd slept. So too did Graham Tooley, not in his little cottage in Ongar, but on a sofa in his office. It was an uncomfortable night but he wanted to be around in case Quinney needed help, not only that, he'd never seen the police get down to business, and he didn't intend to miss out. He awoke with a foul taste in his mouth, yuck, his own fault, he'd have to keep a tooth brush in the office. He struggled across to the open window. Good God! The Superintendent was up already, jogging round the White Tower, but where was the noise and the smell of cooking coming from? The noise he decided wasn't too bad, a folk singer who knew his stuff, but the smell made his mouth water, made him realise he was starving. He shoved his shoes on, dashed along the corridor and into the adjacent flat. As he opened the door the rendering of *Danny Boy* ceased. Bob Quinney grinned at him,

'Good morning Graham, you ready for coffee and toasted bacon sarnies?

'Can't wait. You'd make much more lolly as a chef.'

'I doubt it, my wife calls me Alfred the Great.'

A few minutes later, Byrd, panting a little less than usual, joined them. The fragrance of freshly ground coffee didn't surprise him, nor did the sight of bacon sandwiches. It was what he expected of his sergeant.

The traffic from Oxford to London along the M40 was nose to tail but Georgina had managed to keep moving until she reached the Chiswick flyover. There she sat for half an hour while the emergency services were called to remove a lorry which had jack-knifed. She tried calling Byrd on her intercom, but all she heard was Quinney's voice fading away amid the crackling waves. Dickybird would be furious with her. Strange man, she thought. Blows hot and cold. On the rare occasions when he's behaving like a human being he has a certain charm, but mostly he's a demanding bastard. Wonder what he's like at home? She resigned herself to the wait and the inevitable diatribe when she arrived. It couldn't be any worse than Pete's outburst this morning when he'd realised she was packing an overnight bag. She didn't know whether she'd have to stay or not, but it would be stupid to go unprepared. What did Pete want? A little yes-woman with a nine to five job, who dutifully went to the office each day and who returned in time to cook his evening meal, and who would be there at weekends to do his washing, take his clothes to the cleaners, and generally serve as his valet? Pete was clothes conscious and vain. He'd made up his mind to get to the top, and getting to the top in his book was to be seen at events, immaculately dressed, with the right people, of course. She had to admit he'd done well. He was now a deputy branch manager at Lloyds Bank in Oxford, and this year the Chairman had taken the manager and his two deputies to lunch at The Randolph where he'd made it clear that Pete was in line for bigger things.

While she sat in the traffic snarl-up she faced the problem realistically for the first time. They'd grown apart, they had different goals, and neither would give. She knew there were times when she could have been home a little earlier, when at the end of a long day she'd stopped on for a beer with the lads because she felt exhausted. She'd only just realised the job had never been exhausting, it was the thought of going home to do another day's work that produced the fatigue. They had to part. Pete needed someone who would swan around with him, someone who would go to Silverstone, play bridge and give dinner parties. The joy had evaporated, the joy of those two first wonderful years, and now, if she were honest with herself, her only regret would be leaving their lovely home on the banks of the Isis in the heart of Oxford. It had been an incredible bargain because they'd put the deposit down before the builders started work. Now she supposed it would be worth at least £150,000, but she wouldn't ask Pete to sell up. She owed him that. She'd make her own way, find herself a pad in Kidlington, a small flat with low overheads.

Byrd heard the outer door open and close and then footsteps which stopped outside his office. His anger increased. Georgina knew the score, she knew the motorway would be busy. The least she could have done was call in, let them know where she was. He was ready to blow his top. There was a sharp rap, and the door opened.

'About time,' he yelled.

Pierre Gambon put his head round the door, 'We didn't arrange a time, did we?'

'Sorry! Sorry! Sorry! Mr Gambon. I've been waiting for a member of staff. What can I do for you?'

'Boot's on the other foot, isn't it? Didn't you ask me last night to give you a bit of background about the Martin Tower?

'Yes, yes I did, and I believe it's important. Do sit down and have a coffee. It will reduce my blood pressure.'

Pierre smiled to himself. Nothing in life ever caused him to lose his rag like the bearded policeman who sat facing him. He often felt annoyed, furious even, but he channelled it into a quiet sarcasm which gave him a great deal of satisfaction.

'Why don't we walk round the Martin and have the coffee afterwards, while you ask questions?'

'Suits me fine,' said Byrd quietly.

As they strolled across to the Martin Tower Pierre explained how little had been known about it prior to the 1500's, and how, from the mid-16th century onwards there was a plethora of documentation.

'James,' said Pierre, treating Byrd as though he were a student, 'you must understand that renovation and rebuilding hasn't stopped since William the Conqueror built the White Tower at the end of the 11th century. The Martin has had its full share about which I won't elaborate. It would take a week. However, the most memorable historical story concerns the imprisonment of the 9th Duke of Northumberland, one of the richest men in England, who was a prisoner here for fifteen years. Prisoner, you must understand James, is a relative term.'

Byrd slowly followed the erudite historian up the stone steps to the ramparts taking care not to miss any sign of alterations made over the years.

'This area of the ramparts,' said Pierre, is known as Northumberland's Walk because he had it repaved and used it for his constitutionals. Now come and view the accommodation. The good duke had a suite of rooms, a library, a great chamber, a withdrawing room, and two dining rooms – plus accommodation for some of his twenty servants. The rest stayed overnight in a house he rented on Tower Hill. He furnished all his rooms, and the Constable of The Tower allowed him to bring in his own catering staff, for which he paid a premium. His provisions which cost him £1300 a year, real money in those days, included partridge, plover, teal, woodcock, salmon, apples, pears, cream, parmesan and oysters. His cellar was always well stocked with claret, canary wine, and rhenish. He dabbled in alchemy, chemistry, had his own still, prepared simple tonic medicines and distilled whisky. So you see there was good reason to call him the Wizard Duke.'

Pierre smiled as he waited for Byrd to examine doors, cupboards, windows and thick walls. 'In what flights of fancy are you indulging, Mr Byrd? What are you actually looking for?'

'Wish I knew, but whatever it is it's not here.'

'If you're looking for treasure it would be nothing more than a few clay pipes.'

'Why?'

'Because Northumberland was one of the first men in England to smoke. He and his household puffed their way through eleven pounds of tobacco a week and over twelve hundred clay pipes a year.'

Byrd laughed, 'No wonder King James hated him. Wasn't it James who wrote a dissertation abominating the use of tobacco? But I can't believe that's why he was imprisoned?'

'No. There were three reasons, quite unrelated to tobacco. First of all Northumberland was angered at the way his friend Raleigh was being treated by James. Secondly, he was offended at the harsh treatment the King was meting out to Catholics, and thirdly, he made the mistake of inviting his kinsman Thomas Percy to dinner. Percy was a leading gunpowder plotter so naturally Northumberland was suspected, tried and incarcerated.'

They made their way down to the basement and found a group of children crowding round the rack while a teacher explained its functions.

'I've never understood,' said Pierre, 'why children become engrossed in the horrors here.'

'Ask the Grimm brothers, they knew, and made a fortune out of it,' replied Byrd, whose attention was centred on a wooden panel. Could that be what the anonymous workman was looking for, he wondered?

Pierre interrupted his line of thought. 'Tell me, how does Northumberland being imprisoned here, Colonel Blood stealing the Crown Jewels, and the Crown Jewels being saved in 1845 help your case?'

'On the face of it, they don't, but is there anything else I should know?'

'No, I don't think so, but there is one subject, Superintendent, on which I'd like to take issue.'

Byrd noticed the change of role. He was no longer James, a student in need of instruction, but Superintendent, and by the tone of Pierre's voice, an adversary. 'And the issue?' asked Byrd.

'The destruction of a valuable artefact belonging to The Tower.'

'Ah! You're thinking of the chest?'

'Yes. What are they going to do with it? Burn it? Bury it? Drop it in the ocean?'

Typical of the historian, thought Byrd. 'What the police are going to do,' he said slowly, 'is find out exactly how Steve was murdered, and put the criminal inside for life.'

'But I thought he was killed in a fight?'

'Injured, I believe, and that's what I'm out to prove, and if we allow these builders a certain amount of leeway they may lead us to both the killer and to the cache where the rest of the papers are hidden. They may enable us to discover, and this should interest you, how the auction room activities are master minded.' Byrd was annoyed with Pierre's approach.

'It's often said our courts treat the destruction of property more seriously than the destruction of life, but I can assure you the police don't take that view.'

'You've made your point,' said Pierre as they emerged into the bright sunlight. 'Now, if you don't mind I'll forgo the offer of coffee. I've got a mountainous pile of work on my desk.' Pierre strode away, stopping suddenly, remembering something he'd missed.

'Superintendent,' he shouted, 'I forgot to mention The Mint.'

'Mint! But that's over there on the west isn't it?'

'I'm talking about The Irish Mint which was here in the Martin. Probably has no import but if there's anything else you want to know give me a buzz.'

At the scene-of-crime office the control room door was open and Byrd could see Georgina and Bob Quinney bending over the fax reading an incoming message.

'It works, it works,' said Georgina.

'Of course it works, anything I touch works.'

'Bighead,' she retorted.

Quinney laughed, 'Now let's see if Charley is behaving himself.' As they moved round to the computer, Georgina stiffened. She knew she was being observed and knew when she turned round she'd meet those piercing dark brown eyes which could see through any subterfuge. Now for it.

Byrd was angry. The team was too small to cope with an investigation which seemingly had so many strands, and Sergeant Mayhew had the effrontery to be late. He was about to let off steam when he remembered how she'd worked on her days off, not even mentioning the fact.

'I'm sorry,' she said as she turned to face him, 'there was a traffic hold-up on the Chiswick fly-over, check it if you like, and interference on the radio.'

His anger evaporated. 'Forget it, bring a pot of coffee into my office and the three of us will discuss the modus operandi.'

She nodded and smiled at him. For a brief second there was a flash of understanding between them, broken by Inspector Pollard's entrance.

'Did I hear coffee?' he asked.

'Your timing is masterly,' said Byrd. 'Make it coffee for four, Georgina.'

Frank Pollard welcomed this diversion. A few days away from the Yard would be better than a holiday. Maybe he could do a bit of legwork for a change? Ever since the Met had set up the Art and Antique Fraud Squad he'd been chained to a desk, and to be shot of the infernal machines would make a pleasant break, get his weight down too.

They sat down round a couple of card tables and watched as Byrd produced a scrappy bit of paper from his shirt pocket, which he straightened out.

'I've made a note of nine moves we need to make. We'll go through them slowly and decide as we go who does what and when.' Quinney produced his notebook; he was used to these scrappy bits of paper, and the sooner everything was on the computer the happier he'd be.

'Number one,' said Byrd, 'find Yeoman Miller and ask him to point out the workman who showed interest in the Martin.'

'That's my job, isn't it,' said Bob Quinney, 'because neither Georgina not Inspector Pollard were at the meeting last night?'

'Yes, it is, but you'll have to be nippy about it. Don't forget you and Georgina have a tryst outside The Tower gates.'

'Tryst!' said Georgina to whom it was news.

'Yes, we'll be sitting in my battered Fiesta awaiting the departure of a Transit van which you've followed before, and which we'll be following to the death.'

'Too late for that,' said Byrd drily. 'Now the second move is to find out who is the owner and real boss of Cantries. You could cover that tomorrow morning, Georgina, if it doesn't conflict with anything else, and be early, please.' Damn! He'd decided not to mention her tardiness.

'I've brought my overnight bag with me.'

'Good, we'll get the Colonel to find somewhere for you to bed down. Third point. I need the names and addresses of the three workmen who have been employed on the site by Cantries.'

'I could do that,' said Georgina, 'while I'm tracking down the owner of Cantries.'

'Excellent! Number four entails finding out whether Anstey-Lloyd's only account is with the Midland; where he is spending the next month, and what his job was before he masqueraded as a foreman. Over to you, Frank.'

'Finding out where he banks in this country will be no problem. I've a contact who's helped us out before, but the holiday enquiries might be better left to you or Sergeant Mayhew, seeing as how you're both known to the janitor.'

'That's true. I'll take that on board and get along there today, and at the same time find out what he does, officially, for a living. Five. We need to keep an eye on Charley Austin. Dr Reader couldn't quite gauge Charley's reactions when he was given the post mortem findings on his brother's death. I have a . . . .'

'You have a feeling, sir, we know the feeling, sir,' sang Bob Quinney.

Even Byrd joined in the laughter, but he'd heard the song before.

'Six is your baby, Frank. We need to have details, in depth, about sales of documents in this country over the past five years. I mean historical documents, not Byron's love letters to his sister.'

'I've jumped the gun, Jim. After your first visit to the Yard sheer curiosity drove me to investigate. It's a long story, do you want to hear it now or after this meeting?'

Byrd looked at his watch. 'Let's hear it now, let's all hear it now.'

'What I've turned up may have no bearing on this case, maybe another ball-game altogether. But it can't be coincidence that six of our great country houses, places like Longleat, Hardwick Hall, and Blenheim, have all been astounded at the papers relating to their families or property which have come up for auction. All of them have sent their curators or administrators to examine saleroom lots and all have come away convinced that the papers they examined were their own property. They returned to base, to the libraries or wherever their archives are kept, only to discover their own papers safe and sound. The documents, in all cases, were almost identical but for the odd word here or there, as though the document had been written twice in order to have a copy. No photo-copies in those days. May make sense. Only one of our landed gentry had the wherewithal to purchase a lot at auction.'

'Who was that?'

Lord Landsmuir of Kilhaven. He makes his money from letting out fishing and shooting rights in the Tay Valley. It must be big business these days because he's never short of a bob or two.'

'You mean we could see both versions at Kilhaven?'

'Yes, Sir.'

'You're a Scot, Georgina, where's Kilhaven?

'South of Perth, sir, near Auchterarder.'

Byrd didn't have to think twice. 'Good, book me on a flight to Edinburgh leaving about 8 o'clock tonight, and while you're doing that Bob will top up the coffee.'

Ten minutes later Byrd was booked on flight XK324 to Edinburgh leaving at 8.40p.m. with accommodation at The Royal Scottish. As soon as Bob produced four more steaming mugs of coffee the meeting continued.

'Seven. We'll deal with as it arises, but one of us will have to liaise with the Professor when he's making his rounds of the auction houses. Eight. I want you, Frank, to contact the Dutch Police, ask for more info on Van Den Hoorn and tell them we've something to share. And, Frank, leave your uniform at home, wear something casual.'

Frank grinned. He knew it was going to be a holiday, a busman's holiday, but no matter.

'And lastly, number nine. When Sir Elwyn Rees has eased the way I'll be calling on Inspector Laguerry at the Deuxieme Bureau in Paris. Now my friends, stand not upon the order of your going'

'But go at once,' riposted Georgina. She too knew the Scottish play.

While the four policemen were drinking their coffee and mapping out their moves, Robin Kilmaster sat looking at Brenda and Catherine Morris-Jones while they discussed the figures on a piece of tapestry which Catherine was working. They debated whether the faces should be worked in petit point with wool or with embroidery silk. Brenda appeared totally engrossed. He couldn't fathom why, after the initial shock, she had calmly accepted the fact that Steve was dead. Such an unnatural calm. He didn't want to face a tearful woman but this apparent serenity was unnerving. She appeared to be living in the past and in the future not allowing the present to exist. One moment she was talking about the interminable time it had taken Steve to paint the house and his dogged refusal to instal an additional loo, and the next moment she was talking about the sights Harry had yet to see. She wanted him, so it seemed to stay for ever. It's protection, he thought, insulation against loneliness, but we all know she's never liked the house, so why doesn't she return to her little cottage in Cropredy? He couldn't know that Cropredy would be far lonelier than The Tower. A sister, who never talked, watched T.V. all day long and went to bed at 9 each evening. Neighbours who worked all day and spent every evening in The Red Lion. Here in the Tower, Brenda had friends and interests.

'It's Harry I want to talk about,' said the Colonel at last.

'Is he all right?'

'Yes.'

'Is he still here?'

'Yes.'

'Then I'll go home,' said Brenda firmly.

Neither Catherine nor the Colonel knew what to say.

'I'll go home now. I've some shopping to do if Harry is staying.'

'Don't make any decisions yet,' said Catherine. 'I think you should see Harry here. Why bother to go home at all? I'll give him a call.' She had the phone in her hand when Brenda stopped her.

'No, Catherine, don't ring him. I'm going home.'

'Very well, then, you go back home with the Colonel, talk to Harry and then if you change your mind you can come back here.' Better, thought Catherine, to let the Professor do the explaining.

Lawrence leapt to his feet as Brenda unlocked the door. This was the moment he'd been dreading.

'Do sit down, Harry, I'm going to make some tea.'

'Not just yet, Brenda,' said Robin Kilmaster quietly. 'You sit down, Harry has quite a lot to say to you.'

Brenda sat down and looked at the two men. Both were strangely silent and uneasy.

'What's the matter, Harry?'

'Brenda, Brenda my dear, I'm deeply sorry about Steve, and if there's anything I can do . . . . you must let me know, but I'm afraid when you've heard what I have to say you'll want to see the back of me.' He didn't know how to begin. Through the open window he saw children taking snaps of the ravens, and heard their laughter as the birds squarked their disapproval.

'You see, I have a confession to make.'

'What have you done, Harry? You haven't broken the Worcester vase, have you?' She looked at the pain on the face of the man standing by the fireplace. 'You needn't worry, Harry, there's always more where that came from.'

'No, no I've not broken anything, it's worse than that. I've destroyed the faith of two generous people,' he corrected himself hastily, 'I've destroyed your faith in me. You see, I'm not Steve's cousin. I am not Harry Johnson.' She looked at him bewildered. 'Harry Johnson and I changed places. I'm sorry to have to say this, but he didn't want to visit England, and changing places seemed a good idea at the time.

'What are you talking about, Harry?'

'I'm saying that I'm a heel. You've both been wonderfully kind, and I've taken you for a ride. I never thought it out, thought how a relationship, a cousinly relationship, could develop. I'm sorry. I'd like to make amends, but I don't know how, and I guess the best thing to do is get out of your hair.'

Brenda looked at him for some moments in silence. At last she found her voice. 'If you're not Harry Johnson, who are you?'

'I'm Lawrence Berkeley.'

'Oh,' shrieked Brenda, 'You're Harry's boss, the Professor.'

'Yes, yes, for my sins I am.'

'No wonder you ran rings round Steve when it came to history.'

'Not intentionally, Brenda, but I guess once a teacher, always a teacher.'

'You mustn't go, Harry, I mean Lawrence, there's so much more to see.'

'You're not angry, you forgive me? Is that what you're saying?'

The two men looked at each other, the one perplexed, the other relieved.

'Colonel, it might be an idea if I take Brenda across the road for lunch. Explain everything more clearly, find out when she wants me to leave.'

'I don't want to go out to lunch and I don't want you to leave.' It was a cry from the heart. 'You've no idea what this house is like at night. I'd rather have someone here.'

'Brenda,' said the Colonel softly, 'we have a lot of business to discuss, but it can wait until you feel strong enough to face it. I'll call round in the morning, see how you're bearing up, but do feel free to ring me at any time, and I'll let Mrs Morris-Jones know you won't be returning. He nodded at Lawrence and walked back to his office. Events in the Tower never ceased to surprise him.

22

'Another sandwich, Georgina?'

'Yes, why not.' She helped herself from the plastic box balanced on Quinney's lap. 'You've come well prepared. Sandwiches and orange squash. Can't be bad.'

'My wife's a provider, a mother-figure, treats me like she treats the children.'

They were sitting in the Fiesta with all the windows open, the hottest June day, so the weathermen said, for fifteen years. The sweat was pouring off the pair of them, Georgina mopped her brow with a handkerchief but Bob caught his in a plastic mug.

'It's so humid, I wish the storm would break. It's worse than a Turkish bath,' moaned Georgina, as she mopped her face for the umpteenth time.

'Hold on,' said Bob, 'I think we're in business.' He saw Little Tich, in the mirror, who was on duty at the gate, give him the thumbs up. 'Shove the food on the back seat, and give me one of the peaked caps.' He was already moving when she popped it on his head. A trilby changed her from a long haired beauty into a young man, if seen from a distance.

Bob drove round the block and was in position when the Transit emerged. The Fiesta slid in behind and followed it up Tower Hill.

'Good God,' he said, 'it's turning left. Our leader's intuition has let him down for once. He was positive the chest would be jettisoned further down the river. As they crossed London Bridge the heavens opened, the thunder directly overhead reverberated and echoed round the tall buildings.

'That's better,' said Georgina, as she wound the window up. 'It's much cooler, almost bearable. We're going south west aren't we? Where do you suppose we'll end up?'

'Being builders they may know of some building work in progress where our dummy can rest peacefully imbedded in concrete.'

'You've been reading too many thrillers. Blast! That's another sign I've missed. Did you catch the last one, Bob?'

'Roehampton, and Kingston. They've picked up speed. I have a feeling they're on home ground, like a horse scenting its stables.'

'Look out,' yelled Georgina, 'they're taking the right fork. My God, we're back on the river.'

'The Lower Ham Road, I know it well, did some courting down here when I was with the Surrey force.'

'Why are they slowing down?'

'Don't know. Well I'm damned, they're making for that cabin cruiser.'

'Don't you think, Sergeant Quinney, that you owe our leader a silent apology?'

'I reckon you might be right. Take a look through the binoculars Georgie, while I get as close as I dare. What can you see?'

'Madcap.'

'What!'

'That's what the cruiser's called. They've stopped right alongside. Now they're getting out.'

'How many of them?'

'Three. Two workmen and Anstey-Lloyd.' She watched as the foreman leapt aboard the Madcap. Immediately another man's head and shoulders appeared in the cockpit. 'Take a look, Bob, do you recognise that man?'

Quinney took a long look. 'No, don't know him, but I'll not forget him, quite a distinctive face. Anstey-Lloyd's now shouting to the men standing by the Transit. Looks like he's telling them to open the doors. Yes, that's what they're doing.'

'Hey, wot you looking at mister?' A bedraggled child's piping voice could be heard above the rain. Georgina wound the window right down.

'If I were you I'd go home and change those wet clothes.'

'Mum's not in till 4 o'clock. Wot you doing?'

'We're taking a look at the ducks on the river.'

'Get rid of him,' whispered Bob.

'Can't I see the ducks?'

You see them every day. Here, take this 50p and go and buy yourself an ice cream.' She shoved the coin in his hand. There was no 'thankyou' and no 'goodbye'. He'd gone like the wind.

Bob put the binoculars on the back seat.

The action was quite clear to the naked eye. The two workmen carried the chest, camouflaged in a dust sheet, to the stern of the cabin cruiser. The fatter one of the two managed to clamber on board in an effort to help Lloyd and the stranger to take the weight. As he did so a sudden gust blew the dust sheet off, each man made a wild attempt to grab it but they were too late. It blew across the river disturbing the ducks huddled together on the opposite bank. For a few seconds the chest was visible and then it and the three men vanished below their sight line.

'Damn! Damn! Damn.' said Bob.

The lone workman, who was now drenched, closed the doors and climbed back into the van making no move to drive off.

'He's waiting for Anstey-Lloyd, isn't he?'

'Yes, I reckon so. We'll stay put, Georgina. You'd better let control know what's happened.

'Calling Treasure Seeker, come in Treasure Seeker.'

'Treasure Seeker listening.' Frank's south London accent was even more pronounced over the phone.

'Object has been transferred. Now aboard Madcap, a cabin cruiser, moored alongside the towpath on the Lower Ham Road in Kingston. Can you get the river boys or Kingston to keep an eye on it?'

'Will do. How many aboard the boat?'

'Not sure. Suspect's leaving now with a driver, which means there are at least two men on the boat. We're on our way.'

'OK. Understood, good hunting.'

The rain eased as the Transit and the Fiesta set off in convoy. How peaceful the scene was, thought Georgina, the cabin cruiser tethered at its moorings, the ducks now minding their own business, no sign of the dust sheet, and no small brat taking an interest. No one would ever believe that a 16th century chest containing a dummy, in the likeness of a yeoman warder, had been taken aboard the Madcap. W323AKJ was still ahead, driving carefully, not drawing attention to itself. Despite the heavy traffic Quinney managed to hang on to the van's bumper, until they reached the traffic lights at the bottom of the hill approaching Clapham Common, when suddenly, without using its indicators, the van took a right turn. Quinney cursed as the lights changed to red. Georgina closed her eyes as he swerved round after it amid a barrage of blaring horns. When she opened them she could still see the van, but now there were three vehicles between them.

'He's going left, Bob.' The traffic ground to a halt. Georgina didn't think twice. She jumped out of the car, ran past the stationary traffic and up the side street. She was just in time to see the van turn into a ramshackle shed. There was no need to run any more. She took off her trilby, hoping nobody would give her a second look. They didn't. She walked slowly up the hill and passed the shed. The faded legend told her the business belonged to G.K. Wilkes, Car Sprayer.

Quinney caught up with her as she reached the top of the hill, but she was totally unaware of him until he hooted. Her attention was elsewhere.

'What's the matter?' he asked as she climbed into the car.

'My heart leaps up when I behold . . .'

'I know. I went to school too. Where is it?'

Over there on the west side of the common. They both gazed at a brilliant double rainbow.

'It's a good omen,' said Georgina.

'Not if we've lost the bloody van, it's not.'

'No, we haven't. It's having a respray.'

'What!'

'I've a theory Bob, let's go back and try it on the Superintendent.'

Mick Thomas, his wife and Byrd were sitting in the caretaker's cubby-hole drinking tea.

'It's a bit hot and stuffy in here, Governor, we could have a cuppa in our kitchen, but I like to know who goes in and out.'

'That's OK Mr Thomas, I'm here to pick your brains, not laze in an armchair. You said a few days ago that Mr Anstey-Lloyd was planning to go away, but you weren't clear where he was going. I just wonder whether he might have said anything since, about his movements?'

'Well, he never actually tells us much, but we usually manage to work things out. That's our life, you understand, like you might do a crossword or play chess, we try and work out where the people in this building go and what they do. Gives us a laugh, if nothing else.'

'You're quite a philosopher, Mr Thomas.'

'Oh no, I'm nothing like that, but when we turn Miss Marples or Poirot on we try to solve the case before they do, but of course writers always cheat, they use too many red herrings.'

'Does Anstey-Lloyd use red herrings?'

'No, I don't think so.'

'Yes, he does Mike.' Mary Thomas was quite emphatic. 'Don't you remember he said he was driving to France, and I'd seen his plane ticket to the Bahamas only the day before? I reckon he only drove to the airport.'

'So where do you think he's going next week, Mrs Thomas?'

'He could be going anywhere on the Continent because he's booked on the Hovercraft from Dover to Calais, but he's not going alone because the ticket is for two passengers.'

This is a bonanza, thought Byrd, it gets better and better. They must read everything they lay their eyes on. Best not to interrupt the flow. He looked at her expectantly.

'Two passengers, must mean he's taking the foreigner who's staying here at the moment.'

'He's rude that one,' said Mick Thomas. 'Never a thank you, but we always know when he's coming because Mr Anstey-Lloyd

200

asks my missus to get in extra rolls, milk and cheese. Seems his visitor drinks a pint of milk for breakfast followed by slices of cheese and rolls. Funny breakfast, isn't it!'

'Not funny,' said Byrd, 'not funny if you're Dutch or Danish. And you've never heard him speak?'

'Once,' said Mrs Thomas, 'on the phone, when I was cleaning the kitchen. Sounded German, you know, like we hear in old war films.'

'Any idea what Anstey Lloyd's job is?' asked Byrd looking in Mick Thomas's direction.

'No.'

'Hazard a guess.'

'We thought for a time he was an antique dealer, dealing mostly in clocks.'

'What changed your mind?'

'He's too fond of them,' said Mrs Thomas, 'wouldn't part with them at any price. Then we thought he might be a stockbroker, but the hours were all wrong. After that Mick thought he must be a director of one of the big banks.' Mick interrupted, 'Sort of sleeping partner, put his name at the top of the notepaper and let other buggers do the work, but we discarded that idea recently because he started going out at 7 in the morning and returning about 6. We can't imagine what he's doing.'

I can, thought Byrd grimly. 'You don't think he's a property developer, do you?'

There was a decided change in the atmosphere. Mrs Thomas gave her husband a frightened glance, and he shrugged his shoulders. Byrd waited for a few moments while their unspoken dialogue continued. 'Come on now, everything you say to me will be treated in the strictest confidence. It'll go no further, I promise you.'

'Well,' said Mick at last, 'I was up there one day cleaning the windows for Mary, her wrists aren't all that good, arthritis, you know. I shouldn't have done it, I know, but I looked at some papers he'd left in his desk. I don't really understand solicitor's jargon, but I'm pretty sure he wasn't into property development, though we couldn't work out why he was buying up two bankrupt builders.'

201

Byrd could have hugged the man, instead a smile of satisfaction filled the room.

'Is that what you expected, Guv?'

'Something like that, but it's very good news, Mr Thomas. Now, I don't suppose you remember the names and addresses of the two firms he acquired?'

Mick looked at his wife, 'Didn't you say one of them was in York?'

So it had been Mrs Thomas who'd been rooting around, and her husband was doing the chivalrous thing and covering up for her.

'Yes, it was York, the name, I think, was something like Upworth. No,' she said more decisively, 'it was Unsworth, no idea of the address, though.'

'And the builder's in East London?' prompted Byrd.

'Oh, that's easy,' she said, 'it was Cantries.'

If the Superintendent had been wearing a hat he would have thrown it in the air. Instead he was more circumspect. 'You've both been a tremendous help, more than you know. Now one last question, what chance is there, do you think, of spending a few minutes in the hall of his flat? I haven't a warrant, you understand, but it would short circuit the matter. Can it be done?'

'Yes,' said Mick at once. 'My missus will take you up in the lift, and leave the outer lift door wide open. If he returns, unexpected like, I'll give a short buzz on the fire alarm in his apartment. Very short, you understand, because it don't half carry. Don't want to put the fear of God into the old ladies on the third floor. If you hear the alarm, close the doors and walk down the stairs.'

'Congratulations, Mr Thomas, you'd make an excellent copper.'

'Go on, Mary, don't hang about,' said her husband.

The dough bin was still full of blankets, but the smell was stronger than ever. He knew what he'd find. He lifted the false bottom by putting his fingers through the holes and pulling. Sure enough his instinct hadn't let him down. There were two yellowing documents, emitting the same sort of smell which had assailed him when he opened the Professor's case. But where were the rest? He hastily replaced the blankets and they let themselves out of the apartment. It had taken four minutes flat.

It was late afternoon before the team reassembled in the scene-of-crime office. Byrd was exuberant.

'In the last few hours we've taken massive strides. Now is the time for rejoicing, now would be the time for the Colonel's champagne. In fact, why don't we ask him to join us while we unravel the strands?'

Quinney smiled to himself. He loved his irascible boss, but never more than when he was on a high because his exuberance lifted them all.

Robin Kilmaster was out of his office and across to the Waterloo Block in a flash to join them round the two card tables.

'Now,' said Byrd, 'we'll get Frank to summarise all the information that we've been throwing at him during the day.'

Frank cleared his throat, 'I'll begin with the one matter that hasn't been resolved. We've had no luck in identifying the workman who showed an interest in the Martin Tower, because Barney is *hors de combat*, a touch of food poisoning possibly, but he should be about again tomorrow. We've been much more successful tracking the builders. Anstey-Lloyd and two of his workmen loaded the chest as expected, and drove it down to Kingston where they offloaded it on to the Madcap, a cabin cruiser. Kingston Police are keeping it under surveillance. One of the workman stayed on board the Madcap and the other drove Anstey-Lloyd to a pretty grotty car-spray firm in Clapham where they dumped the Transit. The two men left by taxi. We now know that Anstey-Lloyd bought up two bankrupt builders who ran very small operations. One is Cantries, and Unsworth may be the name of the other one in York. Informants not to be named. We also know Anstey-Lloyd, and his house guest, will be leaving the country tomorrow, travelling by Hovercraft from Dover to Calais. It's possible that the guest could be a Dutchman. Two of the missing papers are also in his flat hidden in a dough bin, a sort of blanket chest, which is in the hall. The Dutch police have faxed us a picture of Kees Van Den Hoorn, but it's a bit blurred. Lord Kilhaven has agreed to see you tonight, sir. Any time between 10 and midnight will suit him. I gather he needs very little sleep. This will give you a chance to catch the 8 o'clock flight back to Heathrow in the morning. He'll have all the documents laid out ready for inspection.'

'Marvellous! Bloody marvellous,' said the Colonel. 'Now tell me what you're going to do?'

Byrd had it all worked out. 'First of all I'll be flying from Edinburgh to Paris in the morning, not London, so be a dear, Georgina, and rearrange my flight.'

Good God, she thought, he must be in a benevolent mood, never called me dear before.

'It's essential,' he continued, 'that we find the workman, so if Barney is still under the weather you'll have to take shots, tomorrow morning, of all the workmen as they arrive, say it's for security reasons, and then he can identify the man from his sick bed. Tomorrow, Georgina, when you call at Cantries' registered office, you may find the birds have flown. We do need the names of his workmen so do what you can. Incidentally, Colonel, Sergeant Mayhew needs a bed for a few nights. Can you help?'

'No problem, I'm sure the Chaplain and his wife will only be too happy to oblige, and what about Sergeant Quinney, where's he staying?'

'On a camp bed in my quarters.' That was news to Quinney, but he said nothing.

'Now then Frank, let's see the fax from Holland.' Byrd looked at the image of a bespectacled man, black hair receding at the temples, thin lips and a large nose. 'Oh yes, I've seen this gentleman before, at an auction in Geneva where he sat unnoticed, so he thought, at the back of the hall'. He passed it to Georgina.

'Good Lord! Bob, take a look at this. Isn't that the guy we saw aboard the Madcap?'

'It most certainly is. Who are we looking at, sir?'

'Kees Van Den Hoorn, who is, at the moment, staying with Anstey-Lloyd and travelling with him tomorrow on an afternoon sailing. Couldn't have been better timed.'

'Why's that, sir?'

'Because by the afternoon Inspector Laguerry of the Deuxième Bureau will, I hope, have informed his colleagues about the arrival of the two men at Calais. Once Anstey-Lloyd's wheels are on French soil we can rest assured his progress will be recorded. With both men, probably, on their way to Switzerland it's crucial to have the Professor seen browsing around Christie's in Geneva. He'll have to put his skates on, there's a sale in two days time.'

'He's looking after Mrs Johnson at the moment,' said the Colonel.

Byrd looked flabbergasted. 'Hasn't she been told yet?'

'Yes, but she doesn't care two hoots about all his play-acting nor the fact that he's not her late husband's cousin. Her problem is the house. It always has been, and I can't think why Steve never asked to be moved. She sees ghosts, talks to them, I'm sure it's all in the mind, but there's no doubt she needs company and if the Professor goes off to Switzerland she may suffer delayed shock, which so far she's avoided.'

'Why don't I stay there?' asked Georgina. The men looked at her surprise. 'In fact I will stay there. I'll let the Professor know you want to see him about the Swiss trip and I'll talk to Mrs Johnson as soon as we've finished this meeting.' No one tried to dissuade her.

'The Governor will be thrilled to learn of the latest developments. Should have brought the champagne with me.'

'There's no time for that, Robin,' said the Superintendent. 'We'll drink the champagne when we've discovered who's masterminding all this.'

'What! Do you mean to say it's not Anstey-Lloyd?' They all looked at their leader in astonishment. 'No, it's definitely not Lloyd, but at this stage it's imperative that the case is not discussed with anyone outside the building. We're missing a clue which may be staring us in the face. There is someone, a consummate organiser, knowledgeable both in business and art history, a ruthless person to whom the door of many of our stately homes is opened without question. We must find him or her.'

There was silence while they all chewed on that unexpected morsel.

'Didn't you say,' asked Bob, looking at Georgina, 'that you had a theory?'

'Yes, I did, but it doesn't look so promising, not now. Difficult to establish a Q.E.D.'

'Come on, Georgina, that's what we're here for, let's be having it,' said Byrd.

'It seemed to me,' she said hesitantly, 'after seeing the van go in for a re-spray that it could carry the builders anywhere in the country. A new colour, a new name. While the builders were in situ in stately homes, they could help themselves to manuscripts, easier to shift than silver or pictures. On the other hand, now that I've given it more thought I can't see Woburn or Chicheley opening their doors to itinerant builders, unless as you say there is one person who is accepted and above reproach.'

'Your theory merely underlines what I've been saying. We have to find X who is persona grata at Blenheim, Longleat, Hardwick or wherever he likes to appear.'

Robin Kilmaster shook his head. 'I can't believe any chairmen or secretaries of institutions like the National Trust or English Heritage would be involved in anything like this.'

'Colonel, right now, we haven't time to place all the chessmen on the board. We know there are several pawns, but we're looking for the black king, who may be here among us. Let us pit our wits, play a game or two when I return from Paris tomorrow night.'

The two sergeants looked at each other, both with the same thought. Did their leader suspect the Deputy Governor? It made sense, he was in a position to manipulate the game, but the vibes were all wrong, thought Georgina, he lives and breathes the Tower. But who else is there?

206

23

While Byrd was winging his way northward Quinney was having a noggin in the Warders' Club, Pollard was on his way home, Georgina was settling herself in at No 5, the Professor was on his way to Gatwick, and the Colonel sat in his office, alone, surrounded by box files, doodling. The remains of a half a box of matches showed considerable resources had been used in lighting his pipe which, together with a generous malt whisky, helped him to concentrate his thoughts.

The problem on paper looked easy. At the top of the page he'd drawn a black king, below the king were two black bishops which he named Lloyd and Van Hoorn, below the bishops two black knights with question marks alongside and underneath the heavy brigade a myriad of pawns. Like James Byrd, he thought, I'm beginning to believe it is someone in my own organisation, and judging by the looks which passed between the two sergeants I'm suspect number one. He chuckled to himself. It wouldn't be the first time the Constable of the Tower and his Deputy had been suspects. Wish I'd had the sense to ask Graham Tooley to stay on. Between us we could have gone through these papers with a fine-tooth comb. It's no good I'll have to start all over again.

He placed the box files in order ready for re-checking all estimates and contracts issues over the past five years, but the first job was to take another look at the list of security passes issued to workmen. All appeared to be in order, all had the address of each man and the firm for whom he worked. Half a minute, go easy, that's odd! Those two brothers, who reputedly hated each others' guts, both lived at 23 Hanslope Road, Walthamstow. With mounting excitement Robin Kilmaster realised he'd probably discovered the identity of the two black knights. Now for more careful appraisal of the records. Two hours and two whiskies later he noticed one small item. On all contracts for work over the past five years there was a time clause, except one. He peered at it more closely. Yes, the time clause had been deleted and initialled. 'Eureka,' he shouted to the empty air, 'We've got you, you bastard.'

Byrd closed his eyes, not because he was tired but in the hope that his companion would cease her endless chatter. He knew about her husband, her children, her grandchildren, her dogs and her constipation. Eventually she got the message and he was able to concentrate on his chess problem. Just before touch-down he realised there was one possibility they'd missed. He'd ring Robin before he left for Paris in the morning, tell him to take a look.

The plane touched down at 2150 and within minutes Detective Superintendent Byrd was in a taxi and on his way to Lord Kilhaven's stately home. He'd forgotten how long the summer days were north of the border, how one day faded into another when neither bird nor man wanted sleep. Maybe that's why the honourable lord thought nothing of seeing him between 10 and midnight? When he arrived it was light enough to see every pinnacle of the baronial pile.

'As you'll not be staying the night, sir, would you like me to wait? asked his driver.

'Yes, if you don't mind killing time for an hour or so.'

'Och, I'll take myself round the garden and have a wee smoke.'

208

'You've been here before, then?'

'Many, many times, sir, especially in the grouse season. You'll have to give a mighty knock on the lion's head, sir. They could be doing with a bell but that would be too new-fangled for his lordship.'

The knocking brought a buxom housekeeper to the door who led him through a maze of corridors to his lordship's study. Byrd had expected to find a healthy middle-aged man who shot and fished with his paying guests and whose reputation for contentious questions in the Lords led to long debates. Should have done my homework, he told himself, I'm definitely slipping. The man who rose to greet him was frail, eighty if he was a day, and crippled with arthritis. Only the voice, a light, decisive baritone, and the unspectacled dark brown eyes, were untouched by age. Lord Kilhaven weighed up his visitor for a few seconds, before deciding he approved of the swarthy bearded policeman who looked every inch a Celt.

'You could have led the attack at Culloden, Superintendent.'

'On which side, sir?'

The dark brown eyes twinkled. 'Well, I'm sure if you'd been rooting for us we'd have won the battle. Now sit down and tell me why you're interested in these papers which, as you can see, my secretary has set out for you.'

'It's a long story, sir, and I'll start at the beginning.'

The old man listened without interrupting until every twist and turn in the saga had been told.

'An amazing anecdote, Superintendent. I can guess what you're going to ask me, so we'll dispense with the questions and I'll tell you what you need to know.'

For an old man, thought Byrd, he's amazing. No wonder he fires broadsides in Westminster which have them fleeing in all directions.

'Yes, we did have builders around the place for quite a time. They did a considerable amount of work on the interior of the building. Small builders they were, and this job saved their bacon, or so I was told. They did several minor jobs in the library. A bit of woodworm in two of the panels, window frames to be replaced, and some re-wiring before the ceiling was repainted.

All our ancient documents, which neither I nor my brothers have really battled with, were kept in a locked chest in the library. We were saving the job of classifying them for our old age.'

Byrd laughed out loud.

'You can laugh, young man, but other interests have kept me fully occupied. It's only this year that I've had time to sort through a fascinating pile of literature; remind me to show you the papers relating to Culloden before you leave. Now the manuscript you're interested in, the one I bought, resembles, as you said, another document which we possess. Slight, almost infinitesimal differences. It's a longish deed, covers nine pages, setting out what a 17th century Laird of Kilhaven expected his progeny to do in the event of his death. That's why it wasn't surprising to find a second copy, not if each child had to be given one. My secretary and I have perused, with great care, both documents, and I must say that if the one I bought is a forgery it's a bloody marvellous piece of work and whoever did it should be able to find more gainful employment.'

'I doubt if anyone could match the fee he must have received from the sale of your document,' said Byrd drily as he crossed to a large table, turned on the angle poise lamp, and stared at the first page of both copies.

'Incredible,' he murmured. 'Which is which, sir?'

Lord Kilhaven was amused. 'You see what I mean? The one on the right is the one I bought and the one on the left, the original.'

'That's where I think you're wrong, sir. For the people we're trying to nail this is big business, they would never risk presenting Christie's or Sotheby's with a forgery.'

'What are you saying?'

'I believe your original was taken away and copied, and then the forgery, not the original, was returned to your chest. Think back, sir, did the builders return to do any checking?'

'Yes, yes, I believe they did. Something to do with the sockets. White were easy to obtain but we insisted on brown, didn't show up like a sore thumb on the panelling. Yes, I'm sure they came back to finish the job.'

'Were you here?'

'No, spent a month with my son in the south of France. Good for old bones, don't you know. Now, young man, what I propose to do is invite an expert to give me a definitive opinion on these documents and send you the results.' There was a sharp tap on the door and the housekeeper entered carrying a tray. 'Your cocoa and biscuits, sir.'

'Thank you, Mrs Duncan, now you get to bed, don't wait up.'

'Very good, sir.'

'My nightcap, Superintendent, never miss, could be it contributes to my longevity, you never know.'

On the journey back to the Royal Hotel in Edinburgh the driver gave his passenger a bloodthirsty account of the warlike Kilhaven family during the Jacobite Rebellions. Strange, thought Byrd, he's talking as if it happened yesterday. It was only then he remembered the old man hadn't shown him the Culloden Papers. Of course! The housekeeper had brought his lordship's cocoa and given his visitor marching instructions in a most diplomatic manner.

24

Sleep hadn't dulled the Colonel's excitement, which came bubbling over the phone.

'You're bang on, James, I spent yesterday evening going through the contracts. We've nailed him, it's crystal clear.'

'Well, what are you waiting for, Robin? Get the champagne out.'

'We'll all celebrate tonight, but it will be vintage this time.'

It took longer to get from the airport to the Deuxième Bureau than it had taken from Edinburgh to Orly. Byrd was impatient. He wanted to get the morning meeting over, make the contacts he needed and get back to the Tower where things were really beginning to move. While he was sweating it out in a taxi Georgina was in Hackney calling on the registered office of Cantries. The trim little house with a wooden garage alongside was hardly what she'd been expecting. She rang the bell and waited, so too did a fluffy tortoise-shell cat. Almost immediately the door was opened by a small grey-haired woman with no eyes for her visitor.

'There you are, Tommy, you naughty cat. Where've you been

212

all night?'

Tommy rushed past them both, straight into the kitchen, he knew where his food was.

'He doesn't love me,' said the woman, 'only comes home for his Whiskas, then he'll be off again.' Bit like me, thought Georgina.

Over a cup of tea she discovered that Mrs Atkins' husband, Gordon, had been dead for over two years. Angina so the doctor said, but Mrs Atkins didn't agree. 'It was overwork that finished him off, trying to keep the business on its feet. Haven't got used to being on my own yet, don't suppose I ever will. Like Tommy, you see, Tommy was his cat, never mine. He was a stray, thin as a lath when Gordon brought him home. He called him Tommy Atkins, said he'd still soldier on. That's why he goes out so much, still looking for his master. Now what did you come about, Miss?'

'It's about the sale of the business, Mrs Atkins. Could you tell me when it was sold and to whom?'

'Mr Smith bought it soon after Gordon died. Gave me a good price for it, you know. He was very fair. Bought all the equipment too and the van.'

'Did you know the business is still registered at this address?'

'Yes, Mr Smith said it would take time to change everything and if I got any letters to hang on to them. Porky would collect them. In fact, Porky still parks the van here.'

'Porky! Who's he?'

'One of the workmen my husband employed. He was the only one who agreed to carry on working for Mr Smith.'

'Why not the others?'

'I don't think Mr Smith wanted them but they all say he was too bossy. My husband was easy going, you know, they didn't like the change.'

'Can you give me Porky's full name and address?'

'He's only round the corner in Frampton Park Road, don't know the number, but it's the house with the gnomes in the front window. I think his name's Dennis, Dennis Robinson.'

'Thanks Mrs Atkins.'

Sergeant Mayhew walked round the corner, said hallo to the gnomes and rang the bell, nothing happened so she knocked. It was some time before a pretty fair haired woman came to the door, at least she would have been pretty if she hadn't been crying. Her eyes were swollen and bloodshot, her skin mottled, and her hair unbrushed. Georgina wanted to run away, leave the young woman with her grief, not intrude, but she had to see it through. She became aware of the neighbours staring at her, some openly, others half hidden behind net curtains. What had happened?

'I am terribly sorry to worry you at a time like this; you are Mrs Robinson, aren't you?' The young woman nodded. 'May I come inside for a moment and talk to you?'

She led the way into the front room. 'Do sit down,' she whispered. The ruddy faces and the smiles on the faces of the gnomes seemed unusually grotesque in the face of such grief.

'You're from the police, aren't you?'

'Yes, but how did you guess?'

'They said they'd send a woman constable to sit with me for a bit, see if I remembered anything, anything that would help.'

'Help with what, Mrs Robinson?'

'With Denny's death.'

Georgina took a deep breath and stepped into the hall, closing the door quietly behind her. 'Come on, Mrs Robinson, I'm going to make you a cup of tea.'

'You don't look like a constable.'

'I'm not, I'm a sergeant.'

'But the Inspector who came this morning said he'd send a woman constable to sit with me.'

'Why, Mrs Robinson, what's happened?'

'They found Denny in the river, drowned,' she burst out sobbing, 'but he could swim, he was a strong swimmer.'

'Haven't you any relatives who could come and stay with you?'

'No, they're all in Australia.'

'What about neighbours, then?'

'No, no, I don't want them.'

'Hush now, hush, I'll stay with you until the constable arrives.'

214

'Why are you here?'

'I wanted to talk to your husband about his job, but what I'm going to do right now, Mrs Robinson, is make that tea.'

'Yes, yes, that would be nice.' She followed her visitor into the kitchen.

'He didn't like the job. It was all right to start with, but two or three weeks ago something happened. Something he wouldn't talk about, but he shouted a lot in his sleep and when he was awake he was on edge the whole time. He talked of leaving Cantries . . . ' Her voice faded.

'Why didn't he? asked Georgina gently.

'I think he was afraid.'

The doorbell rang. 'Sit down Mrs Robinson, I'll answer it.' She threw the door wide open expecting to see the constable, but standing there, saying nothing, was the last man she expected to see.

'What do you want?'

'I've just heard about Denny, so I've come to see Anna,' said Charley Austin quietly.

Georgina didn't move.

'She is here, isn't she?'

'Yes.'

'I need to see her.'

'She's hardly in a fit state to see anyone.'

'What is it?' asked Anna as she walked into the hall.

'Someone asking to see you. I'll ask him to go, if you like.'

'Anna,' said Charley as he pushed past the sergeant.

'Oh, Charley.' He put his arms round her and ushered her back into the sitting room.

It's better, thought Georgina, to say nothing, pretend I don't know who this man is, and listen.

'Who did it, Charley?' asked Anna her voice trembling.

'That's what I intend to find out.'

'Denny had something to tell you. He'd been meaning to tell you ever since Jimmy's funeral, but he kept putting it off.'

'Have you no idea, Anna?'

'No, except he kept saying "Jimmy needn't have died" as though he was blaming the hospital. Perhaps that's what he was going to tell you?'

'Perhaps!' said Charley grimly.

At that moment the door bell rang. This time it was W.P.C. Allen, a capable looking young woman who smiled at Georgina. Sergeant Mayhew introduced herself and asked only one question, not in the hearing of the two people closeted in the back room.

'Are you positive the dead man is Robinson?'

'Yes, wearing a silver heart on a chain round his neck. *With love from Anna* a marriage token. It was all he had on him but we recognised the work of a tattooist working in Stratford East. He confirmed that he'd tattooed a Dennis Robinson about two or three years ago. Described him perfectly.'

'I'll go and sit in the car, and tell Austin, the man talking to Mrs Robinson, I want a word with him pronto.'

'OK Sarge.'

Georgina left wondering how many more workmen were destined to die before this case was solved.

Charley Austin opened the passenger door. 'What do you want with me, Sergeant Mayhew?'

'Since the constable has told you who I am, I'm sure you can guess. A few minutes conversation is all I'm asking.'

'And if I don't feel in the mood for a chat?'

'Then you'll be asked to step along to DHQ and see a Superintendent who may want more than a few words.'

'All right, if that's how you want to play it.'

He pushed the seat back and stretched his legs. He's a different man, she thought, from the one who cossetted Anna. He's going to be difficult.

'Let me ask you, Mr Austin, why you are showing such an interest in the Martin Tower?'

'No more than any of the other towers. They all fascinate me.'

'Are you something of an amateur historian?'

'No. It's the stone work that interests me.'

'Is stone masonry your only talent?'

'No, I can . . . ' He stopped abruptly. 'Yes I guess it's the only thing I'm any good at.'

'Have you any idea what Dennis Robinson was going to tell you once he'd plucked up the courage?'

'What do you mean, plucked up the courage?'

'He was frightened, Mr Austin, shit scared, wanted to leave Cantries but hadn't the nerve. Can you tell me what he was hiding?'

'I've no idea.'

'And you've no idea what he was trying to tell you?

'No.'

'Well I'll tell you. Your brother died because of a sub-arachnoid haemorrhage . . . '

'I know that.'

'. . . brought on, not by a fight, but by being viciously thrown on to a pile of stones again and again.'

'Who says so?'

'That's Superintendent Byrd's hypothesis'.

'My God!' whispered Austin, 'I'll get the bastard, if it's the last thing I do.' He hammered his knees with his fists. 'If it kills me, I'll get him.'

Sergeant Mayhew carried on relentlessly. 'Dennis Robinson died because he was going to tell you what actually happened to Jimmy and a Yeoman Warder in the tunnel under 2A. Both men are now dead.'

'I'll get him.'

'No, Mr Austin, with your help we'll get him.' She looked at his grim face and clenched fists. He'd be willing to talk, she'd put money on it.

'I suggest we both return to The Tower, and, during your lunch hour, why don't you make your way to the second floor of the Waterloo Block? Use the entrance on the north side. You might feel like making a statement.'

He nodded. 'I'll make a statement all right. I'll finish that bastard.'

'Bienvenu à Paris, Commissaire. Pourquoi vous êtes ici?' The two men shook hands in Inspector Laguerry's office overlooking the Seine.

'Je suis ici pour discuter un cas qui pourrait vous occuper.'

'Your French, Monsieur, is excellent, but let us speak in English, it will give me some practice.'

'D'accord, Inspector. I'll be brief and explain why I'm here.'

'Could you not have phoned, Monsieur?'

'Yes, but you French have an evocative word for the merging of like minds – rapport – which, I believe, can only flourish if face to face. We didn't achieve rapport in Switzerland where we met as strangers, and parted as acquaintances. You were most circumspect about your reasons for being in Geneva, but I now know, Inspector, that we were both on the same errand. This time we meet as colleagues with precious little time left to us to accomplish what needs to be done.'

'You mean, Monsieur, that the bird will fly?'

'Exactly.'

'In Geneva, Monsieur, I was interested in the sale of a small Pisarro, and papers which passed between Napoleon and his officers during the Battle of Marengo. Both lots were sold by the same unnamed source.'

'Van Den Hoorn?'

'Oui, Monsieur. What a pity we didn't talk in Geneva. You, I seem to remember, were interested in a letter to Charles I, the poor unfortunate who lost his head.'

'*Uneasy lies the head*?'

'Ah yes, in both our countries.' Laguerry rose, crossed to the window, all the time staring at the river, as though it gave him inspiration. 'We're nearly at the end of the trail, Superintendent. Any day now the Dutch are ready to pick up, as you say in England, the master mind behind years of ingeniously planned theft. Van Den Hoorn is a genius, monsieur.'

'Van Den Hoorn may be a genius, Inspector, but he is not the master mind. The brain behind all this is a Briton. The Dutchman is merely one of his lieutenants.'

'There must be some mistake.' Laguerry frowned as he turned round to face Byrd. 'We've spent five years building up this case and acquiring sufficent evidence to indict Van Den Hoorn. Now you tell me he is *sans importance*.'

'No, no, Inspector, he is most important, but he is not the master mind.' Laguerry felt his case falling about his ears. After five years of careful planning and painstaking work this brash, bearded Englishman was pulling the ground from under his feet.

'Then who is behind all this, and how long have you been working on the case, monsieur?'

'Nearly four weeks, Inspector.' Laguerry sat down slowly. Why was his liver playing him up again? He'd cut out his nightly bottle of wine, on doctor's orders, but the doctor hadn't told him how to cope with shocks like this. Byrd knew only too well what the Frenchman was thinking and feeling.

'Inspector, we can't prove anything without your cooperation which could bring this case to a successful conclusion and help us to put a murderer behind bars. If you are prepared to help us, we could land this fish.'

'All right, Superintendent,' snapped Laguerry, 'what are you suggesting?'

'This afternoon a car with two passengers will be on the Hovercraft from Dover to Calais. An Englishman by the name of Anstey-Lloyd and your old friend Kees Van Den Hoorn, I imagine they will be making tracks for Geneva where a Christie's sale takes place in two days time. We already have Professor Berkeley in position. He's an American, ostensibly hoping to buy historic papers for Princeton University. We're expecting him to be involved in private transactions with our two friends. Now, Inspector, could you arrange to have the car followed from Calais?'

'Of course, *pas de problème*. Tell me, monsieur, is this Anstey-Lloyd the brains?'

'No. That's where we again need your help. Once they've discovered Berkeley is on a marketing expedition they may phone the boss for instructions.'

'What is your relationship like with the Swiss Police?'

Laguerry smiled. 'I have a certain rapport with a commissaire in Geneva.'

'Good. Then it could be possible to arrange a tap on their hotel phone?'

'Of course, but intelligent criminals normally use phone boxes, less chance of being overheard.'

'Yes, it's a gamble. I rang my office as soon as I stepped off the plane and told them to put a check on the suspect's phones.'

'Phones?'

'His office and his home.'

'When, monsieur, do you think we'll be able to arrest these men?'

'Within the next 48 hours. Easier for you to make the arrest in France when they're on their way home. The Swiss Police could delay the procedure and we don't want the top man forewarned. Once they're under lock and key and indicted for murder we'll put pressure on the Swiss Banks to reveal the state of their accounts, which I'm sure will make interesting reading. Now Inspector, I need to reach the airport by 10.45 if I'm to catch the 11 o'clock to Heathrow. It's a relief to know I'm leaving this matter in your capable hands.'

Gallic pride was restored, the two men shook hands, and Byrd was on his way. The meeting had taken thirty five minutes. God! he was parched, could have done with a coffee.

At five past one Charley Austin put his nose round the door.

'Come in and sit down, Mr Austin. Help yourself to a sandwich. Milk and sugar in your coffee?'

'No sugar. Such hospitality, Sergeant. Didn't know the police ever bothered with a man's needs.'

'Don't let's waste time sparring, Mr Austin.'

'Is that what you call it?'

'We all have the same objective, so why don't you tell us your story before we take a statement?'

'Oh yeah, I'm not daft. You'll record it just the same.'

'Of course, but it's easier for you to do it off the cuff.'

'And make it easy for you to put me inside.'

Frank Pollard interrupted. 'If you're turning Queen's Evidence I doubt whether you'd ever see the inside, even for a night.'

'I might need protection.'

'That's different, but we'll tackle that problem when it arises.'

'Pity you didn't tackle it earlier. My brother, that Yeoman fellow, and Denny Robinson might still be alive.'

'If you talk now you could prevent more deaths.'

Georgina looked at Charley's tanned healthy face. An attractive man, grey eyes, a tinge of red in his dark hair, an open countenance, a honest face, not the sort of man one expected to be mixed up in all this.

220

Charley's story was a long one and he told it without interruption.

Quinney, whose feet were killing him, was listening in the control room. In desperation he took off his shoes and socks and put his feet up on the spare chair. He turned the volume down slightly and settled down with his sandwiches and coffee in reach.

'Jimmy and I,' said Charley, 'were inseparable. We did everything together, played snooker, went to football matches, athletics meetings. It was just the same at school despite the fact that Jimmy was two years younger than me. It was at school we discovered we could do this copperplate writing. It's out of fashion these days, but we had a headmaster, Mr Watkinson, who was a bit of a nut. He'd take us to the British Museum and get us to copy old manuscripts which he used to display on his study wall. We won prizes for it, and we designed the certificates he gave out by the score, and we had to write in the winners' names. It became a bit of a bind, and we missed out on other subjects. We were also good at wood carving, but there was no work so we turned our hand to stone masonry knowing we could always find a job. We took to following our favourite football team. When the Spurs went abroad so did we, always the best seats. It cost us but we didn't have anything else to spend our money on, at least not until the Olympics in Mexico. We desperately wanted to go, but couldn't raise the ante, then a couple of months before the games Anstey-Lloyd called on us at home. We didn't know him from Adam, and we've still no idea how he came to hear about us. He asked us to copy three old manuscripts, said he'd give us a grand for each one. We didn't need to be asked twice. We managed, at that late stage to get tickets, and off we went cock-a-hoop. When we got back he was waiting for us. Told us what we'd been doing, told us our forgeries were now in place in three stately homes, but wouldn't tell us where. He didn't blackmail us, not exactly, but he said we were now part of his organisation. Jimmy was to join his firm as a labourer, and he told me to apply for a job with Rush and Jones who were looking for stone masons. He said it would be easier if a story got around The Tower that we weren't hitting it off, that we couldn't stand the sight of each other. He also said there'd be a lot more money available. We were tempted and fell for it. It seemed such a gradual process at the time, but looking back on it I realise how fast Anstey-Lloyd worked.'

Bob was enjoying the story, and didn't hear Byrd enter the room.

'What the hell are you doing, Sergeant?'

'Sorry, Super, sorry, my feet are killing me. Here listen to this, sir.'

'Who is it?'

'Charley Austin.'

The Superintendent sat down on Bob's footrest and sniffed. 'Pretty pungent, your feet. Turn the sound up a bit.'

Charley's voice came over clearly.

'A few months later we were both working here in The Tower. He asked me to take a close look at the stone work in the Beauchamp and Martin Towers.'

'Who's he, Bob?' whispered Byrd.

'Anstey-Lloyd.'

'There was no holding him,' said Charley angrily, 'after he'd found the tunnel under 2A. He was too greedy, expected me to examine the stonework in other towers, signs of doors or cavities which had been filled in and could be concealing secret cupboards or passages. He swore the Tower had a lot of hidden assets. When that bugger Smith, or Anstey-Lloyd, or whatever he calls himself, was out of the way Jimmy took me down to have a decco at the tunnel. They'd already unearthed two chests of papers. The first one had been emptied, a bit at a time, but the second was left until Smith, or Anstey-Lloyd, was ready for it. These papers have to be treated carefully and storing them is quite a problem, especially as Lloyd didn't want to flood the market. He really didn't need us any more. He didn't have to have manuscripts forged any more, he'd got enough of the real thing which nobody could lay claim to. Then a funny thing happened. I was in the Martin Tower taking a close look at the stonework when I saw the architect who's in charge of all the renovation taking an interest in the basement near where the rack's on view. He'd obviously seen me with my notebook at the ready. "Found anything of interest?" he asked. I shook my head and off he went without another word, before he could ask me what I was doing? On the following day Jimmy had a fight with someone in the tunnel. I didn't know until you told me today,' he said looking at Georgina, 'that a Yeoman was involved. Now Jimmy's a peaceable fellow, not really a fighter, but when he's roused he's quite capable, I mean he was quite capable of giving someone a going over. I reckon he must have been a bit punch drunk otherwise Smith could never have finished him off. Denny must have been down there at the time, must have seen what was happening, and that's why he's dead too.'

'Who on earth is Denny?' asked Byrd.

'One of the workmen, sir, found drowned this morning, near Teddington Lock.'

Byrd was livid. 'Why the hell didn't you call me? No, don't answer, Sergeant, I'll hear this through.'

Charley was shouting. 'Denny was a really nice guy. He wouldn't have hurt a fly, but Hodges is still around, and that bugger is bloody going to tell me what's been going on, even if I have to threaten him with extinction.'

Byrd leapt to his feet and dashed into his office.

'You'll not be threatening anyone, Mr Austin. I have a much better idea. Now listen to this.'

25

Lawrence Berkeley hesitated before entering *le magasin des fleurs de Genève*. He'd not sent flowers to anyone since his mother's death, but he wanted to make amends and do something for Brenda. He couldn't forget her stricken face, nor escape from the pain in her eyes. She needed protection and love, which she wouldn't get from a deaf sister who watched the box all day long. There was an innocence there too, unusual in a middle-aged woman, a quality which recent events could easily destroy. What to send? Not red roses, that would be too much. He settled for pink and white carnations with a simple message. *I'm sorry, Lawrence.*

He returned to the Geneva Hilton, disappointed that his meanderings hadn't created any interest. Everything the Superintendent had suggested had been carried out to the letter. On the previous day he'd spent a pleasant hour in the auction rooms before wandering leisurely round private galleries, occasionally asking the price of a picture. It was while gazing in rapture at a snow scene by Pissarro that he made up his mind to accept the Cambridge offer – a three year exchange – yes, he'd enjoy

224

the Chair of History at King's. It would give him a chance to settle a little matter with Professor Kettle. Vengeance would never be sweeter. On the second morning he'd been a bit more outgoing, talked loudly in a shop specialising in 17th and 18th century books. After that, back to the hotel where he'd sat in the public lounge reading and re-reading Christie's catalogue until he knew the damn thing by heart. They certainly made a good job of it, and if he were a millionaire . . . OK, Superintendent, I'm giving up. I'll do the crossword instead. He was half way through, thinking about 28 across, *A diversified musical carthorse*, when a man, whose face he knew only too well from the photographs Byrd had provided, joined him. Kees Van Den Hoorn pointed to the catalogue, 'Bargain hunting, my friend?'

Lawrence finished writing in *orchestra* before taking stock of his companion. 'There are no bargains in this life, sir, not when one is hunting for the near-impossible.'

'So what are you looking for?'

'Historical acquisitions for my university in the States.'

'Are you a Vice-Chancellor, or do they call you presidents in the States?'

'President, but I'm of a lowlier calling, merely a humble professor.'

'So how do you find sufficient funds for these artefacts you hope to acquire?'

Lawrence laughed, 'Oh, the greenbacks are readily available from a benefactor who doesn't know what to do with his money, but finding the goods is another matter.'

'Perhaps I could help?'

The Professor gave a sigh of relief, carefully folded the *New York Times* and gave the Dutchman his full attention.

While the Professor was carrying out his orders to the letter so too was Sergeant Mayhew. She'd made contact with Jeffrey Watkinson, whose life-long hobby was collecting manuscripts and old papers. His warm hazel eyes bored into her soul, much more like a father confessor than an ex-headmaster. He was deeply perceptive and discovered more about her in half an hour than Pete had managed in five years, neither was he reticent about himself. His pension, she gathered, didn't stretch far but it is surprising what one can pick up at sales, especially off the beaten track. He took her into his garden where passion flowers and honeysuckle vied with sweet smelling roses in their effort to cover an unsightly brick wall. Georgina sat with the old man, sipping sherry and watching the red admirals circling round the buddleia. She felt a curious sensation of repose, as though she'd known him all her life.

'You're asking me what I remember about the Austin boys?' He gazed at the butterflies for some minutes before returning to the present and the question. 'They were born out of their time, Sergeant, out of their time. They should have been reared in a fifteenth century monastery and left to illuminate the scriptures. They were masters of their craft, but these days who wants to wait for months for something a machine can do in five minutes?' Georgina didn't answer. 'I can show you examples of their work from the time they arrived at my school until they left. Work which, when I feel the world is moving too fast towards final extinction, I spread out before me and find peace. Does this make sense to you?'

'Yes,' she replied quietly.

'But that isn't what you came to hear? You want to know how they became involved with these criminals who led them away from the straight and narrow, and I'm afraid that is something I can't answer. Who are these men?'

'I doubt whether their names would mean anything to you. One is a Dutchman living in Holland, and the Englishman who is at present in Switzerland calls himself Bill Smith although we know his name is Anstey-Lloyd.'

'Anstey-Lloyd,' he murmured, 'that rings a bell. Nice man he was, an honest upright man. Loved the boys, visited the school, and on one occasion presented the prizes. Pity there aren't more members of Parliament like him.'

Georgina couldn't contain her excitement. 'And did he ever see the boys at work?'

'No, not actually at work, but he knew their work because at the end of the ceremony we presented him with a bible suitably illuminated on the inside cover by both boys.'

'Mr Watkinson, you're marvellous, you have provided a missing link.'

'More sherry, Sergeant?'

'No thanks, I must take the good news.'

'But not from Ghent to Aix,' chuckled the headmaster.

Charley positioned himself at the end of Fentiman Road by the mini-supermarket. From where he stood, it was possible to see who went in and out of the Council flats. It was an interesting mix of people in this area of Vauxhall, though he didn't know that at the time. Victorian houses lavishly converted into flats in which half a dozen M.P.'s resided, all snug within their Laura Ashley-covered walls; a conductor of a London Orchestra; several artists; publicity executives; media people and in the GLC flats ladies who did for them, kept their accommodation clean, washed and ironed, and put the rubbish out on Mondays. Charley would hear all this later in the evening.

Ralph Hodges' only relaxation was darts and imbibing Scottish nectar in the Fentiman Arms. Always, first things first. Two or three games of darts before he became too inebriated to throw straight. Charley gave him an hour before sauntering into the pub and straight to the bar without apparently noticing Hodges.

'Wot'll it be, luv?'

'Half a lager for starters.' He wandered round the spacious bar looking at the photographs of old London before deciding where to sit. Best near the door, he thought, where Hodges couldn't fail to see him.

The game of darts was taking all Hodges' concentration. He was good, thought Charley, but a man with that weight and those biceps ought to be a boxer. Little interest was being taken in the prowess of the two men at the board by the regulars, it was something they expected, an exhibition they saw most nights. The game ended with Hodges' adversary buying him a double whisky. So that was the drill, thought the silent man sitting near the exit. As Hodges sat down at his normal table he caught sight of Charley. A succession of expressions flitted across his face. Charley Austin had never been his favourite person, least of all now. He'd not set eyes on him since Jimmy's funeral, which Lloyd had forced him to attend. At last he made an effort, half smiled and shouted across the room. 'Hallo there, long time no see.'

Charley grinned back. Now was the time. The Superintendent had said something about taking the current when it served or lose our venture. A bit high flown, the language, but he knew what was meant. This was his chance. First another half of lager and a double whisky, before making his way over to Ralph Hodges table.

'Congratulations, Ralph, you throw a bloody good dart. Have this one on me.'

Hodges relaxed. 'Don't mind if I do; mud in your eye, Charley.'

'How's business, Ralph, and what are you working on now?'

'The boss is away for a few days so I've got some time off, he owes me anyway, but you know the set-up, we've never any idea where the next job will be. Smith keeps us hanging around for a couple of weeks and then off we go to one of them 'ouses belonging to the gentry. Can't complain, we always get paid, work or no work.'

Six double whiskies later Ralph Hodges was talking. He had enough money now to buy his own place. Sheila wanted to move out of the area, but he was going to stay. He'd taken the boss's advice and was buying one of the refurbished flats in a Victorian house next to the flats.

'It's £120,000, wouldn't have thought about it, Charley, but the boss says it will be an investment and if I'm ever down on my luck I've something to sell.'

The man listening said little. He was hearing what he expected to hear, but he'd soon have to ask the crucial question. The Superintendent had been quite specific. Better do it now, he thought, before he's too far gone. 'Ralph, you remember the little punch-up Jimmy had with that Yeoman chappie in the tunnel. We know what happened to Jimmy, but what happened to the Yeoman?'

Hodges shook himself and sat up when he realised he'd been set up. This was no chance meeting. His rugged features became ugly and menacing. 'Wot d'you want to know for?'

'I'm interested, Ralph. Wouldn't you be if the bugger had killed your brother? I hope he got what he deserved.'

'Yeh, yeh,' said Hodges, as he thought about it for a moment. 'Yeh, I guess you're right.'

'Did Jimmy manage to finish him off?' whispered Charley.

'Nah, he didn't. Jimmy wasn't a hard man.'

Charley smacked his companion on the back. 'So you did the job for me?'

'Not me, chum. Smith did it himself, nothing to it, just suffocated 'im as he lay on the deck, and then we put 'im in one of them chests we was emptying.'

'You mean you had a ready-made coffin?'

'Not 'alf. Bit of luck that was.'

'But you weren't so lucky when you tried to move Jimmy.' There was an edge to Charley's voice which the befuddled man beside him missed. 'You slipped, didn't you, and dropped him on to a pile of bricks?'

'Yeh, that was rough on poor Jimmy.'

Hodges saw the hatred in Charley's eyes, and too late realised the enormity of what he'd said.

'Ere mate, are you saying we topped Jimmy?'

'Yes, that's exactly what I am saying.'

Hodges struggled to his feet. 'You'd better cut that out man. 'Ow did you find out, anyway?'

'Jimmy talked before he died.'

'He wot!' Hodges grabbed the man in front of him whose sole mission was vengeance. Despite being half cut he realised he was being threatened. No, worse than that! If this guy talked he could find himself inside on a murder rap.

Everyone in the Fentiman Arms stopped talking. They knew Hodges could be belligerent when he'd had too much, but they'd never seen him like this. He yelled at Charley, 'You'll keep your bloody mouth shut, otherwise I'll finish you off.'

At that moment Byrd, followed by Quinney and two uniformed constables, entered. Hodges threw Charley to the ground and rushed to the back exit straight into the arms of two more burly constables. After a struggle they managed to overpower and handcuff him before marching him out to the waiting black maria. Byrd helped Charley to his feet.

'You feeling OK?'

'I'm fine, but I was beginning to think you'd left it too late.'

'The timing was perfect. Sit down, you need a brandy, and what's more I'll join you.'

Charley carefully removed the minute microphone and wires from his shirt pocket. The tape recorder had been carefully hidden by a bulky denim jacket at least two sizes too large for him.

Byrd lifted his glass. 'To you, Charley, and if you're ever out of work, you could always become a private investigator.'

'That'll be the day,' grinned Charley.

Big Ben struck nine as Byrd and Quinney drove along the Albert Embankment on their way back to The Tower. The last stroke heralded a message over the intercom from the control room. Sergeant Mayhew's voice, sounding unusually subdued, reported that she'd seen Mr Watkinson who'd now solved the problem of how Anstey-Lloyd had discovered the talents of the Austin boys, and Colonel Kilmaster, armed with a magnum of champagne, was awaiting their arrival. There was also positive news from abroad, news Byrd had been praying for. Professor Berkeley had made contact with the Dutchman, and would be arriving back in London the following day to take a look at some antiquarian manuscripts.

Quinney laughed, 'You're making headway, sir, you've earned the champagne.'

'We've earned the champagne,' corrected his boss, 'but you wouldn't think so, listening to Mayhew. She should be over the moon imparting such earth-moving information, but she makes it sound like the run-of-a-mill report on a parking offence.'

'She has a domestic problem, sir. She made up her mind this morning to leave her husband and the gorgeous house they have on the Isis. Over the weekend she'll be taking a look at a small furnished flat I've recommended near DHQ. I just hope she's doing the right thing.'

'I'd no idea there were problems. Someone else on the horizon?'

'No, nothing like that. It's the usual occupational hazard. The job and the marriage don't mix.'

'Poor Georgina.'

More bleeps. Frank's voice this time. 'Treasure Seekers here. How long will you be?'

'Just crossing Waterloo Bridge. Be with you in ten minutes. What's the problem?'

'Message from your wife, sir. It will keep.'

'No need. I'll ring her now.' He tapped the digits and waited. Damn! there was no answer. Didn't make sense at this time of night. Kate was always in bed by 8.30. He realised how much he needed to see them both, hear them both, be reassured. Too many days had passed since their brief visit to The Tower and he realised with some compunction that he had not spoken to them since. I'm letting this case take over my life, he thought. It consumes me through my waking hours and when asleep I dream of nothing but tunnels, chests and state papers.

When they reached The Tower, Byrd made straight for the control room.

'Where's the message from my wife, Frank?'

'I didn't write it down, sir. Thought you wouldn't want it on your desk for all to see.'

The Superintendent stopped in his tracks. No, it couldn't be. It happened to other people not to him. Stephanie, had she carried out her threat? Had she left him, or had Kate had an accident? 'All right, Frank,' he said at last, 'what is it?'

'Mrs Byrd rang to say you'd done nothing about their holidays, as promised, so she and Kate have gone down to Poole to spend three weeks with a cousin of hers she hasn't seen for years.'

'What! Cousin? I didn't even know she had any relatives in Poole. What's his name and where does he live?'

'She didn't say, sir, she didn't mention his name, or leave a telephone number or address, so I took the liberty of checking.'

'Go on.'

'I remember reading in the Police Gazette that you'd married a Stephanie Delo. It wasn't too difficult to have all the Delos in Poole abstracted from the Telephone Directory. My lad at the Yard did it in double quick time. There are nine but I struck gold on my fourth attempt. A Mr Keith Delo is expecting his cousins

231

there tonight. Sounded quite an old man, sir, so I guess he must be a first cousin once or twice removed, so perhaps that's why you've not heard of him. Here, Jim, take this, it's his address and telephone number.'

'Thanks Frank, thanks for that. I'll ring now.'

'You'll not get them yet. They caught the 7.30 coach from Oxford, not due in Poole until 10 o'clock.'

'OK. That's taken a load off my mind. I can at least look as if I'm enjoying the champagne. Join us, Frank, we have a lot to discuss.'

'Half a second, sir, something's coming through on the fax. I'll be with you in a moment.'

'Well done, well done, James,' said the Colonel as they all sat down.

'Everything seems to be falling into place. We must let the Governor know immediately.'

Byrd half smiled at this show of exuberance. 'Just a little premature, Robin, but I think a meeting tomorrow morning wouldn't come amiss. We'll need to talk with the Governor, our two white knights, Sir Elwyn and Sir Charles, Hamish Campbell, and Pierre Gambon with Sergeant Quinney in attendance to take notes.'

'Very well, I'll see if they can all manage 10 o'clock, a civilised hour, this time.'

'By tomorrow I am hoping it will be possible to present a flawless dénouement.'

'But we know who it is,' said the Colonel quickly.

'Yes, but knowing isn't proving, so let's keep our ideas to ourselves, for the moment.'

Quinney winked at Georgina. This was his boss, running true to form, never letting on until he was certain. It was an annoying trait but he'd learnt to live with it, and in this case he was pretty sure he too knew the answer.

Frank Pollard entered waving the fax which had just arrived. 'Here you are sir, it's a verbatim report of a conversation recorded late this afternoon.'

'Read it, Frank.'

'Geneva 1700. Anstey-Lloyd rang a London number 071–332–0090.

'Is the boss in?'

'Who shall I say is calling?'

'Jeremy Anstey-Lloyd.'

'Just putting you through, sir.'

'Told you not to call at this time of day. What is it?'

'Couldn't wait. Have a buyer. Professor from Princeton University. Particularly interested in Stuart literature. Will pay up to £40,000 for letters. More for state papers.'

'We've plenty available, but tell him we can only produce three papers for inspection. We don't want to flood the market. Make sure he's genuine.'

'Kees has already checked through a contact in New Jersey.'

'OK then. Tell the Professor he can see some stuff in London on Thursday, at the Waldorf. That gives us two days to clean it up. Bank draft in dollars, as usual, to our Swiss connection.'

'Do you want me back?'

'Yes. As quickly as possible. Leave Kees to cope with prospective buyers at Christie's.'

'Hand me my jacket, Georgina.'

They all looked at Byrd in astonishment as he tried each pocket until he found a scrappy bit of paper which he'd taken from a message pad in a luxurious West End flat. He held it up to the window, and said 'Snap, 071–332–0090. Excellent, that is all we needed. Inspector Laguerry has produced the goods. Frank, send him a fax straight away. Ask him to pick up Van Den Hoorn, when he's on his way home after the Christie auction. He usually stops off at Dijon, has a lady friend there. Let Laguerry know we'll deal with Anstey-Lloyd, and tell him we have identified the brains behind the organisation. An arrest is expected tomorrow.'

'Admirable! admirable,' said Robin Kilmaster as he released the cork and carefully filled five glasses with a fizzing honey-coloured liquid.

'To a modern Sherlock Holmes and all his merry men.'

26

Major General Featherstone-Bonner delayed his departure to France to preside over the second meeting in Queen's House; Sir Charles Suckling cancelled his golf; Sir Elwyn Rees-Davies escaped a boring General Purposes Committee Meeting; Pierre Gambon asked Angela Burne-Jones to give his morning lecture to a group of schoolchildren; Hamish Campbell agreed to attend prior to his weekly inspection, and the Deputy Governor and Superintendent Byrd were accompanied by Sergeant Quinney with his notebook at the ready.

'Welcome to this meeting, gentlemen,' said the Governor with a smile.

'Colonel Kilmaster tells me Mr Byrd has solved this unusual case. Needless to say, I'm sure we're all agog to hear how this has been achieved, so take the floor, Mr Byrd.'

'Thank you, sir. If, because of the many strands, you find my dénouement a little convoluted, please stop me and I'll elucidate.'

The Governor nodded.

'I'll start with 5, The Green, gentlemen, because it is the key which has unlocked every aspect of this case. A few months ago, as you already know, Steve Johnson discovered a secret panel hidden behind an armoire in the kitchen which led to cellars under his lodging. The cellars are all part of a complex of tunnels stretching from Legge's Mount to the Bell Tower. One tunnel links No 5, The Green with 2A, The Casemates through an ingeniously camouflaged wall containing a hidden arch. Steve Johnson had, over the past few months, discovered coins struck here in the Royal Mint during Henry VII's reign. What he virtually ignored, according to Professor Berkeley, were two chests full of documents.'

'Good God, Colonel,' exploded Hamish Campbell, 'why wasn't I informed, and who, may I ask, is the expert trespassing on Mr Gambon's and my preserve?'

'Let the Superintendent finish, Mr Campbell, I'm sure all will be made clear.'

Sergeant Quinney noticed that Campbell's annoyance resulted in a slight twitching in his right eye. A distinctly nervous twitch.

'Steve Johnson's wife,' continued Byrd, 'was never told about this tunnel, although subsequently we've discovered she knew Steve had found some coins, and realised that there must be a tunnel under the house. On Professor Berkeley's first night as their guest while Brenda was out rehearsing *Blithe Spirit*, he was shown the tunnel. As you all know, gentlemen, apart, I think, from Mr Campbell, the Professor changed places with Steve's cousin Harry, but this, fortunately, has stood us in good stead. He saved many of the papers and, during the past 24 hours he has been instrumental in linking the Dutchman with the Tower documents.'

'If I may interrupt again, sir, said Hamish to the Governor, 'I wish to record a protest. The DOE should have been in on all this business from the start.'

'Yes, Mr Campbell,' Major Featherstone-Bonner replied, 'I think you have a point, but let Mr Byrd finish his report.'

The architect eyed the Superintendent thoughtfully. Quite an astute guy this policeman, he had to hand it to him.

'The next link is 2A, The Casemates, which would, I'm sure, have gone unremarked if Steve Johnson hadn't been excavating

235

for coins. Steve and Jimmy Austin, one of the workmen employed by Cantries, came to blows in the tunnel. Steve was a powerful man, an ex-boxer, and Jimmy Austin never had much stomach for a fight. They were unevenly matched, and poor Jimmy was knocked out, concussed. When he came round he saw Hodges pinning Steve down while Anstey-Lloyd throttled him. Jimmy Austin was a mild chap and not one to subscribe to murder, and, in trying to prevent the tragedy, precipitated his own death. Lloyd was in a spot, Jimmy would never keep his mouth shut. He left it to his heavy, whom we now have in custody, to batter Jimmy again and again on a pile of bricks.'

Robin Kilmaster stared at the architect and marvelled at the man's *savoir faire*, but for the twitch which was becoming a little more pronounced no one would ever guess.

'Again we were fortunate,' said Byrd quietly, 'for the Chief Yeoman saw the badly injured Jimmy Austin being carried out to the builder's van. He would have none of it and called an ambulance. Anstey-Lloyd travelled in the ambulance and stayed by the patient's side until the Colonel told him quite plainly to get lost because the accident had happened in The Tower precincts, and the onus was upon him, to make sure that everything possible was done for the patient. We'll never know whether Lloyd intended to finish Jimmy off when the nurses were out of the way, or whether he wanted to make sure Jimmy died before he was able to say a word. However, Jimmy said seven words which eventually made sense, and gave us a glimmering of what had actually happened down in the tunnel. As soon as the ambulance had left the site, Hodges, the man we have in custody, placed Steve's body in one of the chests, covered him with a dust sheet and screwed the lid down. As you know we rescued the corpse and replaced it with a dummy. The chest, accompanied by Lloyd, and Hodges, was transported to a cabin cruiser lying in Kingston, with Robinson doing the driving. Sergeant Quinney clearly saw Van Den Hoorn take delivery, and he also saw the driver go aboard. That was the last time Robinson was seen alive. Lloyd and Hodges drove off leaving the Dutchman to deal with the chest. The river police kept watch and followed the cruiser down to Teddington Lock. They saw the weighted chest jettisoned.'

'What!' said Pierre Gambon.

'Don't worry Mr Gambon, it will be retrieved tomorrow. But what is disturbing, gentlemen, is that the police didn't see Dennis Robinson's end. It's quite clear from a statement made by his wife that Robinson, who'd been friendly with Jimmy Austin, was another man who couldn't live with his conscience. Although Robinson had not been directly involved, his attitude must have been crystal clear to Lloyd so he was faced, yet again, with a man who was prepared to talk. This time he left the killing to Van Den Hoorn who, we think, anchored near the lock until dark before disposing of the body. Robinson was pulled out of the water near Teddington Lock, in the small hours of yesterday.'

'We owe a great deal to Charley Austin who has told us how both he and his brother gradually became enmeshed in the Anstey-Lloyd set-up.'

For the first time Quinney noticed Hamish Campbell's jaw tighten. We're getting to him, he thought, as he doodled over the nonsense he'd written. 'Jimmy and Charley were both good at copperplate, and unwittingly made copies of old manuscripts for Lloyd. Once the copies, or forgeries, were in place in three of our stately homes Lloyd was able to hold the threat of disclosure over their heads. Someone, not Lloyd I think, had been able to filch original manuscripts from historic houses, and at a later date replace them with the Austin copies. To enable the gang to do this Lloyd, from time to time, acquired bankrupt building companies well known in the local areas where the swaps were taking place. Cantries, for instance, was based in the East End, until yesterday when a fire destroyed the premises, but not the records which is what the arsonist had planned. Sergeant Mayhew, and this is not for the record, didn't wait for a warrant, she went in and abstracted what she'd been sent to acquire.'

'Lloyd took on Jimmy Austin as a labourer, and gave Charley orders to apply for a stonemason's job with Rush and Jones. This ploy gave him two useful men on the site. Following Lloyd's orders the two brothers never acknowledged each other. A family feud, if anyone asked. When Charley Austin learned that Jimmy had not died as a result of the fight with Steve, but at the hands of Hodges and Lloyd, he was determined to finish them. It took some persuasion to make him see it our way, and it's thanks to him that we have the whole episode on tape direct from the mouth of Hodges.'

At this point Hamish Campbell caught the Governor's eye. 'Apologies for interrupting, sir, but I have a tight schedule today, and would like to be excused the rest of this meeting.'

The Governor had scarcely opened his mouth when Robin Kilmaster interrupted, 'We'd much rather you stayed, Hamish, there may be points needing your expertise.'

'Very well,' he said grudgingly.

'Hodges' statement taken by DHQ implicates three men in three murders, Lloyd, Van Den Hoorn and himself. What we don't as yet know is how the Dutchman and Lloyd came together. There must be a common denominator. It's possible that their first meeting could have been coincidental, at an auction. Both men have the same fixation, a fetish for acquiring clocks. But I can't help feeling that they're responsible for a case which Inspector Laguerry of the Deuxieme Bureau has been trying to solve since 1988, when a small Braque and a De Shwitters vanished from an exhibition in Paris. They've not surfaced, but we'll be able to bring a smile to the austere face of Inspector Laguerry when we invite him over to take a look at the Braque, loosely tacked behind an uninspiring landscape in Lloyd's flat.'

'Idiot,' said Hamish under his breath.

'We have yet to find the De Shwitters, but that too I imagine is in the flat. However, gentlemen, I digress. Back to The Tower.'

The Governor's mind was elsewhere. 'Now that you have the malefactors, Superintendent, this means that poor Mrs Johnson can go ahead with the arrangements for the cremation of her husband. Colonel Kilmaster, perhaps you and the Chaplain can organise a memorial service in St Peter's Ad Vincula.'

'Yes, sir, I'll put the matter in hand immediately, as soon as Superintendent Byrd finishes his dénouement.'

238

Major General Featherstone-Bonner looked surprised. 'Surely there are no more robberies and no more villains?'

'We have the lieutenants, sir, but we still lack the mastermind behind all this.'

'You mean it's neither Anstey-Lloyd, nor the the Dutchman?'

'No, sir. The man who has ingeniously masterminded the filching of State Papers and the forging of early manuscripts from many of the country's finest houses will be arrested here in the Tower before the hour is out.' There was a grunt of surprise from the Governor, and Pierre Gambon.

'You may wonder why I'm leaving it so late. You could put it down to a quirk, gentlemen, but living in this historical ambience for some weeks has made me think in a historical context. This thief, a thief in the grand manner, has committed treason, stolen State Documents belonging to the Crown, and condoned murder here. I know he has already pinpointed other areas where there may be more papers and almost certainly treasure. I think we should ask him where those areas are before we arrest him.'

'We'll not quarrel with that, Superintendent,' said Sir Elwyn.

'Who is the offender?' demanded the Governor.

'A god-fearing Presbyterian, so he'd have us believe, from north of the border.'

The Governor laughed. 'You could be describing Mr Campbell . . .'

Before he'd finished speaking Hamish Campbell was on his feet waving a revolver in the air. 'Sit down, sit down all of you. The first man to move will get hurt.'

The Major General, always a fearless man, had no intention of obeying orders. He half rose, but his Deputy quickly pulled him down.

'Let him go, sir.' The Governor looked at the Colonel in astonishment. For a man who'd won the MC in Malaya his reaction was surprising, until he caught the barest flicker of a wink. They all watched in silence as the man with the revolver removed the key from the door, and stepped backwards while keeping an eye on them. As the key turned Byrd was already speaking to Mayhew.

'Action stations, Sergeant, he's on his way, and Frank, get this door unlocked, pronto.'

Major General Featherstone-Bonner shook his head in disbelief.

'What are you doing, Superintendent? Why, in heaven's name, did you let him go?'

'He's gone to earth. We'll follow him, find out where he's hiding out, who else is involved and hopefully find the missing manuscripts.'

'But, Mr Byrd, the mechanics for an escape route will have been carefully planned.'

'We have plain clothes men and vehicles at the ready watching every move, ports and airports have been alerted.'

Frank Pollard unlocked the door.

'You're fortunate,' said Pierre Gambon softly, 'that he left the key in the door.'

'He didn't,' retorted Inspector Pollard, 'this is a spare.'

'What an ingenious mind the fellow has,' said Sir Elwyn. 'Think what a contribution he could have made to wartime intelligence. One has to admire his nerve, the brazen affrontery and guts needed to attend this meeting.'

'But,' said the Colonel, 'he had no idea, whatsoever, why the meeting was being called. He spoke to Anstey-Lloyd yesterday, he knew Van Den Hoorn was still in Geneva, and Charley swore not to mention that Hodges was inside, so what had he to fear?'

Beep, beep. Byrd switched on.

'Quickly, sir, he's worked a flanker. The landing stage wasn't covered, and he had a small speed boat waiting. It took off before we could stop him.'

Pierre Gambon gave a snort, hardly able to contain his amusement.

'Didn't you know, Superintendent, that nearly all of those who successfully escaped from The Tower made their getaway by water?'

Byrd ignored him. 'Sergeant, get hold of the River Police, tell them to stop the boat but warn them to take care because he's armed.'

'Have already done that, sir.' He breathed a sigh of relief.

'There's a police launch at the landing stage, Superintendent, waiting for you.'

240

'OK we're on our way. Come on Robin, you too Frank, and Quinney, you get over to the Control Room straight away.

Of the four men left in Queen's House Sir Charles was the most affected by the turn of events. His man, his intelligent unorthodox Superintendent had blown it. Oh yes, Byrd had solved the case but the lack of foresight in allowing Campbell to walk out of the room, lock them all in, which was laughable, and to escape down river, could hardly be regarded as a successful conclusion to what could have been a text book case. On the other hand Sir Elwyn didn't seem bothered. He was smiling to himself.

'You don't look the least bit perturbed, Elwyn, what are you hiding from us?'

'Fate, I think, Charles, may be on our side, but I'd rather not share my thoughts until we hear from your wayward Superintendent.'

Byrd followed by Inspector Pollard and the Colonel leapt aboard the police launch and in seconds they were away, the vessel making 40 knots as they sailed downstream.

'Have you any idea where he is?' yelled the Colonel, trying to make himself heard over the roar of the engine.

'Yes, sir. As soon as we round the bend you'll see a small green speedboat. Poseidon has her in view but is not attempting to outpace the craft.' The engine, after the first thrust, was considerably quieter, quiet enough for the men to talk without shouting.

Poseidon calling Neptune, calling Neptune. The voice came over loud and clear. *Suspect still in sight, 150 yards ahead, apparently unaware that we are interested.*

'Skipper, have them pull out all they've got and tackle the vessel.'

'There's no need to rush, Superintendent, they won't get far.'

'They've already gone too far and I want them stopped.'

The Colonel intervened. 'Why won't they get far, Skipper?'

'Because, sir, the Thames Barrier will be up by the time they get there.'

'You mean,' said Byrd amazed, 'you've given orders to raise the barrier?'

241

'No, sir, we didn't have to. It is tested once a month, at approximately 11 o'clock, depending on the tide, and today is the day.'

'It's 10.45 now – supposing it is delayed?'

'It normally only takes half an hour to do the job because great care is taken not to disturb the river bed, but in an emergency it can be raised in ten minutes. We've told them it's an emergency.'

Robin Kilmaster chuckled, 'This is where our mastermind has slipped up.'

'He wasn't the only one,' growled Byrd.

'Look ahead,' yelled Pollard, 'there's the other launch.'

At the same moment they heard their Skipper ordering Poseidon to stand off while Neptune went full speed ahead.

'Do you want to close now, Superintendent?' asked the Skipper.

'Yes, go right ahead,' said Byrd grimly.

The launch was within a hundred yards of the small green speed-boat when Hamish Campbell, acting as look-out, realised they were being pursued.

'Put your foot down, Charley,' he bawled.

The two vessels increased speed. Both the Colonel and Frank Pollard were enjoying themselves, not at all what they'd been expecting to do before lunch on a brilliant June day. The same couldn't be said for Superintendent James Byrd. Everything had gone wrong. Of course he should have thought of the river. Even now the small boat might disgorge its passenger and that passenger pick up a helicopter and be out of the country before he could sneeze. He'd underrated Campbell and, foolishly, trusted Charley who'd sworn not to contact the architect nor breathe a word about Hodges or Anstey-Lloyd. His intuition had let him down. Charley, he thought, had been out for vengeance, and was more than satisfied, contented even, to learn that Campbell would receive his come-uppance. Why had he changed his mind?

'How much further to the Barrier?' asked Byrd.

'Not far,' said the helmsman. 'As soon as we get round the Isle of Dogs you'll see one of the modern wonders of the world.'

Five minutes later the Superintendent saw, for the first time in his life, the Great Barrier built to save London. It was

242

gigantic, impressive, awe-inspiring. 'Shouldn't think, Robin, that the designers and engineers ever dreamt this structure would prevent a felon's escape.'

They were closing rapidly and as they did so the barrier grew larger and the small green speed-boat smaller, until it appeared as a mere speck.

'Heave to!' yelled the Skipper through his loud hailer.

Hamish Campbell realised too late there was nowhere to go, not even a small gap through which they could inch their way. The Thames Barrier thwarted him as no man ever had. There was no more future for him, no more excitement, no more pitting his wits against the establishment which is what he'd enjoyed most. No more of anything, or was there? He could always control events from inside. They weren't finished with him – yet. A small revolver was no protection now, not against two fully equipped police launches. With a laugh he threw it in the river.

'Stop the engine, Charley. We've had it now,' but Charley affected not to hear. 'Stop it, Charley. There's no way through.'

'No, there ain't, governor.

'Charley, you idiot, I can't swim.'

'Yes, I know that, governor.' Charley opened the throttle and drove at speed towards the central gate.

'Stop it man, stop it, do you hear?'

But Charley didn't seem to hear. The onlookers in the launches looked on in horror as the flimsy craft cracked like an eggshell against the 40mm steel plating. Within seconds there was no sign of the boat, nor of its passengers.

'What the hell was he doing?' gasped the Colonel.

'Carrying out a summary execution,' said Byrd quietly. 'An idea which should have crossed my mind, and an act which I could have prevented.'

'Don't blame yourself, James.'

'But I do, Robin. There have been four deaths in less than a month because my priorities were wrong. Two of the deaths could have been prevented had I not been so recklessly eager to trace the missing artefacts. Four deaths in a search for State Papers belonging to the Crown is not something for the annals nor is it an achievement of which I'm proud. The price was too high, Robin, the human sacrifice too great.'

EPILOGUE

Charley Austin was rushed to the East End Hospital, not mortally wounded, but needing attention to the gash on his head, and a broken tibia. Charley, having fully expected to go down with his ship, was lucky to be alive. Superintendent Byrd sat listening to a garrulous patient, whose grin stretched from ear to ear, and whose off-the-record confession was what he'd expected to hear. No, Charley hadn't said a word to Campbell, and yes, he'd always suspected the architect to be the brain behind the operation. Of course the Thames Barrier effectively prevented Campbell's escape, but there had been other means of achieving his kamikazi objective. Tower Bridge would have served his purpose, but he had wanted to see the bastard's elation when he thought the escape plan was a total success, and then, most of all, he had wanted to see Campbell's mortification when it became apparent that the game was up.

'I don't mind doing time,' he whispered to Byrd, 'but all this is off the record, because my lawyer will tell the court, if it ever comes to court, that I lost both my nerve and control of the boat. Haven't been the same man, you see, since Jimmy died.'

Steve's ashes were blown by a light wind over The Green dusting the spot where three young queens had been beheaded. Two weeks later the community attended his memorial service in St Peter's Ad Vincula. As Brenda entered the Chapel Royal she felt there was no reality, it was like being the chief mourner in an historical film. The Chapel full of the scent of flowers, and the sound of music was drenched in the early morning sun which burst through the east window blinding her. When the music ceased, the Chaplain's lyric tones, which had comforted her so often, brought her back to reality. It was the Colonel's paean of praise for Steve which she found hardest to bear. She wept silently. For Steve, and for herself.

On the following day Lawrence packed his bags and only on the spur of the moment, as he was leaving, did he ask Brenda whether she'd care to spend Christmas in New Jersey. The short Christmas holiday turned into a long holiday, and the long holiday into a lasting relationship. Those two lonely people never professed a love for each other, but with the years their fondness and respect for each other deepened, producing a lasting happiness.

Two days after Hamish Campbell's death, from drowning, Byrd drove down to Poole not knowing whether he was *persona grata* with his wife and daughter. He needn't have worried. Stephanie was heartily sick of hearing the same stories about her great grandfather, told again and again in her cousin's monotone. Stephanie threw her arms round her husband and Kate welcomed him with shrieks of joy. As if from a hat, Byrd produced their passports and said they were off to France on the following day. Three weeks, without a phone, where no one could disturb them.

The white knights, Sir Charles and Sir Elwyn, failed to bestow any accolades upon their unorthodox Superintendent, nor was he promoted. In their book, allowing a felon to escape from The Tower of London, and under their very noses, was almost as heinous a crime as those perpetrated by Constables of the Tower in previous centuries who'd allowed their prisoners to escape. The Superintendent's rating, however, was high with the Governor, Deputy Governor and the Historian of the Tower. They thought his investigation and insight into the case masterly and by retrieving the missing documents had proved that he was a brilliant and intuitive officer. Byrd never divulged his pattern of thinking which led to the discovery. Some things were better kept close to the chest. It had come to him in a flash while playing *Hunt the Thimble* with Kate. He failed to find a white plastic thimble which she'd hidden in the centre of a white hydrangea, hadn't seen it until she pointed it out. 'Like with like,' he had yelled as he lifted his daughter into the air and danced round the room like a Cherokee doing a war dance. The following day he opened the draftman's chests in Hamish Campbell's study. As he unlocked the top drawer, a familiar smell assailed his nostrils. To him the musty smell of centuries-old parchment was like nectar. From each drawer he carefully extracted recent plans relating to work in progress which effectively hid ancient State Papers. Eureka! Unlike the unfortunate Raleigh Superintendent Byrd had discovered his Eldorado, and thus, to his own satisfaction, but not Sir Charles's, completed his case at the Tower of London.

Hamish Campbell had been too greedy. His headmaster at his prep school in Edinburgh had recognised, in the young child, traits which would eventually be his undoing. At the age of six he was organising the children in his class, both at day school and the Presbyterian Sunday school. By the time he was eight he had been dominating his elderly parents. Meals were served in his bedroom where he had a telephone, television and filing cabinet installed. He read vociferously, kept files on all his teachers, and by winning a prestigious design award at the age of seventeen his future was assured. He foolishly precipitated his own demise by refusing to play games at school. No football. No rugger. No cricket. No swimming.

No 5 The Green may never again be used as a lodging. The building which, some say, housed Lady Jane Grey, and for four days a certain German who claimed to be Rudolf Hess, is about to be restored to its former glory and may become much-needed administration space.

Graham Tooley's idea that 2A The Casemates should be earmarked as an additional space for souvenirs, all models of The Tower, may never come to fruition. Archeologists, historians, and architects from all over Britain are already showing a fanatical interest in the subterranean tunnels. They will be digging, delving, researching and arguing for many many years to come.